Some of It Was Real

Some of It Was Real

———

Nan Fischer

BERKLEY
NEW YORK

BERKLEY
An imprint of Penguin Random House LLC
penguinrandomhouse.com

Copyright © 2022 by Nan Fischer
Readers Guide copyright © 2022 by Nan Fischer
Excerpt copyright © 2022 by Nan Fischer

Library of Congress Cataloging-in-Publication Data

Names: Fischer, Nan, author.
Title: Some of it was real / Nan Fischer.
Description: First edition. | New York : Berkley, 2022.
Identifiers: LCCN 2021035582 (print) | LCCN 2021035583 (ebook) |
ISBN 9780593438695 (trade paperback) | ISBN 9780593438701 (ebook)
Subjects: LCSH: Women psychics—Fiction. | Journalists—Fiction. |
LCGFT: Romance fiction. | Novels.
Classification: LCC PS3606.I7666 S66 2022 (print) |
LCC PS3606.I7666 (ebook) | DDC 813/.6—dc23/eng/20211206
LC record available at https://lccn.loc.gov/2021035582
LC ebook record available at https://lccn.loc.gov/2021035583

First Edition: July 2022

Printed in the United States of America
1 3 5 7 9 10 8 6 4 2

Book design by Kristin del Rosario
Title page art: Apple blossom trees © The Len / Shutterstock

This book is dedicated to Henry.
You make the impossible possible.

Some of It Was Real

ONE

Sylvie

The outfit is the easy part. It was chosen by a style consultant hired by my agent to create an image. I slip on a sleeveless black silk jumpsuit with crystals along the edge of a plunging neckline, fasten strappy heels and diamond hoop earrings, and slide a platinum ring whose sapphire stones form an infinity symbol on my index finger. On cue, my stomach cramps and I rush into the bathroom, grip the cold porcelain, and lose a late lunch. Moose whimpers then rests his blocky head on my shoulder. He's a 145-pound Great Dane, but despite his size, he's a big baby. "I'm good. Promise."

A kiss between Moose's eyes; swish of mouthwash then I return to the mirror, sweep my dark brown hair into a glossy chignon. On goes a light coat of foundation, blush, eye shadow, dark gray liner, false lashes, and red lipstick. One final look confirms everything is in place. I swivel my chair and rifle through last-minute reminders. When the phone rings, there's no need to check caller ID. My agent always calls before a show. "Hey, Lucas."

Lucas crows, "We have a deal!"

The news shoves me back in the chair.

"Sylvie? Why aren't you jumping up and down and screaming? We've been working toward this for years."

"Are *you* jumping up and down?"

"I might've shot a fist in the air when Jackson phoned to say we had the green light. Syl, it's a guaranteed ten episodes, more money than we'd hoped for, bonuses, and if we get the numbers, which I'm sure you will, we can push E! for a two-year run. This is *huge*."

"I don't know if—"

"I do—that's why we make a great team."

While we talk, I wander around the dressing room, past a long mirror, a chipped wooden table and mismatched chairs, and a dusty shelf with a drip coffee machine that looks like it belongs in a 1950s diner. My rider—a set of requests fulfilled by each venue—is pretty basic. I ask for a well-lit mirror, a private bathroom, a few bottles of water, and lots of coffee, but don't demand anything fancy, like an espresso machine.

"Sylvie?"

"Connections don't always happen. You know that."

"Then you build a bridge."

"When I started—"

"Syl, what you do? It's incredible. You make people feel better. There's no harm either way. I've told you that since the day we met. You're one of the good guys."

I rest my forehead against the cool wall to quell a nervous heat. "I'm not consistently filling theaters at the shows."

"Your numbers have been climbing fast."

"I've never been on TV."

"I negotiated approval for each episode."

"Who will I read?"

"A mix of celebrities and regular people. Sylvie, if you don't take this opportunity, someone else will. That's just the way things work in this business."

I run through my options. No family support. No real friends. No college education. *And this fits.* At first it was about survival, money, so I never had to go back home. But over the past few years, I've realized that this is the only thing that gives me some semblance of peace. "I'm in."

"Of course you are. It'll take a week for the lawyers to comb through the contract. When it's signed, we'll announce in *Variety*, Page Six, too. Sylvie?"

"Yes?"

"I believe in you."

The first time he said that was my third show after I moved to LA—just a basement club in Venice, but Lucas made sure it was packed and that a few small entertainment papers were there. I was on fire, hit after hit. Finally, I felt like I might be in the right place. After the show, he drove me back to the studio apartment in West Hollywood he'd rented for me. He turned off the engine and said, *I believe in you.* Then he added, *I'm going to make you a star.*

"You still there?" Lucas asks.

Moose leans against my leg and stares up at me. "Is Moose part of the TV show?"

"He even has his own contract."

I kiss the crown of Moose's head and his tail thumps. My first therapist was the one who suggested I get a dog. The young woman who took me around the shelter walked right past Moose, like he was invisible. He ran forward, put a massive paw on the chain links. I pressed my hand to his pads, can still recall their warmth. We chose each other that day. I kept Moose but let that therapist go. Lucas said

4 · *Nan Fischer*

I could hire a new therapist if needed. Even in the early days, he was aimed at the stars. Celebrities can be ruined by all kinds of past relationships and unethical practitioners. Lucas was determined to keep skeletons out of my closet. He also quickly understood that I didn't want to dissect a past that left me feeling like a disappointment.

Now Lucas is right again—a TV show *is* the next step. It doesn't matter how I fell into this profession. Before, I always felt like my shoes were on the wrong feet. This fits, despite my fears. And the bottom line is that what I do helps people.

There's a knock. "It's time," a muffled voice says.

I grab a black marker and slip it into my pocket. "Gotta go."

Moose mouths the enormous, stuffed fuzzy bone he loves and carries it out of the room. On the walk from the dressing room to the wings of any stage, I go through the guided imagery the last therapist I quit designed. It helps me overcome the anxiety that began when I first started going onstage and became crippling as my success grew. Today an image slips through the carefully constructed peace . . .

Pale sand beneath my feet, a blue-green ocean, foam nibbling at my bare toes. Behind me, a castle—ornate turrets dotted with pale pink shells, a drawbridge made from delicately curved driftwood, beneath it, a moat where tiny paper boats rock in the breeze. A wave gathers on the horizon. It grows taller and white horses gallop across its face. When the wall of salt water strikes, the castle will be destroyed and with it a treasure, something precious . . .

The vision disintegrates. Ghostly lips brush my cheek. I know what's coming next. A whisper I've heard intermittently my entire life. When I tip my head, the unintelligible slides away. I crunch an antacid to quell my burning gut then wait for the cue to step onstage and begin my show . . .

TWO

—

Sylvie

Music flows through the theater's surround sound—a symphony of instruments that slowly builds. An intricate dance of multicolored laser lights traverses the empty stage then dry-ice vapor rolls across wooden boards and spotlights turn curls of smoke violet, azure, and emerald. The smoke dissipates, frenetic lights slow their search; the symphony strikes its crescendo. I walk to the center of the stage just as the last notes fade away, wait for the applause to thin and people to take their seats.

One hand on my dog's sleek, black head, I start. "Thank you for coming. I'm Sylvie Young and this handsome guy beside me is Moose. I get a bit nervous before each show and he helps with that, so I hope you don't mind him being here?" There are murmurs of encouragement. "Every psychic has an origin story that reveals when and how we first recognized our abilities. That might be when we predicted a grandparent's passing, delivered a message to the living only the dead could possibly know, or found a lost object, pet, or child. We must then choose whether or not to use our gift." My eyes scan the theater. Almost every seat is taken. "I never planned to be a psychic or stand on a stage. Sometimes where I've landed is overwhelming. Truly. But what's most important is that when someone asks me to connect with those they loved and lost, I will do *anything* to make that happen."

I let this promise settle then continue. "My gift appeared when I was eighteen, living in San Francisco, and had just worked a double waitressing shift, food stains on my T-shirt, the smell of fried food in my hair. On the long walk back to a basement apartment, I stopped in the funky Haight-Ashbury neighborhood to rest on a bench. A few feet away, outside a magic shop named Abracadabra, a young guy read tarot at a rickety metal table. He was flying by the seat of his pants, but he had a gift for weaving stories. After a funny reading, I giggled. The tarot reader laughed, too, we chatted for a bit, then he scribbled a sign that read PSYCHIC $5 on a folded piece of cardboard and dared me to sit in the chair beside him. I took the seat, assumed no one would waste money on me.

"My first customers were sisters. The pregnant one was Bethany. I guessed she was almost nine months along—it wasn't a psychic thing, it was obvious that she hadn't seen her feet in a while." I wait for knowing laughter to subside then go on.

"Am I having a boy or a girl? Bethany asked.

"I rested my hands on the swell beneath the cool silk of her dress. The baby kicked and I jumped, laughed, and the mom-to-be did, too. To give Bethany a good show, I closed my eyes. An instant whooshing sound enveloped me, followed by a river of warmth that flowed around my limbs. The warm water cradled me and I felt my body slowly roll . . . but then something tugged, stopped me . . . The next thing I knew, the tarot reader was shaking me really hard. When I opened my eyes, Bethany was on her feet, arms wrapped protectively around her belly."

The audience is quiet, caught in the story's web. *"Why would you scare her like that?* Bethany's sister demanded.

"Confused, I followed her pointed finger. Scribbled across the inside of my right forearm were the words *I can't breathe.* I turned to the tarot reader. *Did you do that?* But his black marker was gripped in my hand and the writing was mine." Whispers float through the audience. "By then Bethany was crying." I tip my chin and look into the balcony section. "I should've apologized. But when I was little and in trouble, always with my mom, Dad would say that there was a plant that grew inside my belly called a *contrary tree.* Instead of backpedaling, I said, *She can't breathe.*"

I shake my head at the memory. "The sisters left. I eyed the water bottle that the tarot reader had given me. *What the hell is in that?* But it was only water. *What happened with Bethany exactly?* I demanded.

"He explained, *You grabbed my marker, started writing on your arm. I think you have the gift.*

"Of course I didn't believe him. The guy was leaving town and offered to sell me his table and chairs for ten bucks, put in a good word with the owner of the magic shop so I could still work in front of her store. He'd made a hundred and seventy-five dollars reading tarot in just two hours. After a full day waitressing, I'd only made twenty-eight bucks in tips. At that rate, I wouldn't make the month's rent. So I bought the table and chairs, figured I could try for a few hours after my restaurant shifts, vowed to keep things light and lovely, just play around.

"A few days later, I set up my table and nervously waited for customers. They actually came. After my anxiety burned off, it was surprisingly fun. I scribbled messages, hummed songs that burst into my head, and the customers were amazed. I still didn't believe the tarot guy, but I was a crap waitress and it felt good to be good at something, you know?" More than a few people in the audience nod in agreement. They understand that need to be recognized.

"Soon, there were lines just from word of mouth. People came to see *me*. Late one afternoon an old man named Arthur asked if I could contact someone who'd died. He looked so miserable that I agreed and closed my eyes . . . A red barn door materialized. It jumped into my head, like a kid in a classroom with her hand held high, desperate for the teacher's attention. I let the door swing wide and the tang of metal filled my mouth.

"*Anything?* Arthur asked.

"I felt a female energy cross the door's brink but couldn't see a face. The next thing I knew, I'd written a message in the crook of my elbow: *No rush. I'll be waiting. Take that watercolor class old Tiger—M.*

"Arthur told me his wife's name was Maribel and she'd nicknamed him Tiger. She'd been dead six months, and he missed her so much, he wasn't sure he could hold on. After reading Maribel's message, he said that as a young man, he'd wanted to be a painter but had chosen accounting to support his family." The audience draws in a collective breath and I shyly smile. "Arthur kissed the bend of my elbow then walked off with light steps, like he'd sprouted wings." I lower my voice to share, "His smile has never left me."

Crossing the stage, I continue, "Six months later my business was going strong. I'd sprung for a black velvet tablecloth over the metal card table and I wore a midnight blue, sleeveless dress and used a metallic silver marker to draw stars, moons, and planets on the cheap cotton. It was pretty hokey, but I made enough to cover rent, eat more than ramen, and I'd quit waitressing." I admit, "None of this is very flattering, but it's important that you know that I didn't always believe in myself." Murmurs of disagreement ripple through the theater. Each time I reach this part of my origin story and the audience reacts with understanding and belief, I get a lump in my throat.

"One day a woman sat down across from me—pretty with dark blond hair. The man resting his hands on her shoulders had a baby on his chest in one of those trendy slings.

"*I'm Bethany,* the woman said. *You did a reading for me months ago, told me my baby couldn't breathe.*

"I apologized profusely for scaring her. She introduced her husband, Matthew, and I tensed, ready for him to tell me off, probably put me out of business.

"Bethany said, *I came home from your reading and insisted we go to the emergency room for an ultrasound. I was rushed into surgery. Grace's umbilical cord was wrapped twice around her neck. If I hadn't had an emergency C-section . . .* She started to cry.

"Matthew finished, *We wouldn't have Grace if you hadn't warned us. Thank you.*

"He gave me his business card, suggested I get in touch so he could connect me with people who might help.

"*Help with what?* I asked.

"*If you want to be a psychic for a living, do more than just this, then you need a talent agent. My friend Lucas Haughter is a big agent down in LA. I think he'd be interested.*

I confess to the audience, "There was no plan. I just made that phone call. Lucas flew me down to LA and I did a reading for him. He signed me the same day and the rest, as they say, is history."

People have moved to the edge of their seats, ready for me to divulge secrets, solve mysteries, connect them to someone they lost, or turn back time so they can have a second chance. Finished with my origin story, I'm now ready to help as many of them as I can. They believe . . . and some of my story is even true.

THREE

Thomas

I've been to Sylvie's shows before, but never this close to the stage. My orchestra seat, third row, center, cost $500 through TixMix, and the other seat I bought for a friend was $250. I blew what was left of my budget on a cheap flight to Oregon for the next show, just in case. Right now, it's impossible to take my eyes off Sylvie. She's tall, about five-foot-eight, and lithe. Deep red lipstick stains full lips. Long lashes fringe light gray eyes. A single spotlight bathes her skin, reflects back in a golden dazzle. *She's made for this.*

Around me, believers, shiny faces tilted like thirsty flowers, lean forward. Their collective energy could light a city. I'm one of a multitude whose prayers silently float into the rafters of this theater. As Sylvie talks to us, her giant black dog, reminiscent of Cerberus, a fleece bone clenched in his maw, stares into the audience, daring us to misbehave so he can have a snack.

The psychics I've seen all begin with an origin story, just like Sylvie did, then usually launch into a rapid-fire barrage of letters, numbers, messages, and images that force the audience to scramble, search for connections. This is where Sylvie differs. When she talks to her audiences, she chooses her words carefully. And when she's stumped, she admits it, apologizes, and moves on. Also, she's much more creative—humming or singing, contacting the dead by accessing a red door, and going into a trancelike state where she writes on her skin. Sounds scattershot, but Sylvie is extremely believable. That's why we're all here.

"One last thing," Sylvie says. "It's important you understand that I don't have a clear definition for what I do. Psychics use their intuition or spiritual guides to gain information about the past, present, or future. Mediums are channels that deliver messages from those who have passed over. I've been called a psychic-medium, and that's as good a definition as any. But the truth is that I'm not sure why I hear voices, see images, sing at times, or scribble notes—it just happens and I can't tell you how because I truly don't understand it."

Sylvie takes a wobbly breath and the urge to reach out, give her hand a squeeze, tell her that I know she'll try her hardest, always surprises me. That same concern is reflected on the faces of countless audience members. "We are about to embark on a journey," she says. "I hope that whatever happens helps someone. But there's a saying I've always lived by, though I can't recall where I first heard it. The truth has two edges. Make sure you're prepared for the answers you seek. Okay?"

Around me people smile back and say, "Okay." I surprise myself by saying it, too.

Turning to the left side of the stage, Sylvie begins, "Far left . . . five rows back." She moves forward, so graceful she almost floats. "There's a motherly energy . . . she didn't want to die in the hospital. Does that mean something to anyone in this row? Please take your time. I understand that many of you want to make a connection, but it's really important to listen to the details so that you don't mistake someone else's message."

My stomach does a flip as my friend Daryl stands up, runs a hand through sparse gray hair. *Finally*. One of the assistants in the audience races over with a microphone.

Daryl says, "My ma died a few months ago."

Sylvie repeatedly taps her lips. The ring on her index finger sparkles. "Do you collect something . . . maybe pennies . . . no, they're squares?"

"Stamps! I've collected them since I was a kid."

She walks to the edge of the stage, right across from Daryl, the dog glued to her side. "Your mother says she didn't want you to sell them."

Daryl shakes his head, like he can't believe what he's hearing. "I used the money to pay for a home nurse, but I ran out anyway, had to put Ma in a state hospital and still work doubles to pay the doctor's bills." Daryl's voice catches. "I was at work when she passed."

A crease appears between Sylvie's brows. "There's a really young energy coming forward . . . Do you have a sister? She died when you were little . . . She's signing the letter D, then holding up four fingers."

Daryl flinches. "Uh. No. I'm an only child."

Sylvie whisks a marker out of her pocket and scribbles on her palm. She holds up her hand and reads it like she's learning what it says *with* the audience. "D wants you to S-T-O-P. Does that mean anything to you?"

"Ah . . . nope."

"Sorry. Sometimes I get wires crossed. Just know that your mother isn't angry. She says you were a really good son."

The sound of stringed instruments accompanies Sylvie as she traverses the stage, pauses, tips her head back. The music fades. "First row balcony. Do the initials H and F mean anything?"

A middle-aged woman in a striped wrap-dress that struggles to contain her ample cleavage stands. She's passed a microphone. "You're talking about my grandfather, Harold Fairwell?"

"He's showing me strong hands. They're stained black."

"That's him! Always had oil on his hands. He restored old cars."

"There's one he wanted you to have . . . it was a dark color?"

"Blue. Yes! An old MG Midget. But I sold it. He loved that car so much and I still feel guilty about it."

"It wasn't about the car. It was about giving you something to make a difference in your life."

"It did! I used the money to help pay for business school. Got a great job."

For over an hour Sylvie works the stage. She shares messages from estranged siblings, a father lost at sea, a twin who died in a car crash that left his brother paralyzed, a son killed in a ski accident, and a great-aunt who wants her god-nieces to quit their battle over a sculpture, sell it, and split the proceeds. Then she calls on a woman with bobbed red hair seated mid-orchestra. "A brother-figure is stepping forward. He's pointing to his heart . . ."

"That's so flipping wild," the woman says. "My friend, the one who gave me her ticket 'cause she got food poisoning, had a brother who died from a heart attack."

"Please tell your friend her brother is a force, even in the *after*. He wants her to know that he's thankful she's taking care of his daughter." Sylvie hesitates, begins to hum, then pulls a marker from her pocket and scribbles along the inside of her forearm. When whatever spell she's under breaks, she blinks a few times then reads the words scrawled on her skin like she's never seen them before. "'Kel, just because they were yours doesn't mean it was your fault.'"

The redhead gasps. "But you told me it would happen!"

Sylvie tips her head, perplexed. "*I* did?"

"Last fall I came to your show at the Wild Horse Casino in Washington? You asked if the date 'November thirteenth' meant something to me. It didn't, then. You said it would. You were so sure. Have to admit, I left certain you were a sham."

"I'm sure you weren't the only one," Sylvie notes with a wry smile.

The woman shakes her head. "The naysayers are dead wrong. Three weeks later, on November thirteenth, my sister took her life."

The audience buzzes. Sylvie crouches beside Moose, slender arm wrapped around those massive canine shoulders like she needs support. "Is your name Kel?"

"Kelly."

"I'm so very sorry for your loss, Kelly."

"I knew she was depressed. The pain pills were from my back surgery years ago. Doc prescribed sixty of 'em. I only took two, should've flushed the rest."

"She would've found another way. She wants you to know that."

"The song you were humming . . . me and my sis, we used to sing it in rounds."

"What song?"

"An old English tune called 'Rose Red.'" Kelly softly sings . . .

> *Rose, Rose, Rose*
> *Will I ever see thee wed?*
> *I will marry at thy will, sire*
> *At thy will . . .*

Ding dong, ding dong
Wedding bells on an April morn
Carve your initials on a moss-covered stone,
On a moss-covered stone . . .

Ah, poor bird
Take thy flight
Fly above the sorrows
Of this sad night . . .

"Rose, that was my sis's name," Kelly says. "She was nineteen. She'll never marry or have children or get to watch mine grow . . . I miss her so much."

Sylvie's eyes shine. "It's okay to miss the people you loved. But they're at peace and want you to be at peace, too."

My cell phone vibrates and I glance at the screen. The texts are from Daryl.

> Rose's suicide date? WTF?!
>
> AND I had a sister who died when she was
> four years old!!
>
> Her name was Dawn. She was deaf.

I tuck the phone away as Sylvie walks over to the leather chairs in the middle of the stage set on either side of a small table and sits. Moose settles beside her and she rests one hand on his broad back, looks into the audience like she really sees us, and says, "If you leave here today with nothing else, know this: If someone you loved met a violent end, or suffered an illness before passing, that wasn't their *life*. It was all the years before then—every joy, celebration, adventure, and love. Death is only a moment."

Around me, shoulders relax, fists unclench. Some people smile while others wipe away tears. We've reached the grand finale, where one person gets called to the stage for an in-depth read. Sylvie will ask for a personal object to help her. Almost everyone in the audience has brought something. I have a ring in the pocket of my jeans.

There's a collective intake of breath; on the exhale prayers are murmured. Sylvie scans the audience then slowly lifts her arm and initially points up toward the balcony, hesitates, then lowers her arm and points . . . at me.

FOUR

Sylvie

I pick Orchestra, Row C, Seat 23. I almost chose First Balcony, Row D, Seat 37. But Seat 23 caught my eye as I worked the theater, always drawing me back to the part of the stage directly in front of him. It has happened before, where I've been pulled to help someone, but the feeling that this man was the most important person in the audience, that I *needed* to choose him for the final reading, was impossible to ignore. Now he glances left then right to make sure I mean him.

I motion for him to come onstage then watch his progress. He's early thirties, attractive in a boyish, intellectual way, wears a blue flannel shirt, not tucked in, over a white T-shirt, worn jeans, a sport watch, and brown leather boots. A professional of some sort in weekend wear. There's a gold wedding band on his left ring finger, round, tortoiseshell glasses with a mild-enough prescription that it doesn't distort his eyes. A small scar above his right brow looks old, probably from an accident when he was a kid, topped by a mop of dark blond hair that needs a cut. He trips on the last step to the stage—they're always nervous—then pockets his glasses, so they're probably for distance. There are violet crescents beneath his eyes and his posture is curved, slightly defeated. As he draws close, the need for closure rolls toward me in spiky waves.

This is the part of the show where I'm hyperaware. It was a good show, but there were a few missteps. Kelly and Rose made up for them. But the people I didn't connect with, who spent their hard-earned money, showed up, maybe for the second, fourth, or eleventh time, optimistic, will only return if they're left with a sense of trust, for the process, and with me.

"Hi. Um. I'm Theo."

"Welcome. Please have a seat."

Theo glances at Moose. "I'm kind of afraid of really big dogs."

I smile. "That's because you have a cat."

"How'd you know?"

I point to the gray hairs caught on the flannel of his shirt. "Siamese?"

"A mix. Her name is Christopher Robin." The audience laughs. He actually blushes. "We didn't know she was a girl when we got her."

"I didn't know if Moose was a boy or girl when I first spotted him at the shelter," I confide. "I just knew we were meant for each other. Was it like that with Chris?"

Theo's brows jerk then quickly smooth. "That's what *I* call her. Chris. Yeah. We found her on a camping trip in Joshua Tree. She was in a cardboard box. The other kittens, three of them, had already died."

"People can be horribly cruel." Our eyes meet. Theo's are an arresting blue-green.

For a moment I lose the thread, then pick it up. "Chris is lucky to have you." Theo sidles around Moose and slides onto his chair.

"Do you have a personal object for me to hold?" He digs into a pocket, pulls out a white-gold engagement ring. The diamond is cushion cut, about 1.5 carats. The gold has no perceptible scratches or dents and the stone was recently cleaned to a brilliant shine. I glance again at Theo's wedding band. It's yellow-gold and dull with wear. Usually couples choose identical metals and the wear is similar . . . but not always.

"May I?" Theo hands me the ring. "Your wife's?" He nods. "She's passed?"

"Yes."

"You want me to connect with her?"

"Yes. Please."

"The letter C, no, it's a K, is important to you?"

Theo leans forward, brow creased. "My wife's name was Katy."

The audience rustles, excited that I'm on the right track. "Theo, we've reached the part where I say that I can't promise anything, okay?"

He attempts a smile. "Okay."

"Then let's begin." I open the red door and silently beckon. *Katy?* No one comes forward. My fingers press the diamond into my palm, and still . . . *Nothing.* A young spirit finally rushes through, but he's not what I want. *I need Katy.* The energy persists, shows me a leather-bound book with the word JOURNAL embossed in gold on the front. "Theo, does a journal mean anything to you? It's blank?"

He doesn't blink. "No."

Body language experts say a lack of blinking indicates a possible lie . . . but Theo's need for a connection is palpable. Part of him feels walled off, like he's opened the front door, is willing to show me his clean living room, but not the mess in the other rooms. *He's partially shut down from grief.* The male essence slips away, but still, there's nothing from Katy. Sometimes this happens.

I ask, "Is being here really hard for you?"

"I've never been to a psychic before so this isn't, um, *normal*, for me."

"Can I share a secret?" He nods. "It's *never* normal for me."

"Then why do you do it?"

"To help people," I say.

"Is that the only reason?"

He looks so earnest that it's clearly not a challenge, just nerves. "Yes."

"What if you *can't* help me?"

He really needs this. I tug my earlobe, a nervous habit, wait a beat, then nod a few times. "Um, okay . . . There's a female presence stepping forward, but she's faint. Did Katy pass recently?"

"A week ago."

The audience sighs. "I'm so sorry for your loss. Sometimes when people have just gone to the other side, they have difficulty coming through."

Frowning, Theo asks, "How do you know it's Katy? Can you describe her?"

"I never see a face . . . but . . . okay, strange . . . this spirit is showing me a plate of pasta? Is Italian food important to you?"

Theo sits up straight. "We went to Italy for our honeymoon. Katy loved to cook so we took a course, learned how to make homemade pasta." His eyes shine. "It's her. It's really Katy."

The audience claps, thrilled for Theo, but something feels off. Probably, it's me, still rattled after Lucas's call. I turn the wedding ring over and it catches the spotlight, sends a rainbow prism onto Theo's shirt. "Katy is showing me the back of a head. Did she die from a head injury?"

"Kind of. She had brain cancer."

". . . Is the number 3 important? She's referenced it several times."

Theo rubs his eyes. "Three months from diagnosis."

The audience gasps. Lightly, I touch his arm. The urge to keep my hand there, stay connected, surprises me. He pulls back. "Katy wants you to know that she's found peace, but she's worried about you." I place the engagement ring on the table between us and turn to the audience, draw them back in. "No matter how your loved ones died, their biggest concern, wherever they are, is that they've left *you* in pain; that you'll try to live *their* life, not follow your own path."

There's a tic beneath Theo's right eye. "Are you afraid you're not living your own life?" I ask.

"No. I just . . . that idea is sad."

He needs more. I trace circles on the arm of my leather chair. "Katy is showing me a building. Industrial. Lots of dogs, cats, too." I meet Theo's gaze. "Do you work at an animal shelter?"

"Wow! No. But Katy volunteered at one. Helping animals was her passion."

"This is weird. I know you like cats, but did she want to bring home a dog?"

Theo runs a hand through his hair. "Yes—a shepherd-collie mix. Our apartment was too small, but I should've done it to make her happy."

"She understood that you were overwhelmed." *I should wrap this up.* "Could I—would you mind if I held *your* wedding band?"

Theo hesitates then slides it off. There's no indentation or tan line beneath it, but some men don't wear their ring all the time. I put it in the center of my palm and a spirit lunges through the red door. "There's a male energy. He says to tell her *she was right about the rain.* Does that mean anything to you?"

Theo sits back. "Not really. No."

My skin prickles. *Is he lying?* "Was this wedding band handed down?"

"No."

"Bought as an estate piece?"

"We had it made," Theo says and slides it back on his finger. "Both rings."

The audience shifts. *I'm losing them.* "I'm sorry. I must be picking up on someone else."

"It's okay. Anything else?"

". . . Yes. Katy wants you to spread her ashes at the beach you both loved. Does that make sense?"

"It's perfect." Theo leans forward, slides a business card in front of me so smoothly that the audience doesn't see it.

THOMAS HOLMES

REPORTER

LOS ANGELES TIMES

1.444.767.8888

He mouths, "We need to talk."

My heart is slingshot into my sternum then plummets as I realize that the color of his eyes is the identical blue-green as the deadly ocean wave in my vision.

FIVE

Thomas

"Thank you so much, Sylvie. It meant the world."

She smiles warmly. "You're welcome."

I give the dog a wide berth, walk back to my seat. Music swells. The audience applauds, cheers. Not for me, for Sylvie and her *gift*. But I know the truth. She's a fraud. And when my exposé is published, the world will know, too.

As the crowd filters out of the theater, I choose to stay put. Adrenaline flows like I just scored the game-winning touchdown. What she said about the journal and the rest? Those were lucky shots over the bow of a sinking ship. Even a blind man can get a bull's-eye if he knocks back enough arrows. My phone vibrates.

DARYL: Meet in the lobby?

ME: Waiting to see if she wants to talk

DARYL: Did any of it deviate from the script like mine did?

ME: A little

DARYL: I'm still freaked out

ME: Don't be. Either it was a lucky guess, or she figured out you were a plant and has ways to mine information we haven't discovered. I'll find out

DARYL: You really think she'll ask to talk with you?

ME: It's her only chance

DARYL: Have to admit I like her

ME: Halo effect—we assume pretty people are good people

DARYL: Are you sure she's not?

ME: She sells false hope. Money people can't afford to lose for lies

"Excuse me, sir?"

When I look up, one of Sylvie's assistants, a silver-haired guy in a black turtleneck and dark jeans, stands at the end of the row. "Yes?"

"Sylvie would like to meet with you in her dressing room."

I pocket my phone. "Sure thing."

"You must've really made an impression on her," the assistant says as we head backstage then wind through a narrow hallway.

"She doesn't usually meet with people after the show?"

"Never." The guy glances at me. "I'm very sorry about your wife. My dad died a few years ago, pancreatic cancer, so I get it." His face turns beet red. "Not that it's the same thing. I mean she was young, your wife."

"Thanks," I say, unable to meet his gaze.

"Talking to Sylvie about my dad really helped. Hope you get what you need."

"I'm optimistic."

"Here we are." He knocks on the door. "Sylvie? I've got Theo with me."

The moment before cracking a story reminds me of being a kid, flying down a steep hill on my bike, the world streaming by in an intoxicating blur.

"Thanks, Charlie. Please send him in and you can head home."

Charlie gives my shoulder a pat. "Good luck, man. You deserve peace."

Inside the room there's a cracked leather couch on the left wall, to the right, a mirror with light bulbs around the edges. A stool rests beneath a counter scattered with makeup and brushes. Against the far wall is a small, round table with four chairs. Sylvie is perched in one of them. She's changed into jeans, a pale pink T-shirt, and gray canvas sneakers. All traces of makeup have been scrubbed off, hair in a ponytail. Stray locks frame a heart-shaped face. She looks younger than onstage, about nineteen, though she recently turned twenty-four. *She's young to be such a good liar.* In front of her is a mug of coffee but none for me. That's okay. I'm buzzing like I've had ten cups. Between the empty chair and Sylvie lies Moose, haunches coiled, ready to spring.

After the door closes, Sylvie asks, "Should I call you Theo or Thomas?"

"Thomas is my *real* name."

She smiles, but her eyes, so warm onstage, are ice chips. "Have a seat. Thomas."

Game on. I edge around the dog, slide onto a chair. Sylvie takes a sip from her mug. "I'm a reporter for the *Los Angeles Times*."

"So your card said."

"I write general interest articles and some exposés. The last was about a judge who took bribes. He was sentenced to seven years in prison."

"Did that story run in any highly regarded newspapers?"

Her insult comes out so sweetly that it almost could've been mistaken for a compliment. "The *L.A. Times* has won forty-five Pulitzer Prizes."

"Your dead wife must be proud."

She doesn't miss a beat. "If Katy existed, she would be." Moose stalks over to Sylvie, stands beside her. They watch me. It's eerie. I press on. "For the past year, I've been at work on an exposé about grief vampires. They're—"

"People who prey on folks who are depressed or mourning a loss. I'm familiar with the term."

The dog yawns. His canines are very long and sharp. I shift back in the chair. "The piece focuses on three West Coast psychic-mediums—Doug Merrell, Victor Grote, and you."

Slowly she spins her mug. "Famous company. Flattering."

"Glad you think so. Doug and Victor, they've been around for decades, so it wasn't hard to research them. Lots of background information, interviews—some family, friends, fans, as well as victims. Victor even sat down with me."

Sylvie lifts one arched brow. "Did you tell him your name was Theo?"

I chuckle. "No. Lucky for me, Victor believes no press is bad press."

"And Doug?"

"He wasn't as forthcoming. But I already had enough to expose him."

"And how do you plan to do that? What psychic-mediums do isn't an exact science that can be debunked."

"For the past eleven months I've planted audience members at Victor's, Doug's, as well as your shows. Put their fictional sob stories on Instagram, Facebook, and Twitter. All three of you have gobbled those worms off my hook, called on my fakes, and *divined* their stories." I wait for a reaction but there isn't a ripple. She may not have enough of a conscience to be embarrassed.

"That's it?" Sylvie finally asks.

"Hardly," I retort. "Doug had several disgruntled employees willing to share stories and photographs, and Victor's last boyfriend provided damning emails."

"And *my* employees and past boyfriends? Were they equally eager?"

"Your employees are very loyal and I couldn't find any boyfriends. But you've taken the bait I threw out in three of your previous six shows. And today, you bit twice. First with the older guy whose mom died in a hospital, even though he promised to take care of her at home. And second, you chose me and repeated the fiction I posted about Katy."

Sylvie tips her head, like she's listening for advice. It's unsettling. "Why me?" she asks. "I'm no big deal compared to the other two."

"Don't be so modest. Your star is on the rise. Lots of press this year. Celebrity readings. Rumor has it there's a TV show in the works. Plus, I wanted to include a woman and relative newcomer." Sylvie casually scratches behind her dog's ear. I'm impressed by her calm in the face of annihilation.

"You talked to Victor and tried to chat with Doug. Why didn't you call me?"

"Your number is unlisted, as is your address."

"I have an agent."

"Mr. Haughter wouldn't take my calls."

"He's a busy man. Call again."

"I tried a dozen times. And your family in Oregon hung up once they learned I'm a journalist." Her lips compress for a split second. *Does their reaction surprise her?*

"Why not introduce yourself as a grieving widower? My folks are good people, they might fall for that."

She's adept at turning the tables. I'd never tell Daryl, but during performances I liked her, too, despite everything. Her attitude *now* changes that.

"Tell me about the male spirit who came forward."

"Excuse me?"

Sylvie abruptly grabs a marker off the table, scrawls a message on her right arm: *You take the red pill.*

Unsettled, I say, "I have no idea what—"

She continues to write: *You stay in wonderland.*

"I suggest you—"

. . . and I show you how deep the rabbit hole goes.

Sylvie's pupils are so enormous, they eclipse the gray of her iris. A shiver spins down my spine. Keeping my voice steady, I say, "I have no idea what you're talking about."

SIX

Sylvie

I don't know what the message I wrote means. Maybe it's nonsense. But I do know that there's a whiff of desperation to Thomas. *Can it help me?* "You've shared your intentions to expose me. So why are you here now?"

"To offer you an opportunity."

"What opportunity?"

"To tell your side of the story."

I sit back, the picture of calm, while inside I scramble. All those years of revolving therapists, Lucas's unwavering belief, my burgeoning following and many successes, yet five minutes with this guy and I'm a hamster trying to outrun my wheel. I tamp down fear, focus. "Why not interview all the people I've helped?"

"I talked to a lot of them. But they're believers."

I manage a smile and say, "They wouldn't be if I'd failed them."

"We've already established how you succeed."

Draping an arm around Moose, I ask him, "Exactly what do you want to know, Doubting Thomas?"

He opens a notepad, scans it. "I have very little background on you. I'd like you to fill in the missing pieces. You were adopted when you were about six, raised in High River, Oregon, by orchardists. Your high school pal, Holly McConnell, said your biological parents, Becky and Seth Peters, died in a plane crash?"

"That's right."

He looks up from the page. "It is? There's no record of that crash."

Moose is solid beneath my arm, but the room still slips sideways for a second. *He's lying to throw me off.* "Not possible."

He flips a page. "I spoke with a source at the Oregon Department of Human Services. ODHS oversees the foster care program. She read me your file."

"Who was your source?"

"A janitor."

I make a *tsk-tsk-tsk* sound. "You bribed someone?"

"Do you want to know what I learned?" Thomas asks.

A shadow looms behind me. *Every animal senses when they're about to become prey.* Serenely I ask, "What?"

"The only information was your date of birth, birth parents' names, date of arrival into foster care at age four-and-a-half, your adoptive parents' names, and the date you went to live with them at a month shy of age six."

My fingers burrow into Moose's fur. "What's wrong with that?"

"Where do I start? There was no information about how you were adopted or details on your parents, the year-and-a-half you spent in foster care, or names of the families who took you in until you were permanently placed. Foster care files are normally filled with information, doctor's physical exams, dental checks, foster parents' details, and adoption proceedings. None of that was in your file."

"And that proves what?"

He closes his notepad. "That you're a fraud from start to finish.

You've covered your tracks well. What I don't understand but want to is *why*?"

I reach for my coffee. It's cold, the almond milk now separated into yellow flecks that look like pus. I take a sip anyway.

"Sylvie, what are you hiding?"

Rubbing my hands together as if this were great fun, I say, "Absolutely nothing. But if I was hiding something, why on God's green earth would I tell you?"

"I've heard criminals are relieved after they come clean. Their blood pressure drops. They sleep like a baby."

"I'm healthy as a horse and sleep just fine."

"Then I'll appeal to your survival instinct. *Prove* to me there are no skeletons in your closet and that you're the real deal and I'll leave you out of the exposé."

"How would I do that?"

Thomas meets my gaze. "Two ways. First, tell me the truth about your past. Second, you have a show in Portland, Oregon, in one week. Do it without cheating."

I don't let myself break eye contact. "I'm not saying you're right about the *research*, but if you were, how could you be sure I didn't find a way to do any prep before the show?"

"I'd be with you the *entire* time."

My stomach flutters. "And if I don't agree?"

"I'll run with the story I already have—you're a fraud just like Victor and Doug."

"You've already decided that."

"Yeah, but I'm offering you a last chance to prove me wrong."

"And if I do everything you ask and you still don't believe?"

"At least your side of the story will be told."

His silence says he thinks there's no other choice. "Is this an attempt at blackmail? I'm not rich, so that leaves sex." *If he says yes, will I do it?*

"Don't insult me."

I stand. "It's been . . . entertaining. I'd like you to leave now. Please." Moose growls when Thomas walks by him. *Good boy.*

At the door, Thomas pauses. "Don't wait too long. This story will go to my editor soon."

Sweetly I say, "Do hold your breath."

He winks. "You'll call. People about to drown always lunge for a life ring, even if they don't trust the person who threw it."

———————

SEVEN

Thomas

As I step through the entryway of the *L.A. Times*, my cell phone comes alive with the sound of bullfrogs. I answer on the third ring, "Mom."

"Hello, dear. All things good?"

I head to the elevators and push the up button. "Yes. Busy, though."

"It's not a big deal . . . but I'm a little short this month."

I scratch the stubble on my chin. It's been days since my last shave so I could look like a grieving husband at Sylvie's show. "How short?"

"Seven hundred and fifty."

My stomach tightens but it's not like I'm surprised. "Have you paid your rent, utilities, and health insurance for the month?"

"The first two plus phone."

She'd never risk losing the ability to make calls. This month I'll have to push off my own credit card bills. "I'll transfer funds into your account. Please don't let your health insurance lapse, okay?"

"Okay. I'm sorry . . ."

The elevator arrives and I step onto the empty car, push the button for the fourth floor. "It's fine."

"I spoke with a new one. I'm getting closer—he promised. We have another appointment next week."

There's a tug-of-war between my head and heart whenever I talk to my mom. It's not a fair fight. My head always wins—it's hard to love someone who makes you a means to an end. "Okay. Gotta go."

The elevator doors slide open and I step off, take a left, and enter a vast maze of cubicles and desks. This late, there are only a few stragglers. I head down a beige-carpeted corridor past awards and articles framed in black. At the end of the hallway, my boss waves me into her corner office, where floor-to-ceiling windows look out on a cluster of palm trees that edge a busy road. Annie's chair is reclined as she finishes a call, her face and torso only partially visible behind her laptop, two monitors, a mess of files, and empty take-out containers from Pok Pok.

"Gotcha," she says into the phone. "Go get 'em."

Annie hangs up, slides her red sneakers off the desk, opens a gap between her monitors so we can have a face-to-face, then rests a pointed chin on folded hands. Clad in jeans and a navy New England Patriots football jersey, she looks like an overgrown kid playing grown-up behind her dad's desk.

"How's it going, Thomas?"

Annie is one of the youngest editors at the *L.A. Times*. She has a strong résumé. Editor of the *Brown Daily Herald* from sophomore to senior year, journalist at the *Washington Post* right out of college, and three years into her career she was part of a Pulitzer Prize–winning trio. She's also written two *New York Times* bestsellers on politics. Despite all her accomplishments, Annie is still young enough to play my wife in the photos on Facebook I posted of Katy and me. Her shoulder-length auburn hair was hidden beneath a scarf for most of the pictures, though she balked at letting me shave her eyebrows.

My nerves buzz. Despite the fact that my boss is a team player, she's still intimidating. Probably because I worked for only one newspaper before I was hired by the *L.A. Times*, went to a middle-of-the-road college in Oregon, didn't stand out among the journalists who wrote for my university paper, and after my relatively successful article on the judge, had two big missteps. The first was a story about ice skaters and their abusive choreographer that seemed like it had legs but fizzled after a few months—my fault for ignoring red flags. The second one was a huge exposé that blew up in my face.

"Spill," Annie says.

I settle onto a bright yellow Lucite chair and tell her about getting picked by Sylvie and her summons after the show.

Annie asks, "First impressions?"

"There's ice under that pretty surface."

She tips her head back and forth like a metronome then asks, "Anything else?"

"I anticipated cunning, but she's smarter than I expected."

"Do I detect a note of admiration?"

I chuckle. "Hardly. Sylvie is just another con artist and all the good ones have a natural cunning. But I get her appeal."

"So what's your next move?"

I shift on the hard plastic before giving her an answer. "I gave Sylvie an ultimatum. Do an interview about her *real* past and commit to a show without cheating to definitively prove she's not a con artist, or I'll run the story that she's a fraud."

"So you turned on the T. Holmes charm. Be still my heart." Annie grabs her fidget spinner and twirls it.

"She'll call," I say.

"And if she doesn't?"

"It's her only chance to have any control over the narrative."

My boss frowns. "Thomas, you sold me on this exposé based on evidence that Sylvie is not only a cheat, but has *giant* skeletons in her closet that will prove the psychic world's up-and-coming superstar is a *complete* fraud. To be honest, though, this is starting to feel off, like Brezen—big hat no cattle."

Heat crawls up my neck. Senator Stoddart Brezen was supposed to be the story of my career. A source told me that he'd paid underage girls for "massages" and those girls also serviced a network he'd created of powerful people both in politics and entertainment. Annie went to bat for me, got the budget I needed for private investigators, flights, hotels, the works.

I spent eight months pulling the story together but could never get that one, *irrefutable* piece of evidence that would've closed the deal. Then the linchpin, a seventeen-year-old girl who'd sworn Brezen was basically her pimp, recanted. Turned out she was attempting to blackmail Brezen, who was married, over a one-time sexual encounter. Her *friends* recanted, too. My big story imploded. Powerful people were furious. Annie almost lost her job. I'm not sure how she kept me from getting fired.

I clear my throat and tell her, "I've got truckloads on Victor and Doug."

"They're old goats—"

"With interesting backstories and almost a million followers and fans each. Plus, Sylvie fell for the people I planted in her audiences."

"One hundred percent of the time?"

I think about the plants Sylvie never picked, Daryl's text, and my own experience and equivocate. "More than fifty percent. Look, even if she doesn't agree to an interview, I can still use what worked and loop her in with the other two."

Annie chucks the spinner onto her desk. "I told you this before, I have friends who've gone to her shows—people *without* a social media presence, very private people, smart, and they've come away believers. Right now, including Sylvie in your exposé doesn't live up to the *Times'* investigative standards *and* lacks a broad appeal for our readers. The latter is no small thing. Sylvie is young and hot as hell, even if you won't admit it. Cherry on top, she's trending. You need *her* to make this a *big* story."

"You're acting like the *L.A. Times* is as prurient as the *National Enquirer*," I argue.

Annie says, "I'm going to ignore that comment because I know that you're a good journalist and have respect for our venerable newspaper. I went to bat with *my* boss for more time and a higher budget on this one, no small feat given your past two swings and misses." She leans forward. "But let's say you don't get that interview, can't prove Sylvie is a total fake. I'll still print the story without her, albeit buried in the Lifestyle section, but the people upstairs will take notice. So how do we salvage this so I don't have to demote you to obits? We both know that's a one-way street."

She's serious. A vise tightens around my skull. "I could try to find another trending female psychic?"

Annie snorts. "What about making the story more personal?"

I sit back. "As you pointed out, we're a legit paper, not the *Enquirer*."

"Legit papers allow their journalists to include personal stories where appropriate." Annie reaches for the candy jar on her desk and digs out a yellow jellybean, pops it in her mouth. "You could tell your family story. Interview your mom. Share how much she's spent on psychics over the years, how it impacted her . . . and you. Maybe even interview some of the assholes that took her money. It still wouldn't be a front-page story, but it would show my boss that you pivoted, salvaged what you could, and were willing to take a personal hit."

Clearly I'd had one scotch too many after we went to Disneyland together. I rarely talk about my dad's death or my mom's obsession with psychics, mediums, clairvoyants, and whacked-out astrologers in her twenty-plus-year pursuit to connect with Dad. "I don't think that's a great idea."

"Why not?" Annie presses.

"Because the focus of this article is the truth about psychics and mediums. It's not about me, or my dad's death, or my mother's preoccupation. And how is anyone going to believe me if I'm so clearly biased?" I reach for the candy jar, take a handful of jellybeans, then toss the green ones back in.

"Gross."

"I didn't lick them."

Annie makes a face. "Okay then." She picks up the spinner again. "How's life? You getting laid?"

I want to talk more about the exposé but let it go for the moment. The only person I know with less of a social life than me is Annie. A big Friday night for her is spent outlining her next book. It's why she was game to play my dying wife and why we both drank too much after we'd folded up the wheelchair but didn't want to head home to our empty apartments. That's not to say we have a close relationship, she's still my boss, just that we recognize the same empty space in each other.

I wag a finger in her direction. "I'll remind you that I'm the last one of us to have a girlfriend."

"At least I'm on a dating app," Annie counters.

"When's the last time you went on it to get a date?"

"I talked to someone last month. We had phone sex."

"Congratulations."

Annie grins. "Ten bucks I have you beat."

She does. "I've been busy."

"Why not go back to what's-her-name?"

"Thiel?"

"Yeah. Who names their kid a color?"

"Thiel's parents," I say. "And it's not spelled that way. She's moved on." *Almost a year ago.*

"Why?"

I pick out a few more jellybeans. "Why what?"

"Did she move on?"

I shrug. "My job got under her skin. She thought I was on the road too much and put work above time with her . . . I might've missed a vacation, and a few dinners."

"How many dinners?"

"Too many." Thiel's an industrial designer, smart, athletic, and cute as hell. She liked to play volleyball on the weekends, go to salsa clubs, and plan vacations for us. *She deserved better.*

Annie stares at me. "What?" I snip.

"You *are* fairly obsessed with work in general and you've reached new heights with this article."

"Said no editor to her journalist, ever," I joke.

"Get out of here," Annie says.

"Sylvie will call," I announce over my shoulder as I leave.

But I think we both know I might be a dead man walking.

EIGHT

•

Sylvie

"That'll be twenty-nine bucks," the delivery guy says as he hands over my sushi order.

I give him forty. "Keep the change."

"Thanks! Big Friday night plans?" he asks.

"Huge," I joke with a nod at my small order.

"A friend's band is playing at Ray's Room. They go on at midnight. You should check it out."

He's cute—shaggy brown hair, hoodie sweatshirt, and cool vibe. "Maybe."

Halfway down the front walk he turns and says, "Call a few friends. Come to the show. Vincent's band is really, really good."

I wave and shut the door. There are no friends to call. I'm not a total shut-in, I do go to Soul Cycle and hot yoga, and sometimes I even get a juice with people after class. But once they figure out what I do for a living—I used to say *entertainment* like everyone else in LA without giving specifics, but now that I'm getting recognizable, that's harder to pull off—there's a shift. Either they want to know everything about being a psychic, get weird because they think what I do is bullshit, or are afraid I can read their minds. When that happens, I switch class times or studios. I'm currently driving over an hour for my workouts, having exhausted the gyms close by. That said, I do have needs. In the past there have been a couple of casual boyfriends, but as soon as they started to get serious, I broke it off.

I put dinner on my coffee table littered with papers then sink onto the dark blue velvet couch. I live in a two-bedroom condo in Silver Lake bought with my own money. Sometimes it's still hard to believe it's mine, considering the basement apartment I shared in San Francisco and the succession of studio apartments I lived in once I'd moved to LA. Instead of cheap posters, there are a few paintings decorating my walls, and hand-built shelves filled with favorite books. I found the gently used couch and matching chairs by scouring secondhand shops, and I spent a fortune on the chandelier that hangs over an antique dining table I still need to refinish.

Moose pads over, sniffs the sushi, then cocks one brow. "You already had dinner." He licks his lips. "Fine. But only one." Opening the container, I pluck out a salmon roll and he delicately nips it from my fingers. Satisfied, Moose climbs onto the sofa and rests his sleek head on my lap. Instead of eating, I collect the pages on the coffee table—printouts from Twitter, Instagram, and Facebook—and scan them . . .

Mindy recently lost her husband to suicide and his life insurance refused to pay. Her home is in foreclosure and several of her friends are trying to help. Walter's thirteen-year-old son, Billy, is a runaway. I never considered choosing him for the last one-on-one. I don't do kids if I can possibly avoid them. Hal is on a mission to find his high school crush, Gertrude. He has only four Facebook friends so it's unlikely. Daryl was one of Thomas's plants. I rip up his page and move on to Darcy. She's the woman I almost chose instead of Theo, strike that, *Thomas*. First Balcony, Row D, Seat 37. She's a nurse who took care of her sick father. Now she's overwhelmed with guilt that his final days were filled with pain. She wonders if she should've sped up his death with morphine. *I could've helped her.*

I throw all the pages away then wrap my arms around Moose's solid bulk. That reporter has already tried and convicted me. "If he saw my notes, he'd hold a public execution," I tell Moose. My dog lifts one eyebrow then returns to snoozing. "There are plenty of people I help without knowing a single thing about them," I add into his fur. "Back when I first started, there was no need for any of this . . ." *The price of success.*

Lucas reminds me, *I believe in you.*

But Thomas Holmes doesn't. I find a copy of *Theo's* Facebook page and skim his last post:

> *I write this with a heavy heart—Katy, my wife of five years, passed away a week ago despite a valiant fight against the cancer that spread through her brain. She died peacefully. I held her hand and our cat, Christopher Robin, curled by her side . . . Katy was loved by her students, trusted by friends, and valued at the shelter where she volunteered. She never met an animal she didn't want to foster . . . I promised that I'd attempt to connect with Katy through a psychic after she was gone. I don't totally believe it's possible but I love . . . loved Katy enough to try . . .*

Beneath the post are photos of *Katy* and *Theo* at Disneyland, her head wrapped in a scarf, thin body slumped in a wheelchair, in a hospital bed with their cat curled beside her; an old photo from better days of the couple on a hike. *Shit.* I've put off calling Lucas long enough—I get up to pace while I dial and wait for him to pick up . . .

"Hey, Sylvie! We're just putting the kiddos to bed. How was the show?"

"We've got a problem . . ."

"Jiminy fucking Cricket," Lucas says when I'm done filling him in.

It's rare for him to swear. I slide down the wall, pull my knees close to my chest, and rest my thumbs against my temples to dull the throbbing. Moose comes over and settles beside me on the polished hickory floor, oblivious to the bomb dropped, timer set to detonate sometime soon. Shows are tiring—I'm used to that. The heaviness in my body now is a different kind of weariness. I unearth a Tums from my pocket, pick the fluff off, and eat it.

Lucas warns, "His story could kill the TV show."

My chest squeezes but not fast enough to catch my heart before it drops. I didn't know the show mattered so much to me until this moment. *Why?* It's a chance to reach more people, help them. Or is it to prove to my parents that I've chosen the right path? Or maybe it's just knee-jerk instinct, like a beetle caught on its back, legs thrashing even though it's doomed.

"Lucas, I'm sorry. I knew something was off."

"Not your fault," he says. "We'll figure a way out."

My throat tightens at this show of loyalty. I have a history of getting people on my side. Holly, when I was a lonely kid and needed a best friend, despite the fact that she wanted and didn't get more, romantically, from me; Danny . . . I push his wild brown curls and goofy grin away and move on to my audiences, who I also have to win over at *every* show. Lucas falls under the same category. Right from the start he worked to promote and protect me. Even the last guy I dated quickly believed in my abilities—I broke up with him when he mentioned having children someday and the old nightmare resurfaced.

I had the same bad dream throughout my childhood and it has never faded. It began with me walking up to a door that had peeling gray paint, a battered bronze knob. I knew that the door should never be opened; that on the other side monsters loomed, teeth bared, ready to strike. Still, so terrified that I lost control of my bladder, I reached for the knob. Every time I woke, the residue left was the baffling *certainty* that if I ever had my own child, she'd somehow invite death.

Lucas says, "Sylvie, you're too quiet. Do not tell me that you're considering that jerk's offer."

I see Dad's hands, calloused, weatherworn. They point at my belly button and the contrary tree inside. "Thomas doesn't expect me to say yes," I hedge.

"Syl! This is a hurdle, not a cliff. Don't you dare jump."

"Why bring up my biological parents?" This has been what my mind keeps circling back to.

"That jerk is just trying to rattle you. What did your folks say about them?"

"Not much. Their names and that they were killed in a plane crash."

"You never asked for more?"

"I asked once. Mom wouldn't talk to me for a week. It took two weeks before she'd meet my eyes. Dad said the question made her feel like she wasn't enough. I dropped it. My birth parents were dead. It didn't matter." I hold my breath, wait for Lucas to ask, *Have your biological parents' spirits ever come forward? Have you searched for them, on the other side?* He doesn't. Just then a little earthquake, the kind that happens frequently in LA, sloshes the water in my glass on the coffee table.

"So who the heck is this guy?"

I lean back and bump my head against the wall. "After I kicked him out, I did a search. He's written for the *L.A. Times* the past seven years. Before that, he wrote for *The Oregonian*. Worked his way up from Arts and Leisure to Politics to Features."

"*The Oregonian?*"

"It's the big newspaper in Portland. He started there after he graduated from the University of Oregon. He's not married. Lives in Venice Beach. I haven't had time to find much else."

"I'll hire a private investigator, he'll be on the payroll tonight. We'll find out what's in Thomas Holmes's closet."

A black fly with a metallic green body buzzes against the picture window set in the far wall. Beneath the window sits the antique desk I restored. "Why do you think my foster file was so empty?"

"Best guess? They're understaffed, disorganized. I can try to find out?"

"Don't bother." I crawl in front of Moose, curl between his front and back legs. "Lucas, the article will happen, whether or not I agree to an interview."

"Not if I hire a lawyer, threaten to sue for libel if the paper prints anything about you. We'll scare the crap out of them."

"You didn't see the look on the guy's face. For some reason this is personal. Victor and Doug are big deals—hundreds of thousands of Twitter followers, bestselling books, and Vegas shows. Thomas's article will get traction."

"You don't know that—"

"They'll survive but this exposé will destroy my career." My insides lurch. *Then who will I be?* "I don't want this to hurt *your* reputation. If the story is going to be published, tell Holmes I fooled you, too."

"Not a chance, Syl."

There's a roll of half-finished Tums under the couch. I reach for it, pop two, and chew the lemon-flavored discs into dust. It's a struggle not to gag.

"Syl?"

"Did you ever read Edgar Allan Poe's short story 'The Cask of Amontillado'?"

Lucas exhales. "Maybe in high school."

"It was one of my mom's favorites. She loved stories with morals."

"Remind me?"

"It's about an Italian noble named Montresor who decides to seek revenge against Fortunato, a man who insulted him thousands of times. Montresor lures Fortunato into a wine cellar set in the catacombs under his palazzo by offering to let him try a rare Amontillado wine. He gets Fortunato drunk, chains him to the wall, and seals the niche, brick by brick, leaving him to die."

"You're not Fortunato."

"Like I said, you didn't see that reporter's face. What I do is incredibly insulting to him." I exhale. "Montresor's final line is 'In pace requiescat!'"

Lucas asks, "Rest in peace? That's ironic considering he left Fortunato to suffer asphyxiation. What's the moral?"

"I guess don't insult someone and not expect consequences."

"You didn't do anything wrong."

"Lucas, I'm going to do that interview."

"What?"

Lucas's tone is edged with panic. Another earthquake strikes the city. This time the water in my glass doesn't move.

"I do believe in you," Lucas quickly explains. "But this guy is a *journalist*. Come on. He'll never take a leap of faith. He'll *never* understand your process."

My skin is too tight, like I've climbed into someone else's version of me. But still I don't ask the obvious question, the one I constantly avoid. *You believe in* me*, but do you believe I'm a* psychic? It doesn't matter. I down another Tums.

"Please explain why you're willing to take this kind of risk?"

I drill down to the basic question: Can Lucas make this threat disappear? He might get some information from his private investigator, but I'm a good read of human nature and Thomas didn't strike me as someone who'd cave to threats or blackmail. This story is too important to him. At most, whatever Lucas's guy digs up can inform but not protect me. And I don't think a newspaper as big as the *Los Angeles Times* is going to run from a lawsuit, either. They've been around that block way too many times.

"Sylvie?" Lucas asks.

"Hang on, I'm thinking."

So the next question is: Do I want to do something about Thomas's exposé? *Yes.* Can I? Given my history, it's clear that I have the ability to successfully manipulate. I'm not evil or anything, I just understand how useful it is to get people to think what I want them to, and I'm intuitive enough to figure out their weaknesses and what they really want, or need. When all else fails, I'm also skilled at gaining sympathy and creating empathy, two powerful weapons on the path to changing someone's perceptions and, ultimately, their mind.

Thomas will be tougher than most because he's motivated to be skeptical for the sake of his article, and because this story is somehow personal. *I need to figure out why.*

"Sylvie, you're making me nervous," Lucas presses.

"The only options I really have are to either convert Thomas to a believer or capture and kill the story. I can do that." With that, I hang up. Lucas tries me again but I send his call to voicemail and do a quick search on my laptop then pull Thomas's card out, dial his number.

"Thomas Holmes speaking."

"It's Sylvie Young. Is the deal you offered still on the table?"

"Yes. If you're willing to tell me the truth about your past *and* do the Oregon show without cheating."

"And if I prove to you that I'm not a fraud?"

"Then I'll keep you in the story but won't condemn you as a con artist," Thomas replies.

It strikes me that everything in life always seems to boil down to an origin story. "It's a deal . . . if you agree to one detour on the way to Portland."

"What's that?" he asks, his tone wary.

"My hometown, High River, is an hour from the city. You wanted to talk to my parents, so we'll drive out, have dinner with them." *Time with my parents, especially Mom, will throw Thomas off balance and garner sympathy.*

"Agreed," Thomas says, unable to hide a note of surprise.

"Meet me at Union Station tomorrow, two p.m."

"Why not fly to Oregon?"

"Moose is too big. Plus, I love the train. It's relaxing. You can interview me during the ride and make sure I don't do any off-limits research." I hear papers rustling.

"My calendar has your show for next Sunday. Why go a week early?"

I don't know how long it will take me to get what I want. "Don't be late." Heart hammering, I hang up. "Don't think," I mutter. "Pack."

I pull out a suitcase and fill half with Moose's food, the other half with clothes for my show, casual stuff, and sneakers for a run. In the back of my closet, there's a ratty blue duffel filled with the clothes I first brought to SF—hiking boots, jeans, a fleece, red down vest, rain shell. They haven't been worn in a long time, but April in High River is variable. It could be sunshine and sixties or pissing rain and in the thirties. *Will the trees be in bloom?*

My father's deep voice rumbles. *We plant pears for our heirs.* It's an old saying. Some pear orchardists' varieties can take up to twelve years to bear marketable fruit. Their trees are planted for future generations to enjoy and profit.

I'm Wess and Hana Young's only child, their heir. But I left. They probably won't let me in the door. *I'm counting on it.*

NINE

Thomas

Chris won't look at me. The only time she's subjected to her animal carrier is for a vet visit, and I haven't taken her for a long time. Now she's at Union Station in downtown LA after a stop-and-go Uber ride and the indignity of the bright pink carrier Annie gave me after she rehomed her leaky Chihuahua.

I drop my backpack and tote and sink onto a bench alongside the rails, balance the carrier on my knees, and reach in to scratch under Chris's chin until she grudgingly purrs. Half Siamese, half tabby, her long orange-and-white fur is matted in spots, thin in others, and she's lost more weight, hipbones clearly visible. The last thing she needs is a long train ride. "I'm really sorry," I tell her. "I tried to find a cat sitter but it was late notice."

My phone vibrates with the roar of a lion. It's Annie's ringtone. "Hey, boss."

"I'm not going to change my mind," Annie says, all business.

"Sylvie called."

"And?"

"I'm waiting for her at the train station."

"You lovebirds running away together?"

"Funny. If the journalism thing doesn't work out, you should be a stand-up comic. We're heading to her parents' home in High River, then on to Portland to spend some time before her next show."

Annie whistles. "You're serious. Unlimited access?"

"We'll see."

She laughs. "I guess you did lay on the charm. Go get your story."

"Will do. Talk soon." I spy Sylvie walking toward me, gargantuan dog by her side.

"You brought your cat?" she asks.

I slide the carrier off my knees then stand. "You brought your dog?"

She pointedly looks at the green and yellow service jacket on Moose then at Chris's pink carrier. When her beast steps close, Chris hisses. "Call him back," I say. Sylvie snaps her fingers and the dog returns to her side like a witch's minion. They're an arresting pair. Despite my very real fears, I recognize that Moose is a handsome creature. Gleaming black fur with a white patch on his broad chest, perked ears, perfect posture. Sylvie, dark hair in a low ponytail, dressed down in jeans, a white T-shirt, blue blazer, and Converse sneakers, still draws every eye.

Brakes squeal as the Amtrak Coast Starlight pulls into the station. "Have you spoken to your parents?"

"No. Surprise is the best tactic."

Sylvie's expression is impossible to read. "Care to elaborate?"

"Nope."

"All aboard," an Amtrak employee shouts.

"What's your seat number?" I ask. "The sleeper cars were sold out."

Sylvie chuckles. "I got the last one. Come by after you find your seat."

I hold out my hand. "Your computer, tablet if you brought one, and phone."

"Pardon?"

"Rules of engagement."

Her eyes twinkle. "Is this a war?"

"If you want to prove you're the real deal, then your agent and the Internet are off the table." From a contact at TixMix, whom I gifted a case of wine, I know they send out the names of ticket holders to Sylvie's agent two days before her shows. I couldn't crack the other ticket vendors, but my guess is they follow a similar schedule. It's my turn to smile. She slides a laptop and iPad from her suitcase, gives them to me along with the phone from her purse.

Hands on her slim hips, Sylvie asks, "Satisfied?"

"No." I go through the suitcase, try to ignore underwear and bras (they're black and lacy), check her purse, too. She has about a dozen rolls of antacids between the two bags. Maybe all the lies she tells to her audiences have gotten to her.

"Want to frisk me next?"

I match her light tone. "No thanks. Anything in your pockets?"

She pats them down. "We good?"

"How big is your sleeping compartment?"

There's genuine shock on her face. "You want to share my room?"

"If I leave you alone, you'll find a way to contact your agent, production team, or parents."

"Are you always this suspicious?"

Her smile is winsome. This is *her* version of psychological warfare. "It's up to you. My exposé is good to go. We can skip this if it's going to be a charade." My pulse quickens but I do my best to hide that this is a massive bluff.

Sylvie steps onto the train. "All aboard, Doubting Thomas," she says over her shoulder.

I follow her through a narrow corridor. Private compartments are tiny, with two seats facing each other divided by slim tables. "Why are you calling me that?"

"Someone skipped Sunday school," she admonishes.

"Proud atheist."

"*Doubting* Thomas was one of the apostles. He missed the first time Jesus appeared after his crucifixion and wouldn't believe the other apostles until he saw the Son of God for himself. Jesus reappeared and Thomas became a believer. To which Jesus said, 'Thomas, because thou hast seen me, thou hast believed: blessed are they that have not seen, and yet have believed.'"

"I've read about your impressive memory."

"Is that a compliment?"

I shrug one shoulder. "Sure. So, are you comparing yourself to Jesus?"

She chuckles. "Not a chance. I'm just pointing out that, like the apostle Thomas, you don't have the ability to believe anything you can't touch. It's sad, really."

"Save your pity for the people you con," I mutter, uncertain why a crack about my lack of imagination rankles, annoyed that I let it show.

We reach Sylvie's compartment. Thankfully, the sleepers are larger, but with her giant dog, two adults, and a cat, it'll be plenty tight. There's a blue vinyl couch along one wall divided from a chair on the opposite wall by a rectangular table, a minuscule bathroom that converts into a shower wedged in a corner. At six-four, there's no way I'd fit into that shower. The long window between the couch and the seat is table height and rises to wrap a few feet over the top of the sleeping compartment so passengers can see the sky.

Sylvie closes the door, slides her bag under the couch, then sits. Moose hops onto the couch beside her. Seated, he still towers. I set Chris's carrier on the table, wedge my bag into the small spot left under the couch, fill her litter box, slide it beside the toilet, then take the chair across from Sylvie. She makes a face at the litter box. "What? It's not like Moose won't need to relieve himself at some point."

"And when he does, he'll let me know and wait for the next station stop." Sylvie folds her hands over one knee. "So. Here we are. Let's start with an easy question to crack the ice. Why Christopher Robin?"

I play along. "Obviously, *Winnie the Pooh*."

"'Sometimes the smallest things take up the most room in your heart.'"

I'm not surprised Sylvie can quote a popular children's book. Still, there's a wistful look on her face. My guess is that most con artists who've been caught probably wish they could return to simpler times. *What about that wonderland quote?* I dismiss it. That's what these people do—throw out cultural touchstones to hook their prey.

Sylvie nods at Chris. "Are you planning to leave her in there for eighteen hours?"

Moose's eyes are glued to the pink carrier like he's waiting for his next meal to step out of it. His jaws are big enough to wrap around Chris's entire body. He could snap her neck with one shake of his giant head.

"How can I get you to write nice things in your article if my dog kills your ancient cat?" Sylvie asks.

"She's not that old."

Sylvie's eyebrows rise a fraction. "It'll be okay. Promise. Let her out."

The train lurches. We roll out of the station. There's not much choice, so I unzip the carrier. Chris climbs out, pads across the table, sits in front of the window, watches the buildings slide by. Moose silently puts two paws on the floor.

"Did you really get her as a kitten?"

I don't take my eyes off Cujo. "Yeah. But from a local shelter."

"You lied to me about your cat, too? Where's your journalistic integrity?"

I grunt. If she's trying to compare a lie about the provenance of my cat to bilking money from people who can't afford to lose it, clearly I'm on the right side of the line.

Moose now has four feet on the floor. "Call him back." Sylvie ignores me. Moose creeps forward. Chris spins like she has eyes in the back of her head, one paw raised to strike. My mother had her declawed as a kitten. Maybe that's why the dog doesn't blink. I prepare to get mauled. Moose edges nearer until their noses almost touch then backs away like he and Christopher Robin have reached a silent agreement. Chris walks to the far side of the table, the sharp bones of her hips painfully visible, and drops onto Sylvie's lap, curls into a ball. I let out the breath I've been holding.

"You okay?" Sylvie asks with a little smile.

"I'm fine."

She runs light fingers along Chris's bony back and my cat, typically dismissive of strangers, actually purrs.

"Animals like me," Sylvie says. "So I can't be that bad, right?"

I push record on my phone. "Tell me about your childhood . . ."

TEN

Sylvie

I don't have much of a plan yet. Right now I just need to get a bead on this guy. He blushed a little when I asked if he was going to share my room. Buried under the surface are manners—probably raised by a single mother. And he loves his cat so much that he's in denial about her life expectancy. When I run my hand down his cat's side, I can feel how old age has thinned her fur and the jutting of her fragile ribs. Gently, I tickle beneath Chris's chin and she purrs louder. A lump lodges in my throat. *She's holding on for him.*

When I was a little kid, the idea of loving an old pet was alien. Puppies were everything—wiggly, uncoordinated, the epitome of cute. Then my first dog's face sugared, his back end stiffened, and I loved him so much, my heart shattered when we found him dead beneath our porch. For months the fact that he'd been alone when he died, without my arms around him, haunted me.

Thomas watches, waits. I chuckle and say, "Okay, childhood in a nutshell. My parents own an orchard. It's been in our family for generations. I actually went to the same schools my folks did as kids, got solid A's all the way through and my teachers liked me. Skipped class a handful of times but never got caught. Spent four years on the swim team, I was a diver to avoid the grueling practices. Lazy or smart?" I ask with an exaggerated wink. "Let your readers decide. During the summers, I climbed trees, rode my bike, had a vegetable garden. I grew green beans, eggplant, zucchini, and tomatoes. Whatever we didn't eat, I helped Mom can for winter. There were lots of chores— no allowance, just the satisfaction of a job well done. Got my first *real* job at sixteen. I worked in an ice cream shop. My favorite flavor was mint chocolate chip. Sugar cone. No sprinkles."

"Fascinating."

I shrug. "Typical boring childhood in a small town."

"Huh." Casually Thomas asks, "Are you still friends with anyone from school?"

I tug my hair free from a ponytail, take off my blazer, and get comfortable. My T-shirt is pretty tight but Thomas doesn't look at my breasts. *Disciplined or disinterested? Time will tell.* "Seems like you're the kind of guy who does his homework," I say, "so why don't *you* tell me?"

Thomas glances at his notes. "I got in touch with half of your class of seventy-seven kids. Holly McConnell was the only *close* friend I could find. Two guys said they'd casually dated you—nothing more than a few months. You broke it off in both cases. The rest of the people I reached said they didn't really know you."

I trace shapes on the plastic table with nails cut short, painted black from my last show. "I wasn't popular."

"Hard to believe."

"Why?"

"Pretty usually means popular."

It's an opening. I ask, "Would you have dated me in high school?"

Thomas jots something down in his notebook. "You wouldn't have given me a second look. I was a yearbook geek."

"You don't think I liked smart guys?"

He looks up from his notes. "Only if they could help with your homework."

Dead end. "Like I told you, I didn't need help getting A's." I consider cutting my losses but can't help asking, "So what else did Holly say?"

"Other than your biological parents' names and how they *supposedly* died?"

He's already barked up that tree. Why push the narrative? My guess is that it's a rookie move to affect my balance. "Anything else?"

"Huh. Holly said that you took off after high school. Ghosted her."

Thomas says *huh* when he's recalibrating. "She forgot the part about trying to kiss me every time I slept over." Thomas actually blushes. "We did go to senior prom together. I got drunk, finally kissed her back. It was actually nice—she had really full lips. There was some rolling around in bras and undies, but in the end it wasn't for me." Again, his face reddens. I'm on a roll. *Two can play this game—and I'm better at it.*

"Dropping people seems to be a theme in your life," Thomas notes.

Warning bells clang. "How so?"

"Danny."

For a moment I forget to breathe. The origin story I tell my audiences about the tarot reader in Haight-Ashbury, my first customer, Bethany, and the old guy, Arthur, is true. But I never mention that the tarot reader wasn't a stranger—he was Danny.

The train rolls by a field of wheat that sways in the wind. I imagine I'm a single stalk, bending but never breaking. "How'd you find out about him?"

Thomas leans in a fraction. "The same woman still owns that magic shop in Haight-Ashbury. Gigi remembers you fondly—a true believer. She remembers Danny, too."

Taking a moment to trace the bumps of Chris's prominent vertebrae, I say, "I would hope Gigi remembers me. One day I told her she needed to rush home, that her husband was in danger. She found him on the floor, heart attack, called an ambulance, and he lived."

"You said he was in *danger*. He could've been standing on a ladder, using a sharp knife or a saw. You didn't say *heart attack*."

I smile. "Yet still, Gigi is a believer."

"But also a smart businesswoman. You were young, attractive, and convincing—a good way to drum up business for her shop."

"I *was* young and attractive? But at twenty-four I'm over the hill? Not sure where you learned your interview technique, Thomas, but insulting the subject doesn't win her over."

"What I did learn of interest from Gigi," Thomas says, ignoring my attempt to both shame him and flirt, "was that you began your career with a partner."

My stomach drops but I keep my voice steady. "Danny was an acquaintance. Our partnership didn't last long enough to mention. Where'd you find him?"

"I haven't. But I'm still looking."

My pulse slows. "If you do locate him, please let me know. I'd love to catch up."

Thomas nips his lower lip. "Huh. Since you never mention Danny, I assumed he knows that you're a con artist and has dirt on you."

Now I know Thomas bites his lip before he says something mean. "You're way off base, but wherever he is, I'm sure Danny's doing fine. He's a survivor."

"Takes one to know one?"

"Not really. Danny had a rough childhood. Drug-addicted dad, mom took off, lots of shuffling between relatives. I had two loving parents, three meals a day, birthday parties, Christmas with loads of presents, even Easter egg hunts in the orchard. Couldn't have asked for more, really. So. Shall we move on?"

"I'd like to hear how you and Danny met."

I shrug good-naturedly. "Sure. We met at a youth hostel when I first got to San Francisco, agreed to share a studio apartment near Golden Gate Park. Two futons, an illegal hot plate, and a rusty mini-fridge. Danny didn't mind that it was a dump. He always said *every dream had a price.*"

"What was *his* dream?"

I pretend to think about it. "If I remember right, it was to save up money, move to LA, and become an actor. He never graduated high school, worked a bunch of low-paying jobs, so it was slow going. My options weren't much better. As you know, I was a waitress. I can give you the address of the restaurant in case you want to check it out? Maybe my old boss still works there. Vincent. Spoiler alert, he'll tell you I was a crappy server. I once delivered the wrong meals to every customer at a table for twelve. In my defense, once the red sauce went on, a lot of dishes looked the same."

"How'd you and Danny start working together?"

He's a dog with a bone. I consider then decide to go with the truth. "One night Danny came home with a deck of used tarot cards and a battered paperback on how to read them. He thought it'd be a great way for him to make some fast cash." A memory leaps forward and I'm back in the dingy apartment we once shared . . .

———————

We sit on the cracked concrete floor and spread out ornate black and gold cards. I toss Danny the paperback. "Read out a description of each one and I'll organize the cards?"

Cheeks red, Danny hands the book back. "You read. I'll set them up."

"Danny?"

He looks away, says, "I can read. I just need a little time to flip the letters."

"My friend Holly has dyslexia. A teacher in third grade helped her figure it out."

"There were forty kids in my third grade class. My teacher just tried to survive." Danny finally meets my gaze. "You probably think it's stupid, me wanting to be an actor, but Tom Cruise has the same thing and it didn't stop him."

I hold out the half-empty wine bottle I swiped from the restaurant and Danny takes a gulp, passes it back. "You're better looking than Tom Cruise with loads more charisma."

Dimples flashing, Danny says, "You do know I like guys, right?"

I give his hand a squeeze then open the book and start to read. "There are twenty cards that represent a big journey or message. Want to just use those?"

"Simplify. I like it." Danny separates the cards while I go through a short explanation of each and their dual meanings.

"What's that one mean again?" Danny asks, pointing to the first card—The Devil.

Without consulting the book, I can tell him, "Upright, means attachment or addiction. Reversed, releasing limited beliefs."

"How do you remember this stuff so easily?"

"I have an eidetic memory."

"In English?"

"I can recall most everything I read, like a photograph in my brain."

"That's a freaking superpower!" *He sweeps the cards up and shuffles.* "My superpower is that I can improvise." *He pulls three cards, pretends to be deep in thought.* "Sylvie, you have an artist's soul, a painter's vision, and a heart of gold. The cards say that you've broken with your country girl roots to follow a different path . . ."

"As a shitty waitress who gets pathetic tips and has no future," *I half joke.*

Danny suddenly gets serious. "Don't worry, Syl, I've got your back. Always. We'll get out of this dump together . . ."

————

"Lost in the past?" Thomas prods.

"Danny and I had some good times." *He was kind when I desperately needed a friend.*

"I thought you were just acquaintances."

I ignore the barb and gently massage Chris's bony hips. "Danny practiced tarot for a week, then chose Haight-Ashbury to set up shop. It's a lively part of the city—singers busking, funky shops that sell everything from weed to trendy clothes, and great restaurants that draw from the more affluent neighborhoods in the city. He convinced Gigi to let him work in front of her store."

"How?"

"Danny had a contagious grin and nobody could weave a better story."

"How'd you get dragged into Danny's scheme?"

"It wasn't some big con," I explain. "Danny was just charging for *entertainment.* And for the record, I never asked to be pulled in. The part of my origin story about being on my way home from waitressing and needing to get off my feet is true. Danny dared me to sit at his table, pretend I was a psychic. Bethany was my first customer."

"What'd Danny do when Bethany freaked out?"

"Told me that I was a natural."

Thomas leans back, crosses his arms, the picture of a judge who has already decided the verdict. "So you agreed to work as a psychic?"

"Actually, I didn't think it was a good idea."

But Danny persisted . . .

"Do you see a bright future waitressing? Let's make some quick money and both go to LA, become actors. The first one to make it helps the other one. Deal?"

He grabbed my hand, pumped it. "Partners, no take backs."

I laughed. "What are you, four? Okay. It's a deal."

"Eventually, I agreed," I admit to Thomas.

"What changed your mind?"

"I'd come to San Francisco for a different life, and working as a psychic was different." I trace the jagged scar that runs the length of my left palm.

"How'd you get that?" Thomas asks.

"Cut myself on some piece of farm equipment when I was little." I look at him from beneath my lashes. "There's no big secret here. Danny convinced me to join him. I still took some waitressing shifts, but word of mouth spread fast and within a month we had a line of customers." *Mostly for me.*

Thomas scribbles a few notes. "Gigi said that Danny went down to LA with you to meet Lucas Haughter. What happened at that meeting?"

"Danny took the free flight then decided he wanted to pursue acting instead. End of story."

"So why'd you lose touch?" Thomas presses.

I shrug. "It was a normal fork in the road. We were kids. Never saw Danny on TV or in a movie, so I guess he got tired of going out on auditions and left the City of Dreams."

But that's not what happened. There are people in life you wish you could reach back for, like Danny, drag by the scruff to the present, even if they hate you now, for another chance. Sadly, that's not how it works. And if I had that chance, there's no guarantee that I wouldn't do the same thing. I was a kid who couldn't go home, had no options, and my future was waitressing, garage studio apartments, and never having enough money to make ends meet. Maybe that's why there are no do-overs in life. You can't survive if you have to replay situations, hurt the people you love again and again.

The truth is, I screwed Danny over.

ELEVEN

Thomas

It's clear Sylvie is leaving something out. I glance at the notes on my phone. "Okay. Let's go backward. What do you remember from before you were adopted?"

"Not much. Some bunk beds, the comforters were red, cracked vinyl seats in the back of a car, and driving to my new home in High River." Sylvie has a dimple in her right cheek when she grins. "Hana and Wess were on the front step, waiting like it was Christmas and I was the gift under their tree."

"Doesn't it seem strange that you can't recall anything before that?"

"Not really. How much do you remember from when you were a toddler? Are those even your memories or are they stories your parents told you or ones you stitched together from old photos and home movies?" Sylvie shrugs. "I didn't have that."

I drum my fingers against the cold window. "I get where you're coming from. But you have an eidetic memory."

"Maybe there was nothing worth remembering."

"I'd think your birth mother and father are worth remembering."

She twists her hair into a bun, secures it with an elastic band. One lock falls free, frames the side of her face. "You can't have it both ways, Thomas. According to you, they don't exist."

"I said there's no evidence that they died in a plane crash. As for their existence, it's sort of a biological imperative. So far, though, I haven't been able to find out anything about them."

Sylvie dramatically rolls her eyes. "In case I didn't make myself clear before, I don't believe you."

I twirl my pen around a knuckle. "Did you ever try to contact them?"

Sylvie shifts on the couch then crosses her legs, taps her thighs. "No."

"Why not? If they died in a plane crash, then they're on *the other side*, right?"

Her gaze hardens. "Right."

"So go ahead, reach out now so we can clear up this part of your backstory—I'm all ears." Sylvie is silent. I throw up my hands. "Fine. Obviously you aren't capable of telling the truth."

"Wess and Hana are the only parents I've ever known," she finally says. "It's disloyal to make contact with my birth parents."

"Really? That's what you're going with?"

Sylvie scowls. "Plenty of adopted kids decide not to reach out to their biological parents. Just because mine are dead doesn't make the act feel any less like a betrayal."

I shake my head. "Occam's razor."

"Meaning?"

"The most obvious answer is the correct one. Your entire career is smoke and mirrors. You don't have the ability to contact anyone."

"Connecting with people who've passed is not like dialing someone on the phone. It's never a sure thing."

I chuckle. "Nice deflection. I'm sure it takes a very special person. That's why you charge so much for the honor."

"Sarcasm is the poor man's wit."

"Guilty."

Sylvie abruptly stands. "I'm starving. Let's get dinner." Without waiting, she walks out the door and there's no choice but to follow her.

The dining car is empty, tables with white tablecloths set, battery-powered candles in their centers lit. We eat in silence except for the scrape of our forks and knives and the waiter's occasional questions. We both order the chicken and mashed potatoes and skip the red wine. Neither of us wants to be off our game. When I reach for a roll just as Sylvie does, our fingers brush and we both withdraw like we've touched fire.

Once we're done eating, I pull out my phone and set it on the table. "Let's switch gears, okay?" Sylvie shrugs a shoulder, noncommittal. "Can you read *me* right now?"

Her smile doesn't reach her eyes. "Since you like the analogy, think of me as a vampire. I can only read a person if they invite me inside."

In this moment she appears utterly sincere, vulnerable. She really is a *very* good actress. The waiter clears our dishes. Sylvie asks for a container for her leftover mashed potatoes. "Moose likes them?" I ask.

"They're for Chris."

"Don't bother. She's an incredibly picky eater."

Sylvie dabs her lips with the cloth napkin then sits back. "Did I ever make a *real* connection for the people you planted?"

The muscles along my neck tighten. "Look, I have proof you research your audiences. Nothing you say can wipe that evidence away."

"My shows are filled with people who desperately need to hear from someone so they can move on with their lives. If I fail, they go home, stuck in the past."

"Is that a justification?"

Sylvie spins the sapphire infinity ring on her index finger. "So it's black and white to you?"

"Yes."

"I'm not saying I do, but are you certain I research *all the time?*"

"I'm certain unless you can *prove* differently."

Sylvie slightly tips her head, like she's considering my words. "What if I told you that sometimes I draw a blank?"

My pulse ratchets up a notch and I lean forward. "Why?"

"Like I've said before, what I do isn't an exact science. But when I know something about an audience member, it allows me to build a bridge—"

"A bridge?"

"Bits of information about the person I'm reading that let me cross from the *here and now* to the *other side* and attract the deceased, then go further."

"That's one way of rationalizing it. Another is that you hook people in. Excitement gets them to overshare. They think you're psychic when all you've done is memorize Facebook, Instagram, and Twitter posts. That's not called a bridge. It's fraud."

"Despite my memory, I'm not a computer," Sylvie says as she weaves her hair into a braid. "It'd be impossible to do that for an entire audience."

She plays with her hair when she's backed into a corner. "So you make sure you have a handful of big hits and the rest? You throw out enough ambiguous information to snag a few people then read their reactions to make sure you're headed in the right direction. When you strike a nerve, you amplify."

"What about Kelly and Rose at the last show?"

"What about them?"

"A woman I *might've* known something about, *unbeknownst to me*, gave Kelly her ticket," Sylvie says, choosing each word carefully. "I had *no* idea Kelly would be there. How could I? And no clue she'd attended a previous show."

"You recognized her face."

Sylvie shakes her head. "I didn't, though I wasn't surprised an audience member said I'd talked about a specific date. Sometimes dates pop into my mind during an appearance. I share them. But how could I know that Kelly's sister, Rose, was going to commit suicide on that date?"

"Coincidence. Like you said, you throw out dates all the time."

Sylvie leans in. This close I can see three light freckles beneath her left eye. She asks, "What about what I wrote on my arm—*Kel, just because they were yours doesn't mean it was your fault*—or that old song I hummed?"

I ignore the chill creeping down my neck. "There are mentalists in Vegas who make millions doing the impossible night after night. Again, you'll have to *prove* it if you want me to jump on your bandwagon."

We eat our ice cream sundaes in silence then return to the compartment. Thankfully, Moose hasn't eaten Chris while we were gone. They're curled up on the couch a few feet apart like old friends. Sylvie feeds Moose. I pour Chris's expensive, organic kibble into a bowl. She won't even dignify it with a sniff. Sylvie holds up the container of mashed potatoes. "She won't eat it." She ignores me, opens the container, and puts it on the floor. Chris pads over, sniffs, then digs in, eats half the potatoes before taking a break. Even though I know this was a lucky guess, the stupid hairs on my arms rise.

TWELVE

———•———

Sylvie

I yawn then stretch my arms overhead. "Time for bed."

After brushing my teeth in the bathroom, I change into white flannel pajamas and unbutton the top two buttons in the hope that Thomas will notice. I'm not sure I can actually seduce him, or even if I could go through with it if he takes the bait. But I need options. My reflection in the mirror looks calm, except for the eyes. They search for a way out of this mess.

I am aware that *everything* I say and do during a show can be explained away. Even Kelly and Rose. My fears find the cracks and rush in. The note I wrote on my arm was pretty ambiguous. *What about the song?* I can't explain that one. But are the songs and messages nothing more than incredible coincidences combined with a subject's intense desire? *Is Thomas right that I'm rationalizing fraud?* My reflection in the mirror blurs, like I'm losing definition, beginning to disappear. My heart doubles its beat. *No.* I'm the real deal *and* I help people. And if I use research when I can't make a connection? It doesn't matter as long as my audience believes and gets closure. *I'm one of the good guys.*

When I step out of the bathroom, Thomas is hunched over his backpack. He absentmindedly pushes a lock of hair from his eyes. For a split second I see the person, not the adversary. He's cute, a little awkward, which I'm usually drawn to. We have to sidestep so he can get into the bathroom. I make sure our hips touch. He instantly draws back like I'm poison.

Moose snuggles beside me on the couch as we listen to rustles punctuated by thumps and curses. Thomas is way too big to get changed in the tiny bathroom. I'm glad it's uncomfortable. He comes out in a T-shirt and plaid boxers. He has lean, muscular legs—a runner, or cyclist. There's a small tattoo on the inside of his right arm. TDH. I would've put money against him being the type for ink.

The lower couch serves as the bottom bunk. The upper bunk is a plank released from above the couch with a thin plastic mattress. The train provides cotton sheets and comforters. "I'm the top bunk?" Thomas asks.

"Unless you want to sleep with my dog." The look of concern on his face makes me laugh. Moose growls when Thomas stands on the bottom of my bed to make his own, then hoists his lanky frame up. *Good dog.*

He bangs his head on the ceiling. "Shit."

I hand Chris up to him before she can make a leap that might end badly, then slide into bed. Moose settles at my feet, curling into an impossibly small ball. His breath slows then turns into snores. "Just so you know, that's not me."

"If I have to get up in the middle of the night to use the bathroom, will Moose bite my leg?"

"Not sure."

The sky through the compartment's window is a midnight blue blanket dotted with stars. We must be in Northern California by now, beyond light pollution. "On summer nights, when I was a kid, I'd lie in the hammock on the back deck, wonder if my *real* parents ever looked down from heaven. If I saw a shooting star, I thought it was a message that they were watching over me."

A star falls, its silver tail scraping along the sky's dark blue fabric. I close my eyes and the shimmer remains on my lids for a few seconds then fades away. The train rocks, Moose snores, there's an occasional squeak of wheels on rails. Thomas is quiet for so long that I start to think he's asleep.

"Have your abilities been the same since childhood?" Thomas finally asks.

My nerves flicker a yellow alert. "Like I say in my origin story, I didn't know about my abilities until San Francisco."

"How is that possible?"

I don't know. "Every psychic has an origin story when their gift appears."

"So as a kid you never knew if the telephone was going to ring? When someone was sick or died? Where to find misplaced car keys or a lost dog?"

A memory creeps forward. Icy water stipples gooseflesh. A shiver wrings my spine. "I didn't grow up in the kind of house where magical thinking was encouraged. Early to bed, early to rise, get your chores done, team sports, church once, sometimes twice a week, and only *mom-approved* TV shows and movies."

"Hard to believe," Thomas presses.

His relentless questions make me feel like roadkill getting picked apart by vultures. I roll onto my side, curl up, arms around my legs. "I get it. You don't believe *anything* I say."

"You lied about Katy."

"So did you." Thomas is silent. "I didn't get anything from the wedding ring you gave me. Like it'd never been worn. So I built a bridge, hoping to get to the other side . . . to *help* you."

"I borrowed the engagement ring from a jeweler."

The unfairness makes my skin burn. "And you're surprised I couldn't use it effectively?"

"Whatever you need to tell yourself."

"The photographs? The ones from Disneyland?"

"My boss, Annie."

"The apple doesn't fall far from the tree."

Thomas scoffs, "You don't exactly stand on moral high ground."

I swing out of bed, use the edge of the top bunk to haul myself inches from his face. "Why do you hate me?" He recoils. In the moonlight his eyes are the dark blue-green of the deep sea, where the most dangerous predators hunt. Moose presses against my thigh. His low growl vibrates. Maybe he *would* eat Thomas's leg.

Thomas tries to sit up, bumps his head, swears under his breath, then manages to get his elbow up, rests his head awkwardly in an open palm. "I don't hate you."

"Liar. If you want the truth, then have the courtesy to tell it." I slide back down, burrow beneath my covers, heart pounding. Silence stretches taut.

Thomas finally asks, "What do you want to know?"

"The wedding band you wore. It wasn't new, it had a history."

"How do you know?"

"It was worn, scratched." *There's a man . . . he says to tell her she was right about the rain.* "It belonged to the man who pushed forward, who wanted to apologize about the rain."

Thomas clears his throat. "It was my father's. But you already know that."

"Suddenly you believe?"

"Not likely. You had enough time to dive into my past before we met at the station."

"All I know is that you grew up in Portland and your job history."

". . . My father died in a car accident when I was eleven."

"Was it raining?"

"Yes. But that means nothing. Plenty of people die in the rain. His car skidded on an old bridge, broke through guardrails. He was killed when it struck the water. For the past twenty-one years, my mother has been trying to contact him—on the *other side*. She's blown through all her savings."

I was right. This is personal. "The younger spirit with the leather journal?"

"I told you, no idea."

I don't need to see Thomas's face to tell he's lying. Hope, dormant for much of our conversations, pads out of its cave, sniffs the air. *Find out why. Use it.*

"I don't hate you, Sylvie. I hate what you do."

"I help people."

"Have you ever considered that by giving the easy answers people want, you're stealing their chance to come to terms with loss, grief, and themselves?"

"Have you ever considered that you're the vampire? You tear people's lives apart for a story and you don't care about who you hurt in that process. And FYI? I hate what you do, too."

I beckon Moose, wrap my arms around him, follow the rhythm of his breathing, and summon sleep . . .

I'm a little kid standing on a street that's tree-lined, leaves the size of dinner plates painted brilliant shades of orange and gold. Ornamentals fill bark islands. Red geraniums edge manicured lawns. The air is warm and sweet with the scent of the white roses planted in front of a forest green bungalow. I walk on . . .

Around the corner, there's a second-floor addition being built on the bones of a seventies-style shingled ranch house. This street is dotted with smaller homes. I hesitate then take a tentative step then another. I pass the second house on the right. Boone, a dog with floppy red ears, stands behind a chain-link fence, tail between his legs. An invisible hand in the small of my back pushes me on. The third house on the left is where the Baileys live. Their oldest daughter babysits. The fourth is home to Vince and Ted, who just got married. Fifth on the right is the Haycoxes . . .

I need to stop. Another step . . . another . . . another . . . "Stop!" I sit up fast, heart thumping, and peer into the dark to get my bearings. Thomas hangs down over my bunk, so close I can smell the mint of his toothpaste. "What?"

"You okay?"

"I'm fine." I roll my back to him. He returns to his bunk, bumps his head, swears, then settles. My pulse slows but I'm uneasy. I've had the same dream before. It started when I moved to San Francisco. But I've never *continued* down that street and can't shake the feeling that there was something waiting at the end of it . . . something unspeakable.

THIRTEEN

·

Thomas

In the morning, Sylvie won't engage beyond short answers and we eat breakfast mostly in silence. Maybe she's embarrassed about the nightmare. I watch when she takes Moose off the train at a stop for a quick bathroom break—she didn't lie, her dog is a pro at this train business. Before we arrive in Portland, Sylvie changes into jeans, a dark blue fleece, and old hiking boots.

"Is that the dress code for High River?" I ask.

She shrugs.

Once in Portland, we Uber to the rental car place, a Hertz set in a low-slung outdoor mall, load into a white Suburban, chosen, I assume, to accommodate Moose's size. The silent act continues as we head east, leaving the many covered bridges that span the Willamette River that bisects Portland behind. The Columbia River now stretches on our left, miles of wide, dark waters. A brisk wind sends April's slate-colored clouds skidding across the sky. Now and then there are peeks of blue. Evergreens dot the steep hillsides to the right of the highway, impossibly rooted in scree fields. We pass Multnomah Falls. The massive waterfall, fueled by winter snow and rain, drops over a rock ledge then pounds into a pool at the bottom of a deep ravine. It's beautiful but savage.

I pull out my phone. "Should we call your parents?"

"I told you, surprise is best."

"Why?"

She switches lanes so a Tesla riding our bumper can pass. "If they know I'm coming, they might not open the door."

"That's a bit dramatic, don't you think?"

"Did you ever do anything that let your parents down?"

"I stole once. Dad drove me back to the store, made me return what I'd taken and apologize to the owner." I almost tell Sylvie what happened after I came home, but I haven't shared that I had a big brother, or that he was in the car with my dad and died, too. She's adept at mining for weakness and manipulating. I don't want to give her more ammo than necessary.

"Do you remember what your dad said?"

A strong wind buffets the SUV. I grip the handrail as we're pushed sideways. Waves break on the river's surface, creating swirls of icy spray. "He didn't punish me, which was a surprise. He was *disappointed* and that was worse. Did you ever let *your* parents down?"

Sylvie speeds up, changes lanes. "The last thing Mom said when I left home was that there's a place in hell for ungrateful children."

I whistle low. "Wow. She's religious?"

Sylvie snorts.

"Do you believe in heaven and hell?"

"No."

"Huh. How can you have faith in what you do, connect with people *on the other side*, if you don't believe in heaven?"

"Those words, *the other side*, are necessary to communicate with my audience. I have no idea where we go when we die. I have no idea if there's a heaven, hell, or even a God. There's just *here*, being alive, in this world, and *there*."

It's a great quote for my exposé, but it picks at a scab that has never healed. I can relate to Sylvie's audiences. We all want to believe that the people we loved aren't moldering six feet under. Moose hangs his head over the front seat while Chris is curled on my lap. Playfully, she bats his nose. She's lost more hair on her belly. It makes her look like she's in the midst of chemotherapy. My chest tightens. "They like each other."

"There's no pretext in the animal world," Sylvie says.

"You sound jealous."

"Aren't you?"

I switch gears. "Before I meet them, I'd like to know your first memory of your adoptive parents."

Sylvie wags a finger at me. "Don't call my mom that." A gust hits our car and I grip the side of my seat, relieved when Sylvie returns both hands to the wheel.

"Adoptive? Why not?"

Moose rests his head on Sylvie's shoulder and she kisses his snout. "You only have one chance to make a good first impression."

"So what was your first impression of your *new* parents?"

Slipping a Tums from her bag on the seat between us, she swallows it whole.

"You eat a lot of those. Medical problem?"

"Love the taste."

I grimace. "What was dinner that first night like?"

"My mom made sushi."

"Who gives a little kid raw fish?"

Sylvie chuckles. "My mother is not a macaroni and cheese kind of woman."

"You actually ate it?"

"I was a foster kid. I didn't know I had a choice. That night I used chopsticks for the first time. She rubber-banded them together to make it easier. Dad was pretty quiet while we ate. After dinner he brought a stack of square paper, all different colors, to the table and made origami swans, tigers, pheasants, dogs. He had such big hands but he taught me how to fold those delicate animals. That night we lined our menagerie on my windowsill. I liked him."

She didn't say she liked her mom. "When's the last time you went home?"

"Six years ago."

I circle back to the start of our conversation. "So what'd you do to disappoint your parents?"

Sylvie puffs hot air onto her window. Without looking, she somehow draws a perfect barn in the fog with the tip of her finger. It quickly fades. "They didn't want me to go to SF. They wanted college, preferably University of Oregon to study agriculture, or Cornell, if I could get in, and then a speedy return to High River to help run the orchard and eventually take over."

"Why go to college at all?" Sylvie breathes on the window again, draws a tree. I steel myself, ready to grab the wheel if a gust hits.

"Do you know anything about fruit orchards?"

"No."

"My folks grow pears. In today's economy a pear grown in Chile and shipped to Oregon, that's over six thousand miles, is cheaper to buy than one grown in the Pacific Northwest. Worldwide markets, foreign competition, and increasing production costs will put most orchardists out of business in the next decade unless something changes. They wanted me to study agriculture and business, learn, and help our orchard survive."

"But you left."

Sylvie turns to meet my gaze. "Yes."

"Eyes on the road," I say as she gets dangerously close to the car in front of us.

Sylvie jerks into the passing lane and speeds up. "Backseat drivers have control issues, you know."

"I have *stay alive* issues. You didn't want to be a farmer?"

She passes two cars then returns to the right lane without using her blinker. "Orchardist. And no. It never fit."

"But being a psychic does? Fit?"

She corrects, "Psychic-medium. And yes, more than anything ever did."

"Can you explain?"

Sylvie's mouth twitches sideways. "Have you ever felt like something was missing in your life?"

"Not really."

She looks over at me. "Doubting Thomas, you're lying."

"Okay. I guess I'm missing a girlfriend. Eyes forward, please."

"Chill," Sylvie says. "I went through this phase around nine; it made Mom nuts. There was a story in a *Reader's Digest* at the pediatrician's office about vanishing twin syndrome."

"I'm not familiar."

"It's a miscarriage of a twin fetus early in pregnancy. I got it into my head that I'd been a twin and my sibling had been lost. Asked Mom a zillion questions—I thought that's what was missing."

"Is that why you left High River?"

"Thomas, I wasn't nine anymore and that was a *metaphor* to explain that there was a hole in my life from an early age. I left High River to find a way to fill it."

I notch an arrow, sending it flying. "So just like Holly and Danny, you ghosted your adoptive parents, too?"

Sylvie chuckles. "Maybe you should write fiction instead of being a journalist."

Somehow, my arrow missed its mark. "Why's that?"

"You have a *very* overactive imagination."

She smiles and I register the way the corners of her mouth curve and the fullness of her lower lip. Despite the train ride, I'm no closer to figuring out just who the *real* Sylvie is. All I know is that I'm increasingly drawn toward finding out.

FOURTEEN

———

Sylvie

So just like Holly and Danny, you ghosted your adoptive parents, too?

The accusation stings but I'm careful not to show it. The trick is to keep *him* off balance. That's why I shared my parents' disappointment that I left High River but not how they feel about my chosen profession. Plus, actually *seeing* it will be more powerful.

Danny's voice in my head whispers *every dream has a price.* Shame bites at the lining of my stomach. Danny was right . . .

When I called Lucas that first time, he agreed to fly both Danny and me down to LA. We assumed that was because we were a package deal, and we spent the night in an expensive hotel, where we hit the minibar like locusts and ordered more room service than we could possibly eat. The next morning we took an Uber to our meeting on the top floor of a skyscraper . . .

"Let me do the negotiating," Danny murmured as we nervously sat in reception. *"This could be huge for us."*

But when an assistant, dressed in a tight white T-shirt, black jeans, and high heels came to bring me into Lucas's office, she told Danny to stay put. She'd come get him next. But she never did. When I re-

turned, she told Danny that Lucas was done for the day. Danny kept
his cool until the elevator doors closed and we were alone.

"Did you convince him?" Danny asked.

"Yes."

"What'd he offer us?"

"Representation."

*Danny leapt into the air then hugged me. "Syl, that's amazing! We're
in, kid!"*

"What about your dream to be an actor?"

"This is a huge stepping-stone. I'll get there eventually."

"I . . . He only wants me."

Danny's face crumpled. "So you told him to fuck off?"

"Once I'm established, he's open to helping you, too."

"He's open?" Danny stepped back, eyes wet. "You and me, we had a deal."

"I know but—"

"But you're screwing me over for your shot."

"That's not true!"

"Bullshit. We were supposed to be a team."

"Come on, Danny. We still are!"

"You wouldn't even be here without me."

*"I know. But Danny, I can't go home. I promise that I'll help you if I
can . . ."*

We were both crying when the elevator reached the lobby. Danny
walked away. When I tried to follow him down the street, he ran. I
was too much of a coward to return to our hotel room. By the time I
worked up the nerve to face him, he was gone. I stayed in LA. Danny
didn't return my calls or cash the checks I sent in care of Gigi. He
deserved better from me. *So why'd I do it?*

"What are you thinking about?" Thomas asks.

My voice catches as I say, "I'm looking forward to seeing my parents. I mean, I'm nervous, but hope they've forgiven me for leaving. I've missed them." But what I'm really thinking is that maybe I ditched Danny not because his knowledge about my origin story makes him a liability, but because he's a reminder that there's a part of me that wonders if I'm just someone who takes advantage of both the people I'm supposed to love and strangers.

I get off the highway at Exit 63 and bisect the small town of High River—bracketed in the distance by the jagged slants of Mount Hood and the more rounded, snow-covered Mount Adams across the river in Washington. Shops and restaurants dot the edges of the town's main street. There's an old-fashioned movie theater named Andrew's, redbrick brewpubs, clothing stores, specialty olive oil and wine shops, several pot establishments, a pizza joint called Double Mountain, and a shingled green shack that houses Mike's Ice Cream. "That's where I worked in high school," I say, pointing at Mike's.

After we cross over the narrow river, there's a low lumberyard by a four-way stop. We drive past and head up a serpentine road lined with a mix of old ranches and new homes. At the top, the clouds have blown away and sunshine illuminates the white slopes of Mount Hood. The homes disappear behind us as we drive on, replaced by rows of orchards, their perfectly spaced trees laden with stunning white blooms.

"It's beautiful," Thomas says.

"Yeah. Blossom season. We had a warm winter so they're early this year."

"You said *we*."

"Old habit. First blooms are apricot, they're cold hardy, prolific bloomers, then cherries, their blooms grow in clusters, followed by peaches—those blossoms are tinged pink, then pears." I point out the window. "Pears are the trees with gnarled trunks. To me, they always looked like old women's arthritic hands held up to the sky."

"You know a lot about fruit trees."

"I'm an orchardist's daughter."

We wind along Eastside Road, past red barns and fields where men and women in hooded sweatshirts work in the trees. Rows of grapes dot the steeper hills. I take a left and pull onto a narrow drive lined with shade oaks. To both sides of the driveway are evenly spaced rows of pear trees that climb into the distance—twisted soldiers standing at silent attention. A house rises—white, three stories, leaded glass front windows, planters dotted with bright yellow daffodils on a covered porch. Hanging to the left of the door, an old-fashioned wooden swing rocks in the breeze. There's a fishing rod in a metal stand to the right, olive green waders hung beside it. I see it all through Thomas's eyes—an idyllic-looking place, the stuff of old movies. *Appearances are deceiving.*

I park the rental SUV by a dented blue pickup truck. My shoulders are too high, damp hands clamped to the steering wheel even after the engine dies. I'm wound so tight that if I were a guitar, my strings would snap. *Does Thomas notice?* My dog rests his head in the crook of my neck. *Moose does.*

Thomas asks, "Do they believe? In what you do?"

I nibble my lower lip then look down, but not before he has the chance to register the shine in my eyes. "Maybe now that my career has taken off," I say, "they will . . ."

Memories wing like swallows, dip and dive overhead as I stride up the front path. I try to ignore them, but echoes of a girl's laughter, dizzy somersaults on the lawn, cool sprinklers dappling hot skin, summer's fruits dripping down my chin and elbows, a first driving lesson in the old truck, follow me.

Eight steps up. The porch beneath my boots is painted light gray. Every other spring it gets a fresh coat. I recall the first year that became my chore, how proud I was when I'd finished and Dad said *job well done.* The swing beside the door where Dad and I took in lightning storms beneath a wool blanket beckons with a creak of chains always kept rust-free. I can still feel the warmth of his hand around mine.

Our front door is massive, lacquered dark blue—a project from shop class. Dad and I cut, sanded, biscuited, and glued the wood together. Mom chose the color. I knock. This is an enormous gamble. Thomas's takeaway when the door slams in my face may be that even my parents know I'm a fraud. But the past six years have given me an advanced degree in human nature. I'm betting that rejection will swing his anger to sympathy and even pity for the daughter who disappointed her parents but is still hoping for their approval.

What if they let me in?

Footsteps sound along wide-slat oak floors that came from an old barn. It's Mom's cadence. When I was young, some local kids and I played ding-dong-ditch. Ring a neighbor's bell then run, shrieking, into the fields. My brain leaps up and down, arms wave a signal. *Run!* I rest a hand on Moose's head like he's an anchor that keeps me safe from sailing into the eye of a violent storm. The footfalls reach the door. Mom doesn't look through the side window to see who it is. There are few strangers in this valley.

Except I'm a stranger now.

The door opens—the years haven't changed her much. Posture

erect, porcelain skin, dark eyes unreadable, black hair cut to chin-length. There are a few strands of gray, less volume to her cheeks, but as always, Mom's face is unreadable. She has one hand on the door, the other tucked in a pocket of the striped apron she wears to cook, and waits for me to say something. That was always her tactic—let the other person crack.

Thomas has hung back for a bird's-eye view of the prodigal daughter's return. I say, "Hey, Mom." She doesn't step in for a hug. We're not that kind of mother-daughter. There were no late-night conversations, shared secrets. Sometimes I tried, but Mom is a professional bullfighter—quick steps, dizzying spins, never a drop of blood on her. In a flash, I'm a little kid again; desperate to apologize for things I don't understand, to find favor. My mother has never apologized to me in her life.

Mom says, "Big dog."

"That's Moose."

She looks over my shoulder. "Who's he?"

"Thomas Holmes."

This is a hurdle, not a cliff. Don't you dare jump. The contrary tree inside me stretches its limbs. "My boyfriend." I glance at Thomas, hope he's caught off guard. He's blushing. *Good.*

"He's the reporter who called us?"

"And my boyfriend. He's writing an article about me, what I do, for the *L.A. Times*."

Hana sniffs. "We don't read that one."

"He'd like to talk to you."

"Why?"

"Background." Her lips purse tight. She's five-feet-nothing, bones light as a bird's, but inside she's a lion. "So," I say, loud enough to carry,

"I thought maybe we could have dinner together, spend the night?" *Slam the door. Now.*

"You haven't wanted to have dinner for the past six years," Hana says.

"You never invited me back." *Do it. Please.*

"Your old room hasn't been dusted."

What is she thinking? A few moments ago I was desperate for her to shut me out. Now I hold my breath like a convict awaiting the jury's decree—*death, life, without the possibility of parole, or a commuted sentence?*

Hana says, "Your hair is long."

"It grew."

Mom's mouth twitches sideways, a signal that could mean acquiescence or that her fuse has been lit. "It looked better short." She sniffs. "I'll pull out fresh sheets."

Did I just win or lose? Thomas joins us at the front door, Chris dangling at his side in her carrier. I reach up and tousle Thomas's hair in a pantomime of intimacy. It's thick, soft, and my fingers tingle. "Hana Young, this is Thomas Holmes. Thomas, my mother." They shake hands.

Mom asks, "What's in the pink bag?"

"My cat. Apologies, I couldn't find someone to watch her."

"We have a barn that needs a mouser."

Thomas's face turns the color of white linen washed too many times. "Um. She's an indoor cat."

Hana frowns. I know exactly what she's thinking.

"Where's Daddy?"

"Out with Eddie. He'll be back by dinnertime."

She opens the door wide. It's a step back in time. I know every knot in the worn boards beneath my feet. Walls are adorned with photos of the fields, mountain, pear trees—and me. Did I imagine she'd take them down? *Yes.*

I scan the photographs. I'm seven, driving the old green John Deere tractor for the first time, a grin stretched ear to ear. Eight, dressed as an apiary for Halloween, head poking out of a white box, bees glued to my skin. Age nine, pigtails flying, as I rode my new bike with red plastic flowers stuck to a front wicker basket. Ten, Christmas Eve, Mom, Dad, and me side by side before a tree hung with popcorn, cranberries, and origami animals coated with glitter, plus the ornaments Mom's grandparents made while interred in California during World War Two . . .

Hung at the start of a short hall that leads into the kitchen is the last photo my parents ever took of me—high school graduation. The three of us, me in the middle in a shiny blue-and-gold robe and square cap, the tassel switched to the right side. I'm turned slightly toward Dad. I wanted to tell him that I was headed to SF, not college. That I appreciated him, both of them, the life they'd given me, but needed to figure out where I fit. In the end I was a coward, blindsided them a few days later, bag already packed, one foot out the door. There was a battle, all of us gravely wounded in the skirmish.

There are no photos of me after age eighteen. Is that what happens when parents lose a child? They freeze *before* in photos? Capture their offspring in picture frames, like fences those lost children can't scale, where they're caught in time, always young, sweet, malleable, alive . . . theirs?

The house smells the same, savory not sweet—rosemary, sage, and ginger. To the right is our family room. Comfortable couches with handmade quilts folded on their arms, Dad's worn leather recliner. A big-screen TV, so he can watch U of O football and Mom can catch whatever talk show is currently her favorite. Growing up it was Oprah. Mom would frequently quote her, although the queen of daytime TV's battle with weight was an irritant for a woman who never had a problem with self-discipline. I have no idea what Mom likes now.

Holly and I watched movies in this room, a nest of comforters on the floor, packages of Twizzlers, Dots, and Milk Duds strewn around us. I lost my virginity on the loveseat in the corner to Tristan Orton. *Lost* is the wrong word. I gave it, considered my body similar to a new pair of hiking boots, more comfortable once they were broken in. Holly disagreed, but it wasn't her call. My folks were at the Pendleton Round-Up—the biggest rodeo in the US, held a few hours away. I'd stayed home to work at Mike's. A few months later, Tristan said he was in love with me. I broke it off. Love was a tether and by then I knew that I wanted to fly away.

I glance at the basket of yarn in the corner poked through with knitting needles. *She's still at it.* When I was a kid, Mom made sweaters that I'd wear out the door, a change of clothes in my backpack for the moment I was out of sight. The memory makes my skin itch.

Mom says, "Join me in the kitchen for tea while I scrounge up something for dinner."

Not a question. An order. And she has never *scrounged* up dinner. Her grocery lists are methodical. Weekly meals planned well in advance. I glance at Thomas. He stands in front of a photo taken on the Deschutes River. The salmon dangling in my net is almost as big as me. I was just shy of six, new to the family, on my first father-daughter camping trip. There were hikes with the other duos, a lazy raft down the river, and s'mores by the campfire. The fishing season was catch and release, which meant I had to toss my prize back into the river. That night, after we were settled in the tent, snug in sleeping bags, lights out, I asked Dad if it was the same for foster kids, if I might get thrown back eventually. He promised that he'd be my dad forever.

Thomas doesn't understand that sometimes good people lie, too.

FIFTEEN

Thomas

I didn't tell Sylvie as we drove through High River that I've been here before. My dad took us once, midsummer, on a windy day to watch the windsurfers race along a river that roiled with waves. We also tried to fish but didn't catch anything. It was the summer before Dad and Deacan died in the car wreck. My big brother, who was five years older, insisted we listen to NPR on our way to and from High River. He was already obsessed with the news cycle and politics in particular. I push away the memory, focus on the here and now . . .

We drink green tea at a farm-style wood table in a modern kitchen. Worn soapstone counters, a Sub-Zero refrigerator, proofing oven, and well-used six-burner Wolf stove showcase that cooking is a priority in Sylvie's childhood home. Hana doesn't offer sugar but I force down the pale green liquid. Sylvie cradles the teacup between her hands and watches the steam curl. When Hana offers me a shortbread cookie, I take two to overwhelm the dishwater taste in my mouth. Sylvie takes one but doesn't eat it.

This house isn't what I expected. Every wall is hung with photos. The ones in the kitchen show Sylvie fishing beside her dad, making pies with Hana, ballet class in a pink tutu, rafting down river rapids with her mouth in a perfect O of fear and jubilation. It appears an idyllic childhood. The shot of her graduation in the hallway was the most telling. Unlike her parents, she didn't look into the camera. Did she know she was going to leave then? Would I have had the courage to turn my back on the path my parents had chosen for me? I never faced that decision. After Dad and Deacan died, I was mostly on my own. I have to give Sylvie some credit. It takes strength to embark into the unknown. It also takes strength, though not of character, to perpetrate a scam on Sylvie's level.

Sylvie asks, "How's the weather been?"

Hana takes another sip of tea. "Warm spring. Buds came early. Cherry growers are worried."

I ask, "Why?"

Sylvie spins her cookie on the table. "If the buds come too early and we get a heavy frost, it kills them," she explains. "And if the fruit comes in too early and we get a week of heavy rain, the sugar soaks up the water and the cherries split. That's why cherries are way more risky than pears or apples."

"How long have you two known each other?" Hana asks.

I wait for Sylvie to reply but she raises one brow. *She wants to make me lie.* "A year." That's how long I've been researching my exposé.

"How'd you meet?"

Two can play this game. "At one of Sylvie's shows, right, honey?"

Sylvie smiles. "Thomas came onto the stage for a personal reading. He was married for five years. His wife died, cancer—it was a really, really sad situation. He brought her wedding ring for me to hold, so I could connect to the *other side*."

Hana abruptly stands. She opens the refrigerator door, pulls out chicken breasts and an assortment of vegetables; withdraws a cutting board from an island drawer. She woodenly says, "I'm sorry for your loss, Thomas."

I nod to avoid the lie. Sylvie puts a hand on my arm, gives it a squeeze. The warmth from her palm seeps into my skin. Her fingers are long, elegant. When they ran through my hair, I reflexively leaned in. My face warms at her touch, and I slide my arm free.

Sylvie says, "Thomas needed closure and I was grateful for the opportunity to help. After the show, he came backstage, asked me out for a coffee. We've been together ever since. Joined at the hip, really. I barely go to the bathroom without him." She leans in, kisses my cheek.

I ignore the prickles of heat where her lips touched my skin. Despite what Sylvie does for a living, she's an attractive woman and it's a natural reaction. Instead, I focus on the fact that she's baiting me. I get it, but why taunt her mother?

Hana slides an enormous kitchen knife free from a wooden block. She slices through a yellow onion, expertly chops, uses her fingernails as a gauge. "So you believe in psychics, Thomas?"

Sylvie bats her eyes at me. *She's enjoying this.* "I believe that your daughter believes," I say. Hana slits the plastic wrapping on the package of chicken. "How about you," I ask. "Do you believe?"

She sniffs. "Is that why you're here, Thomas the journalist? To get testimonials from Sylvie's parents?"

I switch directions. "Mostly, I want to know what Sylvie was like as a child."

"What were you like?" Hana asks as she ruthlessly separates chicken fat from meat with the tip of her knife then rips the lumpy, yellow strands free.

"I've told him. Normal," Sylvie says. "But I don't think he believes me."

I ask, "Do you have a favorite memory of your daughter?"

Hana's knife hesitates then flicks the chicken fat into the sink. "Why don't you answer that, Sylvie?"

"Mom is a photographer. She took most of the photos in our house. I liked going into the darkroom with her."

Hana uses the knife to point at a shot of Mount Hood that's hung to her right. The mountain's white peaks are painted pink. "She took that one."

"Careful, Mom. You sound proud," Sylvie chides.

For a moment they're not estranged, just a daughter teasing her mom, then Hana looks right at Sylvie and says, "There's before and after. Your father and I live in the latter. We haven't been proud of you for a long time."

Sylvie's hand darts to her chest, where Hana's mortar-round smolders. Her words on the train come back . . .

Have you ever considered that you're the vampire? You tear people's lives apart for a story and you don't care about who you hurt in that process.

Redirecting the conversation, I ask, "What do you know about Sylvie's *birth* parents?"

Hana scowls. "Why would you ask that?"

One, your last comment was cruel. Two, your daughter lied about her early childhood, claimed she can't recall it. Instinct tells me when I dig up the truth about that, added to whatever I glean from the time I spend with you and Sylvie's dad, and after she bombs at her next show, I'll have irrefutable evidence and Annie will publish my exposé, front page. The only negative is that you'll dance on your daughter's grave.

"When I was doing my research, I couldn't find much about them," I explain.

"I don't know anything about *those people*."

"That's a shame. It'd be really interesting for my readers to know if one of Sylvie's *biological* parents also had her gift."

"All I know is that they died in a small plane crash," Hana says, lips pursed as she slices broccoli lengthwise.

"Where was the crash?"

Hana touches her neck. "Someplace in Oregon." She scrapes vegetables into a glass bowl then pours shiitake mushrooms from a paper bag onto the cutting board. The brown nubbins bounce along the scored wood. Using a damp towel, she carefully cleans them.

"Do you know the name of the town?" Sylvie asks.

I glance at her. Sylvie shrugs like she's just being helpful.

"I don't," Hana tells her. "Neither does Wess. We never asked. When the foster care woman came up the driveway with you, we didn't look back."

She's awfully quick to answer for her husband. "Huh. You mentioned foster care."

Hana slices the mushrooms, skillfully flicks them into the bowl with the other vegetables. "What about it?"

"They don't have much of a record from your daughter's time with them."

"They're overwhelmed, I suppose, can't be easy trying to find good homes for so many kids. A lot of them stay in the system until they age out at eighteen. *They* never have a family." Hana glances at Sylvie to make sure her point landed.

"Loud and clear," Sylvie says with a crooked smile.

I fight the urge to say something cutting to defend her. But this isn't my fight and Sylvie isn't my girlfriend. I'm here for the truth, no matter how ugly.

Pulling a twist of ginger from a silver colander, Hana uses her knife to separate the rough bark from the off-white flesh with short, violent strokes.

"You'd think there would be something," I press. "At least the names of other families she was with before you."

Hana's head snaps up. Her eyes drill into Sylvie's. "Do you recall other families?"

Sylvie shakes her head.

Hana glowers and says, "Then I guess once you left them, they didn't matter to you anymore."

SIXTEEN

Sylvie

Mom glares until I look away. You don't have to be psychic to wonder if she just lied about my birth parents' plane crash. Her body language—the neck touching, pursed lips . . . Hell, even Thomas, who I'm sure has spent the past year studying the tools of a psychic's trade, must've registered it. But Hana Young has always been *brutally* honest, no matter the consequences. I recall her losing old friends over issues of morality, and she never spared my feelings when she lectured about doing the right thing. Thomas's questions felt invasive, insulting, and her physical reactions were pure discomfort.

Mom dismisses us. "Get settled in your bedroom. Dinner will be in half an hour."

Tires screech. *She thinks we're going to share a room.*

"I wouldn't want to be disrespectful," Thomas smoothly says. He sweeps Chris, who has been winding around Moose's legs, into his arms. "I can sleep in the guest room or on a couch."

Mom waves a hand to reject the idea. "Wess and I lost influence on Sylvie's life and respect for her decisions a long time ago."

When Dad took me fishing, I'd repeatedly ask if it hurt the steelhead when we removed the hook. Dad always said no, but as Mom's barb sinks into my flesh and I pull free, I'm sure it did. I hide my flinch, remember, as we leave the kitchen, that it was my idea to come here; that Hana's acid tongue has brought Thomas, whose goal it is to bury me alive, to my defense. Yesterday I never would've thought that possible.

On the stairs, my palm glides along polished wood I once slid down. Photos dot the wall—Mom's extended family at a reunion lined in perfect rows with only the hint of a smile, as if life, even at a picnic, was serious business. Dad's folks posed in front of their trees, both wearing Young Orchards baseball hats—Grandpop Dick with a thumbs-up sign while Grandmom Kate stared into his face like he hung the stars. They died within a month of each other.

Halfway up the stairs is Mom and Dad's wedding portrait—they're both so young, faces unlined. Dad in a dark blue suit, green eyes full of sparks. Mom wore her grandmother's satin wedding dress, high-necked, exquisitely beaded. She looked like a rare, delicate flower. As a kid, I dreamt about wearing her dress for my own wedding. I wanted to be and look like her, but when I hit five-foot-eight in seventh grade, that dream went up in smoke. The other one, the desire to have something in common, took longer to die.

At the top, the first door on the right is a sewing room, bolts of fabric stacked neatly in one corner. Dad's study is across the hall, wood panels, and tomes on agriculture, horticulture, and viniculture, along with the novels of Hemingway, Dickens, Austen, Woolf, Fitzgerald, and Tolstoy. When I needed to get away, I'd curl on the tweed couch while Dad worked, look at photographs of flowers and trees. I dove into the classics when I got older, tales of Gatsby's green light, feminism, Russian counts, and the Spanish Civil War. In this room I almost belonged.

Narrow steps to the right of the study's door lead to my parents' bedroom. Gooseflesh breaks along my arms as I approach. Buried recollections slip through cracks . . . Mom in a leather chair, knitting needles clacking as she waited outside the bathroom for an apology. My memories are a nest of spiders suddenly caught in bright light. They skitter to dark corners.

"Where does that go?" Thomas asks with a nod at the staircase.

"My folks' room."

The door beyond the stairs opens to my old bathroom—black and white square tiles, a tub, and a pedestal sink. My bedroom is across from it, door shut. I'm certain it's been renovated, now an innocuous guest room. Still, nerves jitter. *She wouldn't leave my collection.* Mom isn't sentimental and Dad has no voice inside this house. Moose noses my hand. I reach for the knob, say "Tada!" for comic effect, and swing the door wide . . .

Nothing has changed, like I packed my duffel and left yesterday. The double bed has the same white comforter dotted with pink dahlias—my favorite flower. Mom let me order it from a catalog when I was seven or eight, and I'd refused to get a new one when the seams frayed. The furniture is simple—a pine dresser, matching mirror, and desk all made by Dad. Gauzy curtains are held back from the large picture window on the far wall with yellow ties.

Blue ribbons from diving competitions dot the corkboard above my desk along with photos of Holly and me—homecoming dances, basketball games, paddleboard adventures on the river, camping trips beside glacial lakes. I see those photos, this room, through Thomas's lens—a *normal* childhood. *Was it?* Maybe, on the outside, but something ugly lies beneath the surface, gnaws at the edge of my consciousness like a rat . . . or maybe that's just my excuse for leaving this place, deserting them. Only one item in this room is new. My high school diploma, framed over the desk. Mom must've done that after I left.

"You look surprised," Thomas says.

"I assumed she'd redecorate."

"Maybe she hoped you'd come back."

"Is that lie number four or five?" Thomas's smile is lopsided. For the first time I notice that gold strands weave through his mop of hair.

He chuckles. "I thought my mom was strong-willed, but yours? She's . . . a lot."

I laugh. "That *birth parent* comment? Perfect timing."

"She deserved it."

For a moment my insides warm and Thomas is my *real* boyfriend, defending me. But he's just here for the show.

Thomas nods at the far wall. "Snow globes, huh?"

The wall to the right of my curved bed frame has a six-foot-wide bookcase that I made with Dad in his shop. It holds my collection of old-fashioned glass snow globes—a total of 138. Mom hated them, said they were tacky. *So why'd she keep them?* Thomas slowly walks the shelves and my face burns, like I'm standing here naked. He picks up one with a farmhouse perched on the edge of a snowy ravine about to plunge into oblivion, gives it a shake, snowflakes swirl.

"I collected those."

"Really?" Thomas jokes.

He moves along the row, pausing by the globe with an old man in a dark topcoat and derby. Face furrowed, the picture of concentration, the man dangles two small marionettes, a boy and a girl. When the globe gets shaken, the marionettes dance in the snow and the old guy grins. The globe to its right has a stooped fellow who trudges in the woods with a body rolled into the orange carpet balanced on his shoulder. Only the dead man's feet poke out. "I found that one at an antique shop just over the river in Bingen, Washington," I say.

Thomas picks up the globe at the end of the row. The woman inside holds an infant with both hands, about to drop her bundle of joy into a well. "Usually people collect cheap plastic ones from states," he notes. "These are kind of macabre."

I itch to take the globe he holds, set it back on the shelf. "I prefer *original*. They were all I wanted, for birthdays, Easter, Christmas."

"Why?"

I don't know. "Just a weird kid thing." Thomas returns the globe. I reach out, adjusting it so it matches the others.

Thomas asks, "Why'd you tell Hana I'm your boyfriend?"

"She might not have let you in otherwise. Mom isn't a fan of the *fake news*. Obviously, you'll sleep on the floor."

"Obviously. Your mom is Japanese."

I smile. "Obviously."

"Your dad?"

"White as snow. They can tell you their love story over dinner. It's more of a merger."

"Are you okay?"

He's pretty good at acting like he cares. "Why wouldn't I be? My parents lost their influence on my life a long time ago."

"How's it feel to be here?"

"Like a snake trying to fit into the skin I shed years ago."

His eyes pin mine. "She lied about the plane crash."

Acid pools inside my gut. *When was the last time I took an antacid?* "She has no reason to lie."

Thomas asks, "If she did, do you want to know why?"

The color of Thomas's eyes reminds me of the hungry wave, castle, and mysterious treasure.

"Sylvie? Do you want to know?" Thomas presses.

I tell the truth. "I'm not sure."

SEVENTEEN

Thomas

Downstairs a deep male voice calls, "Hon?"

Hana replies, "In the kitchen."

"I guess we should go down. See him," Sylvie says. She runs a hand through her hair, twists it into a bun, pulls it down, pinches color into her cheeks, then blows out a few times, like she's psyching herself up for a race. "C'mon, boyfriend. If you thought tea was fun, this'll be a riot."

She looks so uncomfortable that I almost feel sorry for her. I suggest, "Let's leave Chris in the room so she isn't hit by shrapnel."

"Good idea." Sylvie sets a large, yellow-striped pillow with tassels on the window seat. "At least she can look out the window."

"I didn't choose to make her an indoor cat." *Why would I care that she knows that?*

Sylvie asks, "Who did?"

"We lived in a city—lots of cars—but my mom really had her declawed to protect the furniture, even though it was always covered." I place Chris on the pillow. She's lighter than she should be, a collection of bones covered in fur. She hasn't eaten since last night and can't afford to lose any more weight.

"We'll bring her rice with lots of butter," Sylvie says.

It's not like she read my mind—obviously I'm worried. I almost tell her that Chris won't eat it, but instead hope she's right. "Do I . . . am I wearing the right clothes?" I'm in jeans, a red-and-black-plaid flannel shirt, and Blundstone boots.

Sylvie looks me up and down. "You look good, boyfriend. Let's go meet Dad. Word of warning, don't ask for my hand in marriage until he's had a few beers."

She stands on tiptoes, kisses me, quick as a lightning strike. Her lips are soft, taste sweet. Reflexively, I kiss her back. A trail of warmth winds from my belly down. I pull away as soon as I can. "What was that for?"

A slanted smile tickles her lips. "So when Dad asks when we first kissed, you'll have to lie."

"You're hysterical."

She wriggles her brows. "Gallows humor. You're a dead man walking."

"Seems like your mom liked me better than you."

"I'm a daddy's girl."

Notepad in hand, I follow Sylvie and Moose out of the room. Despite *not* being her boyfriend, that I'll never ask her father's blessing, that if I do my job right, her career will be torched, my nerves are raw. Sylvie's father might share his disappointment or worse. It makes me wonder what my own father would think of the career I chose, the decisions I've made . . .

Hana and Wess are side by side in the kitchen when we walk in. Wess is maybe five-foot-ten, thin, face weathered, a bump on the bridge of a long nose. Deep lines radiate from avocado-colored eyes. He's in worn Carhartts, a dark gray flannel shirt, knit cap, and patched down vest. I glance at Sylvie—hands jammed into jean pockets, furtively glancing from Mom to Dad and back again like a little kid waiting to hear her punishment.

"Ah. Here are our visitors," Hana says with a flick of a knife in our direction. *Her daughter is a visitor?* Wess's eyes sweep the kitchen, light first on me, then Moose, finally Sylvie. Arms instantly rise to embrace his daughter, but he doesn't move and they fall back to his sides.

"Hey, Daddy," Sylvie says shyly.

"Great Danes were bred to hunt boars. Did you know that?"

Sylvie shakes her head. "His name is Moose."

Her dad asks, "What are you doing here?"

The moment suspends. *Does he hope she's come home for good?*

Sylvie takes a step toward him. It's kind of tragic when he doesn't do the same. Instinctively, I wrap an arm around her waist.

Sylvie says, "Just visiting . . . with Thomas, my boyfriend. He brought his cat, too."

"Is the cat in our barn?" her dad asks. "We're down a mouser. Coyotes got the last two."

Coyotes? The impulse to check on Chris, make sure the window isn't open, even a crack, tugs.

Hana pours oil from a silver container into a wok. "Wess, she's an *indoor* cat."

"Hmm." Wess tugs his hat off, tosses it on the counter, unzips his vest, starts to take it off, then buries his hands in the pockets.

"He's the reporter," Hana says. "The one I told you called last month."

"Pleasure to meet you, sir." Wess hesitates then shakes my outstretched hand.

"Thomas is writing an article about me," Sylvie says.

Wess asks, "Why?"

The chicken hits the wok's hot oil, sizzles. Sylvie explains, "He's fascinated with psychic-mediums."

The silence says it all. "Your daughter is gaining quite a reputation. Her . . . people are drawn to her." *None of that is a lie.*

"Anyway," Sylvie says, "Thomas wants context, like what I was like as a child."

Wess takes a glass from beside the sink, fills it with tap water, and drinks it down in three gulps. "Sylvie was a good kid—never a lick of trouble. Loved being outside, climbing trees, riding in the truck, helping at harvest time. She had a knack—with plants, animals, people, too."

"Huh. You grow pears?"

"Yes."

I say, "Hard work."

Wess meets my gaze and says, "Honest work."

Sylvie's chin pebbles then goes smooth. This visit is taking a visible toll. I know what it feels like to never be good enough, though my mom hasn't expressed her opinion aloud. *Why the hell did Sylvie agree to bring me here?*

"Wess, go on and take a shower. Dinner in fifteen," Hana says.

Sylvie stands in the middle of the kitchen. To get to the front hall and upstairs, Wess has to pass by. At the last second she steps back. *Six years and he didn't hug his daughter. Even my mother wouldn't do that.* "Mind showing me around the yard?" I ask Sylvie and twine our fingers together. At the door she looks down at our hands, waits for me to let go so we can grab jackets. She pulls wool hats out of a wicker bin and we tug them on.

The sun has dropped behind the hills, twilight rapidly fading. It must be around forty degrees, air dense with currents of freshly mown grass, flowers, and dirt. We wander down the drive. To both sides are symmetrical rows of pear trees that stretch farther than I can see. "Your orchard is big?"

Sylvie says, "We have two hundred and eighty acres of irrigated land."

"Is that a lot?"

"Typical orchards only have about seventy acres. Ours is a combination of winter pears, medium-density pears, and Bartlett pears."

I ask, "What goes into growing them?"

"Lots of labor—pruning, spraying, irrigation, thinning, picking. Operational costs include workers' comp, insurance, and overhead expenses." She faces me. "But you don't care about any of that. You want to know if my mom was always a bitch and why my dad didn't hug me."

"Did you expect more?"

She twirls a silver earring in the shape of a teardrop. "I don't know what I expected, exactly. I call for Christmas."

"Do they call you?"

"No."

I think of my own mother, who only calls when she's short on cash. It's becoming clear that once Sylvie left, she was no longer useful to her parents.

Sylvie continues down the drive, boots scuffing along the packed dirt. Moose trails like her shadow. "Mom wasn't always this . . . mean. She was tough, sometimes distant, but there was love beneath it. She taught me to cook, how to take and develop photos, plant a garden. She made Halloween costumes."

"And your dad?"

"As long as I followed in his footsteps we were fine . . . better than fine. We were buddies. They're both really disappointed." Her eyes shine. Quickly, she deflects. "Watch out or they'll toss Chris in the barn when you're not looking."

"Clearly they're not used to an indoor cat."

Sylvie steps into the orchard, wanders down a row, knotty pear trees surrounding us on both sides. Their delicate blooms give off a fragrant perfume, and the turned earth is soft underfoot. "My mom rarely shared stories from her childhood," Sylvie says. "But there was one she'd repeat. In addition to their orchard, her family kept sheep. They had an Australian shepherd, Misty, raised from a puppy to herd them. When Misty was three, she went deaf. Mom's dad put her down. One shot to the head."

"Hana must've been devastated."

Sylvie gives a sideways look. "She wasn't."

"What? Why the hell would she tell her own kid that story then?"

"For the moral. It's a waste to expend resources on something that isn't useful. That dog didn't deserve their love. She didn't even deserve to live." Sylvie heads back to the farmhouse. "Come on. If we're late for dinner, they'll eat without us."

EIGHTEEN

———•———

Sylvie

Admittedly, I was thrown off course when Mom let us in, afraid I'd lost control, but Thomas now feels sorry for me. The story about Misty, which is true, plus Mom's taunts and Dad's discomfort, pushed him along. Goal achieved. Thomas pities me and that's a weapon I can use to manipulate him. But I don't just want his sympathy. I want him to believe. I'm not sure why that matters to me, but it does. I probably shouldn't have kissed him. It was meant to throw him off, but he responded . . . and I did, too. I've read that prisoners become attracted to their captors and he's definitely holding my career hostage. *Do I want him to believe as some kind of twisted revenge, or as validation?*

Dinner is a series of uncomfortable three-word conversations. *Pass the salt. Wess, more rice? Delicious meal, Hana.* Thomas is abysmal at eating with chopsticks, the only utensils Mom provided. After watching him try and fail repeatedly, even with the sticky rice, I finally take pity and say, "Hold the upper chopstick like a pencil, one-quarter of the way up like this . . . Good, now place the other stick against your ring finger and secure it with the bottom of your thumb." I reach over and help him get it right, my fingers pressed against his warm skin. "Okay, now move the top chopstick with your index, thumb, and middle fingers." Thomas tries to pick up a clump of rice but only a few grains make it into his mouth. "It takes some practice." I get him a fork. He eats quickly, eyes down. I almost feel sorry for him. When he's done, he compliments Mom then attempts to hide his fork beneath the edge of his plate.

Thomas says, "Since we don't have much time together, I'd like to ask a few more questions." He pulls out his phone, sets it on the dining table. "Mind if I record?"

"Yes," Hana says. "And I've already answered your questions."

"Mr. Young?" Thomas asks, swapping his phone for a notebook and pen. "It'd be great to hear from you, too."

Dad glances at Mom. She half shrugs. "Go ahead."

"Any favorite stories about Sylvie to share?"

Mom daintily picks up a piece of chicken but doesn't eat it. She's hardly touched the food on her plate, just moved it into different positions. Dad finishes the last drop of his beer—Pfriem, made at a local brewery. Thomas dusted his five minutes into the uncomfortable meal. Any worries I had about my parents spilling too much of my past—things I didn't know or secrets that could hurt me—are long gone. They have even less desire to tell Thomas anything than I do. We just need to get through this dinner, take off in the morning, and never come back.

Dad says, "She always did well in school."

"Especially in biology," Mom adds.

"My high school didn't offer any courses on tarot, psychic readings, or tapping into your inner medium," I quip. I'm not sure why

I'm poking the bears, maybe because neither of them will really look at me.

Thomas tips his beer bottle back even though it's empty. "Another one?" I ask. He flashes a grateful smile and for a split second we're on the same team. The idea of that, someone having my back in this situation, is a fantasy. I made this bed of nails and tonight need to sleep on it.

"Sure," Thomas says. "Thanks."

"Dad?"

"Yes."

I grab two beers from the fridge and pop the tops with the church key hanging on a hook shaped like a cherry. Everything in this kitchen has remained in its place . . . except me. My arm grazes Dad's shoulder when I set his down on the table. It's the first time we've touched in years. He shifts out of reach. Before I give Thomas his, I take a long pull off the bottle. As I hand it over, our fingers graze. I wait a few seconds, force contact, before I release the beer.

Thomas watches me before he says, "I'm looking for more *personal* stories about your daughter. It's hard to get a clear picture of her childhood."

Dad says, "Like all reporters, you want dirt."

Thomas corrects. "I want the truth."

Dad tries to stare him down but Thomas doesn't retreat. I'm both impressed with his level of determination and concerned.

"She helped the pickers during harvest, liked to make homemade tamales with Carla, my manager's wife. We never lost the three-legged race on Fourth of July. She loved when the blossoms came out, used to make crowns out of 'em . . ."

I chuckle. "I made you wear them." Silence drops like a guillotine's blade.

Thomas says, "Huh. Sylvie tells me you and your wife have quite a love story."

Dad glances at Mom. She gives a tiny nod. "My grandfather and Hana's were orchardists in this valley. Then World War Two came. There were several Japanese families in High River at the time, mostly farmers and orchardists. Before they were taken away, interred in camps in California, they signed over their land to neighbors to make sure it was taken care of, not claimed by the government or bought by strangers, while they were incarcerated. The agreement was that their neighbors would return the land once the Japanese were released from the camps. My grandfather and Hana's granddad made that deal."

Dad clears his throat. "Hana's mom was born at the camp— conditions were brutal. Not enough food. No medicine. She almost died. What we did to those people was tragic, a crime, but it was abysmal when they got out, too—lots of prejudice and cruelty perpetrated on folks who were just as American as you and me." There's grit in Dad's voice. He takes a gulp of water and continues, "After three years, the Japanese returned to High River. Some of the folks they trusted refused to return their land; argued that they'd worked it for three years so it was now theirs. The Japanese had signed it over, legally, and given the times and the war, courts weren't too favorable even if they could scrape together the money to seek justice. Many of those good people lost their land. Their legacy."

Dad finally looks at me after his last word. *Legacy.*

"Your grandfather?" Thomas asks.

"Not only gave Hana's family back their land, he helped finance the machinery they needed, their employees, insurance, the works, until they got back on their feet," Dad says.

"Good man," Thomas notes.

Dad nods. "There was a deep friendship and loyalty between our families. Hana's and my parents grew up together. When we started dating, they agreed it was fate at a time when marriage between culturally different folks wasn't universally accepted. We combined our orchards when we married. Hoped to have a large family to pass it down to—"

"But Mom couldn't have children of her own," I finish. "So they ended up with me." My dad's lips pucker like he's bitten into a lemon. Mom gets up, clears the dishes. She rinses plates and loads the dishwasher. I consider helping but decide against it. In ninth grade science I learned that if you place the same poles of two magnets together, they repel. That's the way we've always been.

Thomas says, "My father died when I was a kid, but I imagine he might've wanted me to follow in his footsteps and be a lawyer, too."

"An honorable profession," Mom intones, her back to us.

"Did you think about adopting more children?" Thomas asks.

I applaud. "Great idea! You should've kept at it until you found the right one."

Dad grimaces. "When we started the foster process, we were in our late forties, already considered too old to adopt."

"Then how'd you end up with me?" I needle.

He rubs his mouth. "Luck, I guess."

He's lying. Why?

Dad drains his second beer. "Any other questions?"

I shake my head.

"Huh," Thomas says. "So you never saw any signs, when she was a kid, that Sylvie was . . . different?"

Mom snaps, "I told you, no."

Dad says, "If you're asking if we thought Sylvie could read minds or whatever, the answer is never. She was a *normal* kid. A *good* kid."

The clear implication is that I'm no longer *normal* or *good*. Thomas glances at me. I give him a bruised smile. But this is nothing new. Hearing it up close and personal stings, but it also kicks Thomas even further into my corner. After twenty-four hours with my parents, he just might drop me from his exposé out of pure pity. I'll take what I can get if it means saving myself.

"Huh. Have you ever been to one of Sylvie's shows?"

"Look," Dad says. "Bottom line? What Sylvie does now? We don't understand it. We don't *want* to understand it or watch in person."

"She was raised Catholic," Mom adds like I'm not even in the room. "The first commandment, 'I am the Lord thy God. Thou shalt have no other gods before me.' You went to Sunday school, church, Bible camp."

I snort. "It's not like I'm a witch or worship the devil!"

Mom slams the glass bowl she just washed onto the counter. I'm surprised it doesn't break, shocked that she's actually showing emotion. She whirls, then demands, "I have a question. Did you throw away your morality all at once, or was it like the frog in the pot?"

"The frog?" Thomas asks.

"Place a frog in a pot of water, slowly turn up the heat," Mom says, "the frog won't feel it, realize he should hop out until it's too late and he's been cooked."

"I'm the frog," I tell Thomas. "If we're sharing Sunday school stories, how about the one where the frog falls into a bucket of milk."

Thomas says, "He drowns?" then looks to Hana like he's at a tennis match, waiting for her to return serve.

"Nope," I correct while making a swan out of my cloth napkin. "He keeps swimming, never gives up, until the milk is churned by his little froggy legs into butter, and he gets the hell out of the bucket and never comes back." I set the swan on the table. The napkin hasn't been starched so the bird's proud neck droops. Mom has turned her back again. Methodically she dries the wok.

"Religion aside, do you believe *at all* in Sylvie's abilities?" Thomas asks my parents.

I admire his persistence. Maybe he's trying to get us kicked out. That's never happened before, not even after Mom discovered I was on the pill, but this is a night of firsts.

"No," Dad says. "We do not believe that Sylvie has some sort of gift that allows her to know the future or talk to dead people. We don't hang our hats on nonsense."

So far I've batted away each paper tiger my parents have sent to attack, but Dad's tone of disgust is too much. I'm an intricately folded piece of origami scrunched into a tiny ball, tossed away. The heat in my belly flares.

"We done?" Dad asks. "There's a game on TV."

"Just a few more questions," Thomas says. "What can you tell me about Sylvie's birth parents and her time in foster care?"

Mom turns, looks at Dad, not Thomas. Her hand drifts to her neck. "I told you," she says. "We don't know anything."

Dad adds, "It didn't matter. Once Sylvie arrived, she was ours."

Thomas withdraws a letter from his back pocket. His name is

typed in the center of the envelope. The return name and address printed in the top-left corner is for the National Transportation Safety Board. I move behind Dad as he withdraws the sheet of paper inside and we both silently read it.

National Transportation Safety Board
490 L'Enfant Plaza, SW
Washington, DC 30594
To: Thomas Holmes, L.A. Times

Dear Mr. Holmes,

We have reviewed your request for information about the deaths of Becky and Seth Peters from the years 1996 to 2002 and even expanded that search five years before and after your stated dates. There is no record of a fatal crash involving either a Becky, Rebecca or Elizabeth (common name variations), or a Seth, either married or single, with the surname Peters. Our database is definitive for all aircraft-involved incidents in the United States. If you have further questions we are happy to do an additional search.

Sincerely,
Erin K. Sedgewick

My heart crashes against the wall of my chest like it's trying to escape. *It's fake, just like the Facebook account Thomas constructed for Theo and Katy.* Dad holds out the letter to Mom. She gets her glasses from a drawer, takes the letter, and scans it. My parents exchange a quick look. That's all. No shock, denial, outrage, just a silent look. And in that moment, I know two things: The letter isn't forged, and my parents knew that Seth and Becky Peters's plane crash was a lie.

Mom takes off her readers and returns them to the drawer. "I won't be awake when the two of you leave in the morning," she says. "Wess will already be out in the orchard. Safe travels." She turns her back to us and begins to efficiently scrub every inch of the kitchen counters.

NINETEEN

— · —

Sylvie

The desperate need to escape pushes me outside like a fist to the small of my back propelling me. But first I fill a bowl with leftover rice, top it with a thick pat of butter, and hand it to Thomas before I quit the kitchen. Dad's down jacket hangs on the banister. I slide into it. It's the only way his arms will ever wrap around me. Moose trails me out the door. Dad's musk rises from the coat—sweat, dirt, and sap—it always made me feel protected. Now it makes me sad. I asked for this and don't deserve any pity, but that doesn't mitigate the ache.

A short story we read in junior high comes to mind—"The Man Without a Country." It was about an American lieutenant in the army who renounced his country during a trial for treason. He was sentenced to spend the rest of his life at sea without any news about his country, family, or friends. He died broken, lonely, and repentant. *Will that be me?*

I fall onto the porch swing while Moose wanders down the steps to explore. I'm not worried about coyotes or cougars. He's big enough to scare them away. When the door opens a few moments later, I expect Thomas checking to see if I've found a phone. It's Dad. He sits on the far end of the swing, stares into the orchards. We swing. When I was a kid, we'd hold hands, my tiny one engulfed in his paw. That gave me a sense of permanence, like I was a helium balloon that might float away unless he held tight to the string.

"What's all this about, Sylvie?" Dad quietly asks. "Why'd you really come home?"

To buy time—gain sympathy—manipulate Thomas—save my career—survive. But there's another painful reason. I was afraid to come home before this. Afraid to see if my parents still loved me. It's one thing to call on holidays and have a short conversation; it's another to be rejected face-to-face. Maybe Thomas gave me the excuse I needed to see if the relationship with my parents was salvageable. *It was easier not knowing the truth.* "I don't know."

"Your agent called. Lucas something. I didn't tell Mom."

I stare into the fields, try to see what Dad sees. It was always beautiful, a living quilt of roots, bark, branches, blossoms, and pears, but never seemed mine, like one day my parents would realize a stranger had sat at their dining table for years, ate their food, slept in their bed, and I'd be sent away. "What'd Lucas say?"

"That you might come our way; that there was a decent chance you wouldn't have access to your phone; I should tell you, when the journalist wasn't around, to call him. Sounded like you were in some kind of trouble."

Dad withdraws his phone from a flannel pocket, holds it out to me. The rectangle is warm from his body heat, heavy in my palm. *This is my chance. Lucas will have scraped together every piece of dirt in Thomas's life. I can use it to help take back control, stop him.* A phantom's kiss skims the tip of my nose. I hear the whisper, same as before my last show. For the first time I can tell it's a woman's voice . . .

"Are you going to call him?" Dad asks.

I hand the phone back. *What's wrong with me?* "Maybe later." I take in my dad. There's less than a foot between us but it stretches for miles. Unlike Mom, he's visibly aged. His hair has grayed, thinned, and once smooth, tanned skin is now a network of lines and creases. Gravity has drawn the corners of his mouth into the start of a permanent frown. *Or did I do that to him?* He reaches out, tucks a loose lock of hair behind my ear. The red barn door materializes in my mind. There's a hard knock from the other side. The energy is male, older. I taste metal. *Or am I just imagining that one of Dad's ancestors has come so I can prove to him that leaving was the right thing to do?* Dad's fingers linger on my cheek for a moment then return to his lap. The spirit retreats, the door fades.

"I'm sorry . . . for coming home, upsetting you both."

Dad leans back, pushes off with his feet, and the swing slowly arcs. "When your mom and I married, I made a vow to put her needs first, even above my own; to be her best friend, husband, and defender; forsake all others for her," he says. "I loved you, Syl, still do. But your decision torched our hearts. Mine still has space for you in the remains, but your mother's . . . it was burned to ashes."

"I'm not the only kid who chose a different career than their parents wanted," I say softly. We're talking and the last thing I want is for Mom to come outside and end the conversation. "Why does it have to be all or nothing?"

Dad sighs. "Hana moved heaven and earth to adopt you. She's never been good at showing emotion, you know that, but still waters run deep. She loves fiercely, and I'm not saying this is her best attribute, but when trust and loyalty are broken, she judges fiercely, too, doesn't forgive. She's always been that way."

"It's not fair."

"Life isn't fair, Syl. You turned your back not only on us but also on a legacy that our parents and their parents fought for; that Hana and I cherish." He shakes his head. "Maybe, if we believed in what you'd chosen, but we don't."

"So you agree with her that I'm some kind of sinner?"

"It's not about religion, at least not for me. You know I wasn't big on church." He falters, rubs his chest. "The path you've taken? It's dishonest and immoral, if not illegal. You *lie* to folks for money. Your mom and I didn't raise you that way and we're ashamed of you."

Bow hunters sometimes wound their prey and have to follow a blood trail to finish the job. The animal suffers for hours, sometimes days. At least this was a clean shot. Mouth dry, I ask, "What about the letter Thomas showed you?"

He starts to reach for my hand but then drops his onto his lap. "Head inside now. I'll be gone when you get up. It was good to see you, Sylvie. But don't come back."

The acid in my belly climbs up my throat, blocked only by the massive knot wedged there. "Okay," I manage.

"Sylvie?"

I stop at the door. Hope limps forward. "Yes?"

"Don't dig up the past. There's nothing good there. Focus on the future."

Dad's shoulders are hunched, hands knotted. He looks so much smaller than I remember. "Bye, Dad." Moose has reappeared and follows me inside.

I climb the stairs, one hand pressed to my tender gut. Up until now, steadily eating Tums has been enough to suppress the acid, but I don't think even a whole roll would help put out this heat. Lucas has been on me to see a doctor, but I haven't made an appointment. My second therapist said that when people don't face issues, mend friendships, alleviate doubts, their body reacts and even attacks. She pointed out that some people embrace the pain as if it's deserved. When I told him, Lucas found a new therapist for me.

Right now, I need medication stronger than Tums. My folks might have something in their medicine cabinet. When I reach the narrow wooden steps leading to their bedroom, I pause. Downstairs they're talking, too low to hear. Dad is telling Mom he's told me to leave tomorrow and never come back. Mom agrees. I don't know why I thought he might want me home. Not outwardly welcome me but, before the door slammed, show me that I was unconditionally loved, maybe agree to talk on the phone when Mom wasn't around. Sometimes I'm an idiot.

And the lies about my past?

I wrestle that question into submission. It doesn't really matter if my birth mom was an addict, or if my real father is a murderer, warehoused in some prison, if they're both long dead, or even if Hana and Wess weren't lying about my history but always had suspicions. Dad is right about one thing. There's nothing good in my past or I wouldn't have ended up in the foster system. I need to focus on the future, make sure I still have one.

Thomas pokes his head out of my bedroom. "Sylvie?"

At the end of the hall, I motion Moose inside the room. "Bathroom break," I say and shut the door. With one last listen to make sure both my parents are still in the kitchen, I dart up the narrow staircase.

Their bedroom looks the same. Gray carpet on wood floors lacquered white. Four-poster bed handed down from Hana's grandmother, covered in a quilt of red and blue snowflakes. A worn leather chair sits beside the window, wicker basket beside it filled with balls of white, cream, black, and green yarn, knitting needles stabbed into a half-finished scarf. A white barn door that's hung on an overhead iron track separates the bathroom. I grab the iron handle and slide it open. The grating sound of wagon wheels along the track makes me shudder.

The bathroom used to be pale yellow but is now painted moss green. I cross to the medicine cabinet. There's a box of extra-strength antacid. I turn on the faucet and wash down a pink pill. The mirror reflects a rectangular walk-in shower on the back wall with a glass door. Inside are tiny gray and white tiles . . .

A vision of a little girl, skinny body huddled on that tile beneath a frigid cascade of water, flickers. The room spins like one of those whirling teacups at an amusement park. A sideways shuffle and I slump onto the woven leather stool in the corner. Head pressed between my hands, I search for a spot to anchor myself; like I did the first time I got drunk on strawberry daiquiris with Holly and had the spins. There's a bubble in the paint, low down on the frame of the bathroom door. I pull the door close and put my finger directly on the bubble. It's soft enough that my nail goes through. When I pull back, a scab of paint rips free, revealing the barn door's previous color—brick red.

The panic attack hurtles toward me like an asteroid. There's no time to run . . .

TWENTY

————

Thomas

Hana and Wess's reaction to the letter from the National Transportation Safety Board was a silent explosion. In that moment it was clear they both knew that the plane crash was a lie. And Sylvie recognized that they knew it, too. I thought she might've been in on it, but the way her face collapsed? No one is that good an actress. That moment when you realize your parents aren't who you wanted them to be, or who you need them to be, is devastating. A wave of pity hits. But I'm not Sylvie's friend, or even an acquaintance. I'm a journalist.

I grab my phone, type in some notes. Hana and Wess are definitely hiding a secret. They'd only do that if it was a major one. I have a long way to go, but I smell a much bigger story, though it may be different from the one I'd planned. There's more investigating to do. And even if Annie won't give me the time, if she demotes or fires me, I'll keep going, then sell the piece to another paper. It's going to be that good.

Downstairs Hana and Wess's conversation rises and falls. I can't make out the words, but know the content. They're assholes, but that doesn't change the facts. Sylvie never showed any signs of being a psychic-medium as a kid. Her parents gave her a home, a family, and a future. She ditched them to work her con. They're overwhelmingly disappointed, but also offended. I can't blame them though their delivery is brutal. Still, it's impossible *not* to empathize with Sylvie—it's a horrible thing to know you can never live up to a parent's expectations.

Sylvie has been gone awhile. Is she on the phone with Lucas? Her parents probably have a landline. It doesn't matter. Nothing is going to kill this story.

Moose stalks over. Brown eyes study me like he's picking which limb to tear off first. "Don't get any ideas, buddy. One bite and I'll call the dog catcher, have you locked up." He doesn't react, like he knows I'd never do it. Admittedly, I've gained a grudging respect for Cujo. He's been gentle with Chris and his devotion to Sylvie is obvious. She did rescue him. "Where is she?" I mutter. Moose takes a few steps back, whines. A few more steps then he turns to the closed door. "I'm not taking you out. Wait for Sylvie."

The beast stands on hind legs and grazes his nails down the door, leaving deep gouges in the paint. He scrabbles again. "Stop it!" I hiss. Sylvie's parents will be pissed. *Not my problem.* Moose spins and barks at me. "Fine." I open the door. "Head downstairs, find your way outside if you need to take a whiz. Watch for coyotes." But instead he bounds up the narrow staircase to Hana and Wess's bedroom.

He's not Lassie. I hesitate then take the steps three at a time. Sylvie is on the bathroom floor, curled like a caterpillar. She's hyperventilating, her lips tinged blue. I rifle through cabinet drawers for a paper bag. There isn't one. I cup my hands in front of Sylvie's mouth, press tight to her skin. "Slow it down." Moose whimpers. "You've got this." Her lips skim my palm as her body struggles to apply the brakes. I glance over my shoulder, consider a run for help. *She wouldn't want her parents to see her this vulnerable.* My palms are moist as Sylvie's hot breath forms condensate. Finally she pushes my hands away. Her lips are pale but no longer blue. "Help me get—out of here before they come—upstairs."

She struggles to stand, wobbles, still too dizzy. I slide my arms beneath her knees and back, cross the bedroom in a few strides, and descend the steps as quietly as possible, Moose at my heels, and try not to feel the weight of Sylvie's head against my chest, the side swell of her breast beneath my fingers. I walk down the hall, carry her into her room then shut the bedroom door with a foot and slide her onto the bed. Sylvie hangs her head between shaking knees. "You okay?" Tears patter onto the wood floor like raindrops. Moose creeps onto the bed, more gently than seems possible given his size, lies down beside her. Her fingers burrow into his fur.

Gently I ask, "Sylvie? What happened up there?"

She shakes her head. "I don't know."

I don't believe you. "Then why are you crying?"

"It's just . . . a lot. I assumed Mom would slam the door in my face. We'd head back to Portland."

I settle beside her. "But she let us in."

"I hoped—"

"What? That they'd forgiven you?"

"Maybe." She sits up, face wet. "But they haven't . . . and then dinner. I expected *her* to be mean, but *he* was, too." Tears drip off her chin. "They didn't say a word . . . but that letter is real."

"Yeah, it is. Did you expect your father to tell the truth after he read it?"

"Maybe."

"What reason do your parents have to lie?"

She shakes her head. "I don't know."

"I can think of two possibilities," I offer.

"Yeah?"

"One is that maybe the truth would get them in trouble."

"Like what? They had someone steal me from a mall? Raised me under the pretense that I was an adopted foster child while some family in Indiana still searches for an abducted kid?" She shakes her head. "They don't have it in them to commit a crime like that."

"People desperate for a child have done worse."

Sylvie snags a Kleenex from the bedside table, noisily blows her nose. "If I was kidnapped, there would be no records at all in the foster system. What's the other possibility?"

"That they still love and want to protect you."

She wipes her wet cheeks. "Lucas called before we arrived. My dad gave me his phone when we were on the porch."

I'm surprised at my level of disappointment. *Was I starting to trust her?* "You called him."

"No."

She winds a lock of hair around her fingers, tight enough that it cuts off the blood supply. *Do I believe her?* "Why not?"

Her chin quivers. "I'm not sure."

Sylvie rests her head on my shoulder. The scent of vanilla rises from her hair. The desire to protect her and more overwhelms. I hesitate then put an arm around her, imagine my fingers tracing the curve of her neck . . . *Stop.* I wrote an article a few years ago about male and female scents. How there are certain smells that attract men. *That's all this is.*

I change directions. "You now know for sure that your parents lied—that plane crash never happened. Do you want to find out the truth about your life before you came here?"

Sylvie sniffles. "They're not going to tell us anything."

"Your mom won't . . . but your dad? What if you get him alone? He gave you his phone to call Lucas. He still cares, at least a little bit." Sylvie's tears soak through the shoulder of my shirt and I feel like an asshole for pushing her right now.

"Dad said he's *ashamed* of me."

Anger blooms despite my desire to remain impartial. "You're the only person who gets to decide if you're ashamed. Are you?"

She traces a small rip in her jeans. "And if he doesn't tell us anything?"

"Then we go at it from a different angle. Visit the foster care offices in Portland. Find your caseworker."

Sylvie sits up. "Didn't you get their name when you read my file?"

"My source just left a voicemail. I didn't get to read your file."

"Can you call them?"

"I tried to follow up a couple of times, but she won't call me back."

"Can't we just call the foster office and ask?"

"Their records are all confidential. You would have to go in person, show ID, and fill out some forms to see your own records. But once we get that name, we can ask him or her what happened to you for that year-and-a-half you were in the system. That's information they're far more likely to give you than me."

I take a slow breath to drain some of the adrenaline that comes with being on the verge of breaking a story. "Sylvie, you do realize that your birth parents could still be alive?" She pulls Moose closer. "What's it going to be?" Now I get to find out if she's been bullshitting me.

Sylvie blots her nose then toys with the Kleenex. "On one condition. It's off the record unless I say you can use it."

I hesitate, consider. "Deal."

Grabbing a pillow and the folded quilt from the foot of Sylvie's bed, I look around for a spot to sleep. The window seat has a thin cushion. It's about five feet long, but I doubt I'll be able to sleep anyways.

"Seriously?" Sylvie asks. She crawls beneath the covers. "You sleep on top. And don't get handsy." Her eyes are swollen, cheeks tearstained, nose red, but she's rebounded enough to make a joke.

"I'll try to hold myself back," I say, and am rewarded with a weak snort. Moose follows me to the other side of the bed. "And you have your buddy here ready to tear me apart."

Sylvie's grin makes wrinkles that look like little whiskers on either side of her nose. "Only if I tell him to." She rolls over, her back to me. "Sleep with the angels."

"Do they sleep?" I ask.

She turns out her bedside lamp.

TWENTY-ONE

Sylvie

For a long time I pretend to sleep. My father's warning plays in my head on a constant loop: *Don't dig up the past. There's nothing good there. Focus on the future.* Thomas's breath steadies; his lips send off tiny puffs now and then, like a little kid blowing out candles on a birthday cake. I have the urge to kiss him again, this time for longer, and I angle my head toward him, bit by bit, until I'm so close that his breath glances off my lips. But I don't steal a kiss. It would be another crime he would add to the list. Anyway, I don't want to kiss *him*. I'm just searching for a port in the storm.

I roll onto my side, count the snow globes lining my shelves, a habit from childhood. They look charmed in the moon's glow. The farthest to the left was given to me on the first birthday I can recall, my sixth, about a month after I came to live in High River. I didn't have any friends to invite to the party, so the guests were my new parents; our orchard manager, Eduardo; his wife, Carla; and their kids.

Eddie brought a piñata, Carla, homemade tamales. Mom and Dad gave me stuffed animals—a bear and a rabbit. The Lopez kids gave me their favorite snow globe. I still have it. Inside is a white castle. Tiny figures stand on the parapet's walls. Some hold bows and arrows.

I was amazed the first time I shook the globe. White flakes fell, a drawbridge opened, and a black horse charged out. The drawbridge had a magnet, so after the last snowflakes settled, the horse receded and it closed.

My name was spelled in fat letters on a carrot cake that had nuts. I picked the walnuts out, lined them around the edge of my plate to save for later. Back then, I hoarded food—slid it into my pockets during meals, then into the corner of my bedroom closet. When Mom finally discovered the food, she broke that habit along with the other ones.

My birth parents could still be alive . . .

I've never asked myself if I wanted to find them. They were dead—end of story. The idea that I might have the chance to stare into a face that looks like my own, learn about their lives, childhoods, and what we have in common? Meeting them would be as shocking as winning the lottery without ever buying a ticket. We could have the same laugh, eye color, smile. *Maybe I'll finally belong.* Or they could be horrible people . . . or still long dead. It's like being given a present wrapped in gorgeous, sparkly paper but not knowing if there's a wonderful gift or a bomb inside the box.

If they were alive, would they want me to search for them? Show up on their doorstep? Here I am, the daughter you gave away. Surprise! I'm back! Hey, just wondering what went wrong? Were you sixteen and scared–never wanted a kid–low on cash? Or was it because you didn't love me? Will my birth parents let me in when I knock? Politely refuse and shut the door? *Will they be ashamed of me, too?*

Gently, I put Thomas's arm around me and rest my head on his chest, listen to the metronome thud of his heart. Still asleep, his arm reflexively tightens and long fingers glide down my side. When he unconsciously kisses my hair, a tear slides over the bridge of my nose. It's the little things, unintentional acts of intimacy, that get to me. My love life has been a handful of failed relationships and brief encounters that left me empty. Star-shine glances off Thomas's skin. He has faint seams that radiate from the corners of his eyes. I've never heard him laugh. When I met him in my dressing room, I couldn't stand his face; now I'm drawn to it. A siren wails in the distance, reminds me that this man is my adversary.

I didn't tell Lucas everything about "The Cask of Amontillado." Montresor's family crest was a snake with its fangs embedded in the foot crushing it. The motto was: "Nemo me impune lacessit." It meant: "No one attacks me with impunity." Thomas's article will ruin *my* career. I have the right to fight back, don't I? *Maybe I could be Montresor instead of Fortunato?*

My mind spins through the last twenty-four hours, possible scenarios for the next few days. Regardless of what happens with Dad, am I really considering a show without any prep? Before Lucas, back when Danny and I sat side by side behind a rickety card table, I always did cold reads. People lined up. But it's been six years. I hardly remember that girl. She performed with zero expectations. Now I have both a reputation and a career to protect. Now there's a *show* to perform.

What if I work up the nerve to skip prepping and then, without any bridges, the door doesn't open? Lucas is building my career, and I do think he cares about me, but he won't stick around long if the numbers go south. *He's a survivor, too.* Where does that leave me? My fear that failure meant having to come home seems almost quaint now. They won't take me back. *I'm a tree without roots.*

Exhausted, I slide toward sleep . . .

The sun is warm on my skin, sand coarse beneath bare feet. There's a light breeze that smells of salt and sea. I wear a white dress dotted with pink flowers. A blue-green wave rises in the distance, gathers momentum. I turn to the castle and frantically dig beneath its walls. *There isn't much time.* Sand crystals stick to my sweaty skin. The hole is four feet, then five then six . . . The wave now touches the sky, blocks all but a sliver of sun. It rumbles like a hungry beast, calls my name . . .

I rip clear of the dark dream, sit up. Thomas has moved to the window seat, crunched sideways to fit on the short bench, Chris curled beside him. Both are sound asleep. *Did Thomas wake to find his arm around me? Do I repulse him now?*

Dad's quiet footsteps descend the stairs. The hallway floor creaks as he heads into the kitchen to fill his thermos with coffee. He'll come home at 7:00 a.m. for breakfast with Mom—two eggs over easy, one piece of toast, cherry jam. More coffee. I could slip out of my bedroom, confront Dad by myself. Last night I agreed to press on, with Thomas. If I didn't, he might've thought that I was hiding the truth. Our goals don't align. But if he returned to LA right now, despite whatever pity I've earned with this family visit, his article would probably cast me as an unredeemable fraud.

My chest tightens at that thought. I've spent years burying every doubt, but in two days they've all risen from the dead. Now I've reached a fork in the road. I glance back over at Thomas. *This is a big risk.*

Moose watches me from his curled position on the rug as I creep to the window and study Thomas. When he hugged me last night, I thought I'd gained the upper hand. Looking down at him now, the curve of his lower lip, his broad chest, long lashes on a smooth cheek . . . I'm not sure who is manipulating whom. Yesterday the battle lines were clearly defined. But last night things changed. The only certainty is that I'm walking on quicksand.

I tap Thomas's shoulder. He wakes with a start. "Dad's up. Let's go." Silently we tug on jeans, sweaters, and boots. The front door creaks open, closes with a dull click. Dad always walks through the orchard to Eduardo's first. Together they plan the day. I want to catch him before he gets to Eddie's. Thomas scoops up Chris. Moose follows as we tiptoe through the hall, down the stairs, across the front porch.

The moon is so bright, we don't need the little flashlight I snagged from a desk drawer. We leave our bags by the car. Thomas nods at Chris. "Leave her on the front seat," I mouth. "We won't be long." He opens the SUV's door, slides her in, and shuts it with pressure from his hip. *What would happen if Mom woke now? Would she follow us into the orchard? Stop Dad from talking to me? Would she drag me upstairs, to their bathroom, and . . .*

That first birthday, Mom constructed elaborate sushi rolls in the shape of dragons with fiery red eyes and scaled tails made from avocado, sesame seeds, seaweed. They scared me, like at any moment they'd breathe fire or claw with sharp talons. I slid Carla's tamales onto my plate and Mom's eyes filled. She turned away but I knew she was crying. *I hadn't chosen her.* When it was time to eat the cake she'd baked and expertly iced, I had two pieces, even though I didn't like it. But she only noticed the walnuts I'd picked out of each slice.

"Ready?" Thomas asks. It's cold enough that his breath makes white clouds.

My pulse quickens. "Let's go."

"Where is he?"

I point to fresh footsteps in the dewy grass. Dad is a creature of habit. He chooses a random row, walks slowly, so he can examine his trees for signs of fungus or fire blight, a bacterial disease that can wipe out an entire crop. I lead, Moose by my side, Thomas follows. We could take a shortcut to Eddie's, but this one last time I want to walk in Dad's footsteps. Thomas glances at me, like he can't quite believe I'm here, doing this. *Will he keep his end of the deal?* I didn't, with Danny. If Thomas screws me, it'll be karma back to bite me in the ass.

This walk through the orchard makes me feel like Benjamin Button. The years fall away until I'm a little girl again. I climbed these trees, played tag with Eddie's kids, balanced on tall ladders to help pick. *What would Eddie say if he saw me now?* He watched me grow. Taught me about pears, but also, family. He and Carla have five children. Their home was noisy, messy, filled with energy, fun, and love. Their small ranch stands on the corner where the elementary school bus dropped me off. I'd run in to get a hug from Carla and a snack. Until Mom made a rule I had to come right home. *Is Eddie ashamed of me, too?*

Thomas touches my arm, points. Dad is twenty yards ahead of us, head bent over a tree branch. He's in the same work clothes as last night, but now wears a green down coat over his vest and one of Mom's knit hats, this one striped blue. He doesn't look up as we approach, though by now he's heard us. "Daddy," I call softly then realize we're out of Mom's earshot. "Dad."

"Sylvie."

I swallow hard. "I'd like to ask you a few more questions."

He scowls. "I thought I made myself clear last night."

My heart flutters like a hummingbird's wings. "You lied."

"Ironic, coming from you."

"Think whatever you want about my career—"

"Come on, Sylvie. What you do is—"

"Go ahead, say it," I dare him.

"What you do is a charade . . . at best."

"Fine! You're better than me. Mom's better. Your way of life is the only one that's worthy. Okay? But you both lied about how my biological parents died. I want the truth."

"I told you, leave the past alone."

"I *need* it."

Dad exhales a mist of white. "I don't know the whole truth."

TWENTY-TWO

Thomas

Sylvie asks, incredulous, "How is that possible?"

Wess turns and continues walking slowly down the row of trees. Silently, I take my phone out and trail closely behind Sylvie and her dad. I hesitate then press the red record button, slide the phone into my vest pocket.

"When Hana couldn't have a child, she was heartbroken. Don't give me that look. Being a mother is all she ever wanted. You know that she's an only child. Continuing her parents' and grandparents' legacy . . . it was her heart's desire but also her responsibility to honor them."

Sylvie asks, "Why didn't you go the fertility route?"

"We started down that road. But it was early days for IVF and also, as a Catholic, Hana was torn about the process. She wasn't sure God would approve of circumventing her body's natural abilities. We did two rounds of fertility treatments, they failed, and Hana said no more. She thought it was God's will."

"So you decided to adopt," Sylvie states.

"*We* did not decide. *Hana* did. I was certain that I couldn't love someone else's child."

The impulse to squeeze Sylvie's shoulder hits; to let her know she's not alone. But that gesture would be hollow. *She is alone.*

"Hana filled out all sorts of forms, applied to different agencies. By then we were in our mid-forties. Low on every list."

"But you said you didn't want to adopt."

"Your mother convinced me to *get the fish in the boat* then decide if we wanted to keep it."

"So foster care was the last resort?"

"I put my foot down on that one. Biggest fight of our marriage. An older child was already influenced by parents who could've been drug addicts or worse."

"It's not their fault what their parents did," Sylvie says.

"No, it's not. But children are molded in those first few years. I didn't want to borrow trouble." He tugs off his hat, scratches his head, then replaces it. "Damn hats are always itchy."

"Try wearing the sweaters she made."

Her dad chuckles, and for a moment I can see how they once were partners in crime, buddies.

"So how'd you end up with me?"

"One day your mom packed a lunch, all my favorites, and we went up to Mount Hood for a hike and picnic. She told me that there was a little girl, barely six, who needed us. We could take her on a trial basis. I argued that the child would come with big problems that we weren't equipped to handle, that it could potentially damage our marriage. She reasoned that we had built upon our legacy, created an even more successful orchard, but had no heirs. Didn't I want someone to pass things on to?"

"So it was all about the orchard?" Sylvie asks, a thread of hurt woven through her words.

Wess must hear it, too, but still admits, "That was a large part of my decision." He looks around. The sun glances off the hilltops. "Generations have put their lives into this place. I'm proud of them, and always hoped they'd be proud of me. The idea that we will eventually sell it and someone else will run Young Orchards is a bitter pill to swallow."

He coughs, deep and phlegmy. Sylvie's hand rises to touch his back then falls without contact.

"Hana promised that she'd be responsible for you. If there were problems, she'd solve them. If you were too much to handle, you'd go back."

Sylvie asks, "Did you know how she solved problems?"

Wess squeezes the back of his neck. "I knew from the moment you stepped out of that car and came up the front walk, knobby kneed, eyes pinned to the ground, hair in messy braids, we both loved you. It was that simple. Whatever your mom did to help you let go of the baggage brought with you, to give you a shot at a good life? I don't fault her. Hana always wanted the best for you and our family."

"Did you . . . did you ever consider sending me back?"

"Not once."

Sylvie sharply exhales. "So Mom is the only one who knows about my past, foster care, my birth parents?"

"She doesn't know much." Wess runs a hand over his grizzled chin. "Look, Hana did ask about your past. Anyone would. She was told that if she made a fuss, our petition to adopt could be denied. She pressed a bit more and learned that the story about the plane crash had been created to protect you. That kind of thing only happens if the birth parents were really bad people, reprehensible. The caseworker said she wanted to give you a fresh start, a bright future. She called it divine intervention, *God's work*. That was enough for your mom."

"What was the caseworker's name?" I ask.

"I don't recall," Wess says. "It was decades ago."

He scuffs a boot along the dirt. "Sylvie, if your mom thought that adopting you was somehow criminal or immoral? You know her. She wouldn't have done it. The adoption went through very quickly. Both Hana and I, we felt fortunate for the chance. The idea that I couldn't love another man's child disappeared that first night as we sat making paper animals, your tiny face scrunched with determination. You were my daughter."

Sylvie looks away, sniffs. "I understand. But I need to know where I came from."

Wess demands, "Isn't it enough that you're a Young?"

"It matters. But—"

"But the fact that a journalist wants to write an article about you matters more? Sylvie, you don't even know him. I got the impression from your agent that Thomas doesn't have your best interests at heart."

They're talking like I'm not even here. But her dad is no fool.

Sylvie finally meets his gaze. "It's not about him or his article. That's what started things, but I've realized that I need to know. For *me*."

Wess reaches into his back pocket and pulls out a tattered manila envelope, lumpy at one end. He holds it out to Sylvie. *He was prepared for this; he knew his daughter would try to talk to him one last time.*

"This is all you came with," Wess says. "Your mom kept it in the bottom of her jewelry box all these years. I have no idea what's inside."

Sylvie clears her throat. "Thank you, Dad—"

He jerks the envelope out of reach before she can take it. "Think hard before you open it. You did come with problems. Big ones. I know that much. And the woman who brought you that day said your past was filled with darkness. Sylvie, whatever you escaped was ugly."

A cold breeze blows through the orchard. Sylvie shivers. She holds up her left hand, the faded scar visible in the faint light. "Did I get this here?"

"No. You came with it. You must've been a lefty before it happened. Your mom worked hard to make your handwriting legible." Wess holds out the envelope.

Sylvie takes it. He pulls her into a rough hug, holds tight for a few moments, then kisses the top of her head. "You're freezing," he says and takes off his jacket, helps her into it. She tries to hug him again, but he takes her wrists, presses them back to her sides, then walks away. Sylvie watches until he disappears around a bend.

TWENTY-THREE

Sylvie

My dad walks away and the years spool out.

He read bedtime stories in different voices—*Charlotte's Web*, *Watership Down*, *The Secret Garden*—taught me how to climb a Douglas fir *and* get back down, to drive a 3616 narrow cab tractor, work the three-on-the-tree transmission of our old truck, change a tire on a bike or any vehicle. I know how lightning makes thunder and how to rebuild a hydraulic pump.

During camping trips he explained that I should stand my ground with cougars, play dead if a grizzly attacked, but make noise and fight back with black bears. I can set up a tent, tie flies, catch and clean a fish, cook it on a cedar plank over a fire I make. He effortlessly imparted wisdom about farming. I understand that certain pear crops will bear fruit three years after planting but won't produce a full crop for five to seven years while others take up to twelve; trees should be planted in late winter or early spring in fertile, well-drained soil with good air circulation; rootstocks must be resistant to fire blight and other diseases; birds that eat insects are an orchardist's friend and so are wasps and earwigs that eat insect larva; and field peas can maintain soil moisture during a dry summer.

His wisdom didn't just stem from being an outdoorsman or an orchardist. He modeled how to treat people with fairness and respect by the way he worked alongside the families that helped maintain our orchards. He handled Mom with kindness, Eddie and his family with consideration, and until I left, he always made time to listen and love me. We were a team every Fourth of July race. There was no one else I wanted to sit beside during fireworks. I could always pick out his cheers at diving meets, even when I lost. When I was sad, his hugs were a tonic. He was a whiz at checkers but never let me win—he made me earn it. When Mom attended her club meetings, we'd sneak out for pizza and huckleberry shakes.

But he was far from perfect . . .

Dad kept the peace in our house when Mom and I fought but never questioned her version of the truth or protected me from her wrath. Instead, he made me apologize without hearing my side. He couldn't separate his dreams from my own and didn't have enough room for both. He was prejudiced against *some* Mexicans, though Eddie is his best friend. He voted Republican, no matter what, was a proud member of the NRA, and didn't support gay rights though he told Mom she should pray for *those folks*. He was good, bad, prejudiced, loving, kind, complicated, cruel, and human . . . and a part of my foundation feels ripped away as he disappears around the bend.

"You okay?" Thomas quietly asks.

My eyes burn. "Not really."

Thomas, Moose, and I return to the car. The envelope in my hand hardly weighs more than a feather. "You drive?"

"No problem."

I toss the keys to Thomas, load Moose into the back, and take a moment to kiss my dog's soft forehead. He licks away the salty track that dribbled down the side of my nose. I slide into the passenger seat. Chris climbs onto Thomas's lap, paws pressed to the window, head ticking back and forth. "She seems to like an adventure."

Thomas starts the car. "She's lived for twenty years in an apartment, only gone outside for trips to the vet. She's finally discovered the truth. There's a whole world out there."

"You kept her safe," I say. But it strikes me that the things we do to protect those we love are really for us. Thomas rolls down the driveway. In the side mirror I watch my childhood home grow smaller and smaller until it could fit on the tip of one finger. We reach the road, pull away, and it's gone like a dandelion seed in the wind. Rows of pear trees, *our* trees, follow me, wave in the breeze. I open the window despite the chill and inhale, hold High River, our orchard, in my lungs then let it go.

The envelope from Dad rests on my thigh. I trace the veins that crisscross the paper. Someone once crumpled it into a ball. *Why did Mom keep it?*

Thomas asks, "Are you going to open it?"

"Are you going to keep our deal?" He digs his phone from a vest pocket, hands it over. The record app is open. I press play and listen to the conversation between Dad and me. *If I hadn't asked, would Thomas have used it?* I erase the recording then turn over the envelope. The top-left corner reads: OREGON DEPARTMENT OF HUMAN SERVICES STATE OF OREGON FOSTER CARE. There's a name handwritten in the center of the envelope: Mrs. Hana Young. No address—it must've been hand delivered. The envelope is open—the top slit long ago by Mom's silver letter opener. I withdraw a sheet of lined paper instead of the expected official stationery, read aloud a short note written in perfect, looping cursive.

Dear Mrs. Young,

Bless you for taking little Sylvie Peters into your home. As we briefly discussed on the phone, her parents' plane crash was a tragedy but I believe with your love and GOD's guiding hand, Sylvie can have a good life. As also discussed, leave the past alone and I will smooth the way to a speedy adoption.

"Give justice to the weak and the fatherless; maintain the right of the afflicted and the destitute. Rescue the weak and the needy; deliver them from the hand of the wicked."
—Psalm 82:3-4.

May God bless your family,
Heidi

P.S. G is on board.

I read the letter aloud for Thomas then hold it out so he can verify that I didn't skip anything. "What do you think?"

"That I need coffee." Thomas swings into a Starbucks by the highway on-ramp and merges into the take-out line. "You want anything?"

"Large. Black. And something sweet."

He orders two coffees, a couple croissants and muffins. They're ready at the window when we pull up and he hands them to me then pays the girl. The rich smell of coffee fills the car. I wait until Thomas pulls onto Highway 84, west toward Portland, before I take a sip then share my croissant with Moose, who has already gobbled the morning bowl of food I put on the back seat. Chris delicately eats flaky pastry crumbs off my lap.

"Now you like croissants?" Thomas asks his cat with a smile that finally touches his eyes.

There's a heavy inversion layer today and the low clouds cast the day as gray as my mood. The car's thermometer reads forty-one degrees. Hopefully it'll rain later. That will make the orchardists happy. I nibble on what's left of the croissant but caffeine on an empty stomach has made me queasy.

After he's downed his coffee and a muffin, Thomas says, "The first question I have is why did your mom keep that letter?"

I take off my boots then tuck my coat behind my back, cross my legs. "Maybe it was a memento of my childhood?"

"Those go in a scrapbook with photos of a first step, a letter to Santa, a lock of hair, painted handprints."

"A lock of hair?"

"First haircut."

"Weird." Thomas shrugs. *His* mom must've done that. "Could be because it's all Mom had to mark the day I arrived?"

Thomas taps his hands on the wheel. "You said Hana isn't the sentimental type. Seems like that was more your dad's role."

I struggle to untangle the last twenty-four hours. A knot slowly teases free. "Mom knew I'd try to get Dad alone . . . convince him to tell me whatever he knew." I stare at the letter. "She . . . she gave this to him . . . to give to me."

Thomas switches lanes, glances at me. "Okay. But why?"

All at once, it's crystal clear. "You saw how Hana cooks, methodically washes dishes, and scrubs the counters. Everything in its proper place, no mess left behind. That letter was important to her, once upon a time. But now that she's done with me, she's cleaning house."

Thomas shakes his head. "Wow. That's cold."

He's right, but his judgment pisses me off anyway. "I wouldn't cast any stones, *Theo*. Tell me about *your* perfect mother."

"She lives in Portland, in the Pearl neighborhood, same apartment where I grew up."

Does Lucas know this? Is the private detective he hired already mining that vein? "Are you going to visit her while we're here?"

"Probably not." Thomas glances at me. His cheeks are ruddy. "Sorry about criticizing Hana. It's just . . . I understand what it feels like to be judged by a parent."

"So your mom isn't proud of your career, either?"

The muscles in his jaw bunch then release. "She had bigger dreams." He passes an SUV then pulls back into the right lane. He's a much more cautious driver than I am—signals every lane change, stays within the speed limit.

"Do you hate your mother?" I ask.

"I feel sorry for her. She thinks that people like you can bring back the dead."

I challenge, "What if people like me could, at least for a few minutes?"

"Then, assuming you always believed that your bio parents were dead, why didn't you ever try to connect with them?"

"I told you on the train, it felt like a betrayal."

Thomas shakes his head. "Doesn't ring true."

The answer slips free like a fish off the hook. "I can't."

"Why not?"

"I don't know."

The set of Thomas's mouth tells me he thinks my inability to connect with my birth parents is proof that I'm a fraud. What I don't tell him is years ago I tried. Each attempt brought on panic attacks that burned through me like wildfire. My therapist at the time said it meant childhood trauma. It was easier to drop that shrink than to dig into a past that no longer mattered. I let Thomas's reaction go for now and tentatively press fingers against the lumps in the bottom corner of the envelope.

"What else is in there?"

I turn over the envelope. Pieces of plastic tumble onto my palm. They're toy figures. The smallest is a girl with brown braids. She wears a white dress with pink flowers that look like dahlias. It's the same dress I wore in my dream about the beach and similar to the comforter I ordered as a kid for my bedroom in High River. The one I refused to replace. Beside the girl is a woman in a sleeveless yellow sundress and straw hat. Thomas glances at them and it makes me feel . . . exposed. I push the narrow red and orange pieces around then hold out my hand. "What do you think these were?"

"Turn that big one over?"

I rearrange the pieces. We see it at the same time and say in unison, "A swing set."

"Does it mean anything to you?" Thomas pushes.

I poke at the two figures. The little girl's braids stream behind her. The woman's suntanned arms are held out . . . *The woman was pushing the little girl on a swing* . . . My mind casts its net into the past . . . *cracked vinyl seats beneath my legs* . . . *the long driveway shaded by oak trees* . . . *a big white house* . . . *flower boxes with bright yellow blooms* . . . *my hand clenched around the only things that were mine* . . . *a walk up the flagstone path . . . my new foster parents on the front step . . . the Japanese woman reached for my hand and my treasures spilled to the ground . . .*

I touch each piece of plastic like they're talismans. "I brought these to High River. Mom promised to keep them safe. But I never saw them again."

"What are they from?"

The jagged scar that runs the length of my palm separates the figures. "Not sure." Ghostly lips graze my forehead. The woman whispers . . . I lean in, but the words blow away like smoke.

"Sylvie?"

I ask, "What now?"

"We check into the hotel then we visit the Oregon Department of Human Services, find your caseworker, Heidi, and ask her what the hell that letter was about."

I hear my dad's warning about digging up the past and hesitate. But I've never really tried to understand my own abilities, I've just let them happen, never fully trusted them. Finding out the truth about my biological parents, and my time in foster care, could help answer all my doubts, validate my choices; prove I'm the real deal. And working with Thomas will allow me to at least partially control what we find, lead him to trust me.

"You still game?"

I close my fingers over the plastic figures. "Yes."

TWENTY-FOUR

Thomas

"We have you in a queen room," the young woman behind the front desk informs us. She glances at me, the cat carrier in my arms, and Moose. "Would you like to upgrade to a suite with a separate living room?"

Sylvie reads the name tag on her white blouse. "No thanks, Madison. It'll be cozy for sure, but my boyfriend likes to keep a *very* close eye on me." She winks.

Madison is Oregon winter pale so her blush is visible as it crawls up her neck to the roots of her strawberry blond hair. She types some information into her computer, pulls out a pair of keycards, and slots them into a square, black machine. "We have you in a pet-friendly room." She hands Sylvie the cards. "Would you like help from our bellman?"

I say, "We've got it from here."

"Certainly, sir. Oh. Ms. Young, you have a package and, ah, a bunch of messages." Madison hands Sylvie a document-sized envelope with her name on the front and a stack of yellow slips. "Um, Ms. Young?"

"You can call me Sylvie."

"Really? I'm . . . I'm a big fan of yours. My sister and I have tickets to your show on Sunday!"

Fatigue from the last twenty-four hours flakes away when Sylvie smiles. Several people in the lobby glance over, drawn to her like honeybees to blossoms.

Madison asks, "Do you mind if I pet Moose?"

"He'd love that."

On cue, Moose sits. Madison comes around the reception desk, scratches his chest with rose-painted nails. The gold charm bracelet on her wrist jingles.

Sylvie sways and I catch her around the waist. "You okay?" *She hasn't eaten much.*

She touches one of the gold charms on Madison's bracelet—an old-fashioned trolley car—then covers her ears, winces like she's in pain. "A man gave you that . . . but two figures are attached to it?"

Madison's posture goes ramrod straight, mouth agape. "My brother! He gave one to me and the other to my sister, before he—"

"He's out of the country?" Sylvie asks.

"Yes."

She taps her lips with the tip of an index finger. "You're worried about him."

"Yeah. He's a contractor for the US government, in Iraq."

Sylvie nods then asks, "Has your dad passed?"

"Yes," Madison says, "when we were little. I don't really remember him. But my—"

"Your mom is still alive?"

Madison bobs up and down on the balls of her feet, face flushed. "She is!"

"Your brother, he's more of a father figure?"

"He helped raise us."

Sylvie tugs at her earlobe like she can't quite hear. "Does his first name start with a B or R—"

"Brian! And his middle name is Robert. This is unreal! Brian went into the military at eighteen so he could make money to help Mom with Becca and me. He wanted us to attend Saint Mary's—it's an all-girls' high school. Is Brian . . . is he going to be okay? Over there?"

"Know that Brian is at peace with the choices he made," Sylvie replies. "He loved you, and given another chance, he wouldn't have done anything differently."

"Thank. You. So. So. Much," Madison gushes.

We head across a stylish lobby dotted with wing-backed leather chairs and clashing patterns in bright colors that somehow form a cohesive, hip vibe. When the silver elevator doors close, Sylvie murmurs, "Something happened to her brother. There was a really loud noise, maybe an explosion, and—"

"Skip the theatrics, okay?" I mutter. "They won't sway me."

Sylvie flinches. "What? Are you mad at me?"

Instantly, I feel like a jerk, which makes me angrier. *I'm mad at my knee-jerk desire to help you; that I registered the swell of your hip beneath my hand; liked that I was the man next to you while the other people in the lobby could only look; I'm pissed that you just fed a load of BS to a young woman who's got a damn good reason to be worried about her brother's safety.*

"Say it," Sylvie demands.

Anger scrapes inside my chest like flint to steel. "You just can't resist, can you?" I accuse. "I sense two figures? Madison had already said she had a sister. She intimated that her brother had left before you followed a natural progression. Even I knew, by the look on that girl's face, that she was worried about him, that he's a father figure. Does his name begin with a B or an R? Popular initial for a guy's name—you had a good chance with one, got lucky with two. Basically you played the odds, threw logical assumptions out, took off with whatever hit. That girl is just another mark."

Sylvie's eyes frost to the color of the rink Deacan and I skated on in winter. Flatly, she says, "So we're back to me being a grief vampire."

I slap a palm against the side of the elevator. Moose growls low and I take a step back from him. "Look, you admitted that you don't even know what you're saying to most of them. Numbers, dates, first letters of names that aren't right but women like Madison are too desperate to notice. For fuck's sake, Sylvie, you spoke about her brother in the *past tense*." Sylvie looks away and I'm glad she's ashamed.

The hotel room décor is a clash of yellow-and-blue-plaid furniture, matching bedspread paired with a similarly colored Persian-style carpet. Sylvie silently hangs her clothes in the closet then goes to the desk, drops the folder on it. She sorts through the message slips. "Eleven. All from Lucas."

"And the folder?" My tone is petulant and I hate it.

Sylvie sighs. "It's my prep—names of audience members, research on their social profiles. Lucas must've asked for them early, considering my situation."

"Are you going to look at it?" She glares at me. The truth hits hard. I'm mad at her for being who she is. It's like I forgot for a moment that I'm writing an exposé. I'm pissed off because I've started to like or at least empathize with Sylvie. How could I not, after meeting Hana? They have different MOs, but our mothers both have obsessions—Hana for her religion and orchard, my mother for psychics and the dead. Both women have pushed their children away. *But my job is to be impartial; state the facts. Period.*

Still, it's hard to look at Sylvie and *not* imagine her at eighteen, desperate to escape High River and Hana. When I left for college, I was desperate, too, rarely returned, making any excuse not to be back in that apartment, surrounded by unfulfilled dreams and ghosts.

Sylvie pulls a roll of Tums from her pocket, chews one. "When I was a kid, my dad used to eat those by the box," I say. "Turned out he had a peptic ulcer. The doctor said it was work stress, put him on a prescription drug that reduced stomach acid. It's sold over the counter now. We passed a CVS about a block away?"

She doesn't bother answering. Moose stalks the room. I let Chris out of her carrier and she instantly follows the big dog, sniffs where he sniffed like she's a Great Dane, too, except she's a twenty-year-old cat held together with bits of string and old glue. Her hips hitch with each step, like she's a wind-up toy powered by a twisted rubber band that's ready to snap. I'll put a pain pill in whatever she decides to eat today. I've tried not to give her too many, worried they might hurt her somehow. The pills were prescribed two years ago for arthritis. Chris needs to see the vet when we get back to LA. I've been putting off that visit.

I dial the concierge from our room phone and ask him to get a fourteen-day course of Prilosec, charge it to my credit card. I'd go myself, but that'd mean leaving Sylvie alone with the room phone and that folder.

Sylvie slumps onto a corner of the bed, pulls her hair down, and braids it. She untangles the braid, lets her hair fall free. *Backed into a corner.* My article will protect folks from people like Sylvie, Doug, Victor, but in this moment it feels like I'm the Grinch who tells children there's no such thing as Santa. *The truth is the truth.* I pull out my computer, Google "Oregon Department of Human Services." "ODHS is only a half mile from here. We can walk."

Sylvie pinches the bed's comforter. "Shouldn't we make an appointment?"

"It's a lot easier to move things along in person. Maybe someone there will be a fan like Madison and you can *do your thing* to grease the wheels." She picks up the remote and flicks on the large-screen TV across from the bed. *What the hell is wrong with me?* I'm purposefully trying to hurt her. "Sorry," I say. *Again.* Sylvie doesn't look at me, just scrolls through channels. When the hotel phone rings, I wait to see if she'll answer it but she doesn't move. After the fourth ring, I pick up. "Hello?"

"Please hand the phone to Sylvie," a clipped male voice says.

"It's for you." I hold out the phone and Sylvie takes it from me, turns her back.

"Hello . . . Yes . . . Because I don't have my phone anymore . . . Yes . . . Thomas took it and he's right here . . . He already saw the package you sent . . . I . . ."

Sylvie glances at me then quickly looks away.

"Yes, I hear you . . . Lucas, listen to me . . . No . . . No, I didn't . . . And I'm not going to . . . What? . . . But don't you think it would . . . Lucas, please listen! . . . I can . . . Okay, okay . . . Thanks for the vote of confidence." Sylvie slams the phone into its cradle.

"What did Lucas say?" I ask.

"It doesn't matter. I need a shower. Then we can head over to ODHS."

I itch the scruff along my jaw. "I'll take a quick one when you're done."

She challenges, "You're not afraid to leave me alone in the room with Lucas's folder?"

"I'll take it into the bathroom with me."

Sylvie asks, "What about the telephone?"

"I'll leave the door open when I shower."

"Don't worry," she snaps. "I won't look. Just don't take too long. I want to get to ODHS before everyone is at lunch."

"Look, apologies for coming on so strong."

"But not for *what* you said."

I turn away. We both know my answer.

TWENTY-FIVE

Sylvie

I'm quiet as we walk to the Oregon Department of Human Services, mulling over the information Lucas shared during our brief conversation. Thomas had an older brother, Deacan, who died along with his father. *Why didn't he tell me?* When I read Thomas onstage, back when I didn't have any idea who he really was, a young spirit with a journal came forward. *Could that have been his brother?* Regardless, telling me about his father's death but omitting Deacan's means Thomas has some related conflict or unresolved feelings. I can use that, though I'm not sure exactly how yet. The fact that I have another weapon should give me a sense of power, but it also makes me . . . sad. I always wanted a big brother, someone to look out for me, to care even when my parents didn't. If Thomas and his brother were close, then Thomas lost a best friend, confidant, and protector. That's a wound that never fully heals.

ODHS is spread over a city block. A single-story redbrick building houses the Child Welfare Office. Double glass doors lead to a white linoleum hallway lit by rectangular fluorescent bulbs. A woman with closely cropped black hair sits behind a high counter. Her bright orange dress defies the dismal atmosphere. She taps away, eyes glued to a computer screen. Her name tag: CLEMENTINE WEBSTER.

Clementine glances up. "Can I help you?"

I smile. "Yes. Hi. My name is Sylvie Peters Young and I'd like to see my foster care file."

She slides a form onto a clipboard and hands it to me with a pen. "Just fill this out and bring it back with your driver's license."

"It's that easy?" I ask, quickly filling out the short form.

"Sure is, kiddo. You have rights and we're happy to provide that information. What years are we talking about?"

I hand back the clipboard and dig my driver's license from my purse. "I was born in 1996 and adopted in 2002."

Clementine grimaces. "Ah. That's a problem."

"Why?"

"Department policy is to destroy records seven years after a child is adopted or ages out of the system at eighteen."

"When we called, the woman I spoke to said a lot of the older records are still in storage," Thomas says.

Clementine nods. "True. The policy is seven years but no one actually has the time to regularly sort through all of that mess down there."

I ask, "Could someone check for me?"

Clementine makes a copy of my driver's license then says, "Sure thing. You never know. We might get lucky." She ushers us into a small room. As we wait on opposite sides of a table, Thomas drums his long fingers on his plastic chair. "Quit it." He folds his hands.

Fifteen minutes later, Clementine walks in and produces a faded brown file with a flourish. "Ta-da! Hard to believe the clerk found it. That's practically a miracle. First, that it was still there. Second, if you saw the storage in the basement? It runs the length of this building, tight aisles, a claustrophobic wouldn't last five minutes—total rabbit warren. But your file was right on top of the year 2002! I'll be at my desk if you need anything else."

My fingers tingle as I open the file. There's a single sheet of paper inside that lists my date of birth, 5-10-1996; biological parents' names, Becky and Seth Peters; arrival in foster care, 9-15-2000. The date I was sent to foster parents Hana and Wess Young, 4-12-2002, and my adoption date, 6-1-2002. "It took one month and change for Mom and Dad to adopt me," I mutter. "Whoever Heidi was, she worked fast."

"The average time for foster parents to complete the process of adoption is a year to eighteen months," Thomas says.

There's nothing about how my birth parents died, or who fostered me in the year-and-a-half before Mom and Dad took me in. My early childhood is summarized in one lonely paragraph. I hold up the sheet for Thomas to see. "There's no caseworker's name."

Clementine pops her head around the doorway. "All good here?"

"Quick question?" I ask.

She steps into the room. "Sure thing. Shoot."

"I went from foster care to adoption in about a month. Is that fast?"

Clementine whistles. "Lightning fast."

"Would there be a reason?"

Clementine's smile is a thousand watts. "You're one lucky kiddo!"

"What if it wasn't luck?" Thomas presses.

Her smile dims several notches. "Not sure what you mean. But I wouldn't know. I don't have anything to do with casework."

I give her an encouraging smile then ask, "Does every foster child get a caseworker?"

"Course they do—sometimes more than one. So many kids, lots of sad stories, some pretty violent ones, too, hard for a mind to take, day in, day out. The job has a significant burnout rate so it's normal for a foster child to get passed along to a new caseworker. Why do you ask?"

"There's no caseworker's name in my file."

Clementine steps behind me, peers at the file. "Well, I'll be. You're right." She sighs, straightens the pink belt on her dress. "If you saw the stacks of files our caseworkers have on their desks—you can barely see around them. They're supposed to be responsible for no more than fourteen cases, but the average is about thirty children. Sorry to say it, but they're only human."

"I totally get that," I say. "How long have *you* worked here?"

"Since 2008."

"Do you know a caseworker named Heidi?"

Clementine looks up, mentally scrolls through names, then shakes her head. "Nope. Was she yours?"

"I think so."

Thomas pushes, "Is there anyone who worked here from 1996 to 2002 who might've known her?"

Clementine hesitates then says, "Hang on a sec."

Her pantyhose swish as she strides off. When she returns ten minutes later with a gray-haired, mustached security guard in a pressed white shirt, blue slacks, a gun holstered at his hip, I'm sure we're about to be ushered out of the building.

"This is Max," Clementine says. "He's worked security in this building for, what, thirty-five years?"

"Forty this month," Max says.

He's mid-sixties, built like a retired football player with broad shoulders, a thick neck, bulbous nose, and mole beneath his left eye. "What can I do you for, child?" Max asks.

"I was wondering if you knew a woman named Heidi who was a caseworker between the late nineties to early two thousands?"

Max rubs the back of his head. "If I did, would she be in some kind of trouble?"

"No. I'm the one who needs *her* help."

He pulls at his mustache. "'Cause folks who work in foster care are givers, through and through, not takers."

Irritation flickers inside me but I smile brightly. "Like I said, I have no intention of doing anything that could hurt her."

"Good to hear. Never met a kinder soul. Beautiful woman but she never did marry though a buncha fellows tried. Nope. Totally dedicated to the kids she shepherded. Always went the extra mile, wanted the best for each and every one of 'em. Sad day when we lost her."

Hope splashes into a puddle at my feet. "When did she die?"

Max holds up both hands. "Oh. No! Sorry to make you think that. She retired in 2002. Far as I know, Heidi is very much alive. Saw her 'bout ten months back at a Rotary thing."

"What's her last name?" Thomas interjects.

"Hiddleston. Don't have her number," Max says, "But she lives on the way to the coast. Tillamook, 'bout an hour from Portland, 'pending on traffic."

The idea that I might talk to someone today who knew me, *before*, sends a jolt through my body and the conviction that finding out the truth about my birth parents is more important than I'd ever imagined . . . *but why?*

"Please give Heidi my best if you chat, won't you?" Max asks.

"Will do." I stand. "Thanks for your help." Max holds on to my hand after we shake.

"One of my favorite authors is C. S. Lewis. You ever read him?"

"No," I say. Max's fingers press harder.

"C. S. Lewis said, 'You can't go back and change the beginning, but you can start where you are and change the ending.'" Max gives my hand a final squeeze then releases it. He shrugs. "Always thought that was mighty fine advice for foster kids."

I look over my shoulder before Thomas and I pass through the building's double doors to the street. Max still watches us, jaw clamped tight. Certainty bites hard. The truth about my biological parents is darker than I'd imagined. But I have to know.

TWENTY-SIX

Thomas

When we return to the hotel, Madison is no longer at reception. It doesn't mean anything. The idea that Sylvie prognosticated a disaster on the other side of the world, that Madison's brother was somehow involved, is absurd. We stop at the concierge's desk. The guy behind it is mid-thirties sporting a dark blue suit, red tie, hair slicked back.

He peers up. "Can I help you, sir?"

I ask, "Do you have a pharmacy delivery for Room 816?"

"Let me check." He opens one of the desk's drawers, withdraws a small brown bag. "Here you go."

I pull some singles from my wallet to tip the guy. "Thanks much." My feet stick. "Ah—"

"Yes, sir?"

Don't do it. "There was a young woman at reception earlier today. Madison?"

The concierge's smile slips a degree. "That'd be Madison Farrow. Yes?"

"She was very helpful and I, we, wanted to thank her. Do you know when she'll be back from her break?"

The concierge folds well-manicured hands, lowers his voice. "I'm sorry to say there's been a family emergency. I don't know when Madison will be back to work."

We don't talk as the elevator climbs. Something else could've happened to Madison's family—a grandmother's heart attack, a sister's car accident, an aunt's stroke, a dog's broken leg; it's not Brian.

"She might've just lost her brother," Sylvie finally says.

I bark, "Leave it." But the devastating loss and loneliness I felt after Deacan's death still floods in. My eyes burn. *Stop it*. Over the past year there have been times when Victor and Doug also knew or predicted the seemingly impossible. Each time I figured out how they'd managed the trick. If Madison left work because something happened to her brother, then I'll figure out Sylvie's hoax, too.

"Are you okay?" Sylvie quietly asks.

"Why wouldn't I be?"

Back in the room I sit down at the antique-style desk and put "Heidi Hiddleston" into Google. She retired in 2002, the same year Sylvie was adopted. *Coincidence?* I search the online Tillamook white pages and find only three Hiddlestons: Grier and Barr F. Hiddleston, Vernon and Charles P. Hiddleston, and H. Hiddleston. The latter lives at 10 Lattimore Lane. There's a phone number. I dial and a woman answers on the second ring. Quickly, I hang up. Surprise has served us well so far. I put the address into Google Maps. "I've got Heidi's address and she's home. Ready?"

Sylvie watches me from the couch. Moose lies at her feet chewing a massive rawhide bone and Chris is curled in her lap, purring. It seems impossible that my cat had any more weight to lose, but she's thinner. I trace the nick on my freshly shaven jaw. Being around Sylvie has thrown me off. That needs to stop. I also need to quit being such an ass. "I shouldn't have cut you off."

"Would you rather we wait to talk about Madison until after your exposé runs and my career is destroyed?" Sylvie calmly asks.

I fold my hands on the desk. "Go ahead and say what you need to say."

"You seem to have already made up your mind."

"Like I said when we met, agreeing to an interview, opening up your life means that your side of things will be represented in my article. And if you can prove you're not a fraud, that will be in the story, too."

She lifts one brow. "How's it going so far?"

"The jury is out." My answer surprises me. *Is that true?*

Sylvie shifts forward on the couch and asks, "I'm curious. What do you think about psychics throughout history that have predicted major world events?"

"Like who?"

"Nostradamus for a start. He predicted the Great Fire of London, the French Revolution, and the rise of Napoleon."

I scoff, "Pretty hard to fact-check a French astrologer whose book was published in the 1500s."

Sylvie tips her head, considers. "Okay, how about Jeane Dixon? She predicted that a Democrat would win the presidential election in 1960, and that he'd be assassinated in Dallas on November 22, 1963. That was John F. Kennedy."

"You're leaving out the fact that Jeane Dixon famously reversed some of her predictions, including JFK's."

Sylvie's eyes gleam. "Maybe there was a journalist trying to destroy her career."

Enjoying the light sparring, I admit, "Maybe. But there's a reason the Jeane Dixon effect is named after her—it's human nature that people publicize the correct predictions of psychics and forget about the false ones." I rest my chin on folded knuckles and ask, "Do you know what the 'law of truly large numbers' is?"

"With a large enough sample, anything, even the outrageous, is likely to happen," Sylvie replies.

"*The Simpsons* has predicted *major* world events in its thirty-year run—Super Bowl winners, 9/11, even Disney's acquisition of 21st Century Fox. I don't think Homer is psychic. I *know* that the show has brilliant writers."

Sylvie quips, "So you're saying I'm a liar but I'm brilliant?"

Her smile is impish and I can't help but laugh. "Like I said, the jury is still out. You ready?"

"I guess so." She hands me Chris, dusts cat hair off her jeans. "She's shedding an awful lot."

"That's normal."

"This morning she drank most of Moose's water."

"Normal." *Is it?*

Sylvie crosses to the door. "Okay, let's go find Heidi then."

I have to ask. "What did Lucas say when you spoke with him?"

She turns. "Well, he wasn't at all happy that you were staying in my room."

I joke, "Maybe he's jealous. Are you two romantically involved?"

"Seriously? He's twenty years older than me."

"Have there been *any* since high school? I mean, you're decent looking—"

Sylvie snorts. "Thanks."

"Why couldn't I find anyone?"

"There have only been a few guys, one semi-serious, but he wanted children so I broke it off."

"You don't want kids?"

She twists her hair into a knot. "Nope."

"Huh. So why'd Lucas call?"

Sylvie fiddles with her earring. "To make sure I got the package he sent. I told him that I wasn't going to read it and he gave me an ultimatum."

"Which is?"

"Still off the record?"

"Already agreed."

"Either I find a way to prep without you knowing or he'll cancel the show."

"Can he do that? Cancel your show?"

"Not without my okay."

"You going to give it to him?" Sylvie opens the door. "Are you going to do your research?" I press.

She says over her shoulder, "The jury is still out."

I bite my lower lip. "If you cancel the show or find a way to do prep, there's only one conclusion I can come to."

Moose trails Sylvie into the hall. I scoop up Chris and follow. When the elevator doors open, a couple who must be well into their eighties, both with snow-white hair, his thin enough to see slivers of spotted scalp, hers a stylish wave pinned behind her ears with rhinestone clips, glance at us. They see Moose and the man, with the aid of a wooden cane, reflexively steps in front of his wife.

When the elevator dings on the restaurant level, the two get off.

As the doors slide closed, Sylvie quietly says, "For you, this is all about the article, but for me? It's about *me*."

She's right. This is as much an indictment of *who* she is, as about what she does for a living. And I can't change that. On the way to the car we pick up sandwiches at a little café. I'm driving and still finish mine before we get on the highway. Sylvie picks at hers but doesn't eat much. *She's thinner, too.*

The day hasn't brightened from this morning, as dreary as the mood in this car, the clouds low, suffocating. At some point Sylvie switches on the radio, clicks through bad rock stations, classical music, settles on NPR.

A news anchor says, "NPR is supported by a grant from the Charles Stewart Mott Foundation. Now we return to breaking news and our foreign correspondent Jane Arraf. Jane?"

"Thank you, Andrew," Arraf says. "As we reported a few hours ago, a car bomb was exploded at a US military construction site outside the city of Baghdad in Iraq. There were reports of multiple injuries. We now know there are twelve confirmed dead and ten wounded. The list of dead US servicemen whose families have been notified include: Private First Class Derek Sampson, age twenty-three; Corporal Sharlene Kavitz, twenty-six; Private First Class James Woods, twenty-two; Lance Corporal Wayne McDoogle, twenty-seven; Sergeant Patricia Richardson, thirty-one; and military contractors Lawrence Stemper, thirty-five; Brian Robert Farrow, thirty-nine . . ."

My pulse takes off like a rocket. Adrenaline makes my fingers twitch as I turn off the radio, hand Sylvie a bottle of water, and dig the Prilosec packet from my bag. "Take one. Please." She pops a pill from the silver pack and washes it down with water. "You'll need to take the entire fourteen days for them to work, okay?" Sylvie nods, her eyes trained on my face. I pull into the passing lane, overtake a Prius, then move back into the right lane.

Brian Robert Farrow. It's Madison's brother. She's just lost her big brother. "How'd you know?"

Sylvie runs her fingers lightly down Chris's back. "You won't believe me."

How the hell did she do it? "I'll listen."

"When I touched the charm on Madison's bracelet, there was a loud blast. It hurt. I smelled smoke . . . heard screams."

Sylvie covered her ears, winced.

"I knew there was an explosion but didn't know why, so I asked questions, and you're right, some were leading, others educated guesses. Maybe I should've left it alone, but I rarely do that . . . and then there was a male energy at the red door, very faint. I opened it and he showed me blistered skin, blood . . . he'd died in fire."

I glance at Sylvie as she wipes the sheen from her brow. Despite my certainty that she's a fraud, goose bumps rise on my arms.

"The spirit showed me a heart, broke it into two pieces, and held them out. I guessed those were his two sisters. When I told Madison the part about her brother loving her and that he wouldn't have done anything differently, the spirit's energy changed, he was at peace." Sylvie traces a heart on the fogged window, makes a jagged line in the center. "Go ahead. Explain it away."

The problem is that I can't . . . unless I believe Sylvie is just really lucky at making guesses. But is anyone that lucky?

TWENTY-SEVEN

Sylvie

Thomas's face has gone pale. I consider using the information Lucas gave me about Deacan now, while he's rattled. I could easily fabricate a lie about a young spirit coming through with a message that would lead Thomas to believe . . . but I can't bring myself to do it. Is it because I'm waiting for a more powerful opportunity, or do I want to avoid hurting him *that* way?

Does he now believe, at least a little bit? Maybe, maybe not, but I sit up straighter. My parents have convicted me of being morally bankrupt. Thomas's goal is to expose me as a fraud; humiliate then erase me. They've all chipped away at confidence that has always been precariously balanced. Over the past few days their doubts and accusations seeped into me like poison and it's amplified my fears. One of my early therapists asked, point-blank, if I was a hoax. He said it would explain my anxieties. He told me the only remedy was to come clean, quit the business. Lucas fired him.

Now I stare out the window at the monochromatic gray sky and wonder if this next move, talking to Heidi, will help or hurt me. *Time will tell.* All I'm sure of is that I have to know. When we reach Lattimore Lane, it's a narrow street of small homes, most the size of a double-wide trailer, painted in varying pastels, with white picket fences, flower boxes lined with early tulips, daffodils, and irises. Lawns are postage stamp–sized, well tended.

A group of six women, most with short gray hair, powerwalk down the street; laughter and quick conversation trails behind them. A man in a baseball hat and down jacket works clippers along the top of the box hedge that borders his driveway. Everyone is taking advantage of the cold but dry April day.

My nerves thrum. I reach behind the seat and Moose finds my hand, licks it. His unconditional love is my touchstone. "Good boy." I scratch behind his ears, and his forehead scrunches with pleasure. Thomas has been quiet since our conversation about Madison. I glance over but the set of his jaw tells me he's not ready to talk further about it.

There are moments like Madison's during some of my shows. Things I can't explain, voices, energies that come through the red door; that are real . . . at least to me. After a show it's hard to sleep. I reconstruct every interaction, create delicate origami boats out of them, then rip holes in their hulls and watch them sink. It's not difficult to tear what I do apart. But it's the times when I can't find any explanation for what happened, when a boat continues to float, that keep me going. Kelly and Rose's reading was like that. So was Madison's.

We pull into Heidi Hiddleston's driveway. Thomas turns off the car, but keeps his hands perched over the steering wheel. What does it say about me that I'm attracted to his hands, despite everything he's said to me; that he doesn't believe; thinks I'm a swindler, a vampire, and deserve to be ruined? I don't think it's Stockholm syndrome anymore. Therapist three, or maybe it was four, delved into my dating life. She told me that keeping relationships surface-level or choosing one-night stands was a form of self-punishment. Maybe the attraction I now feel toward Thomas, a man who despises what I do, is a way to punish myself for the people I've hurt. But what about all the people I've helped?

Focus.

Thomas is a reporter, skilled at influencing his subjects. We're evenly matched in that regard. He knows how to mine information. He's a dangerous adversary but could still be a valuable asset. With effort, I look away from his hands.

"I don't think we should tell Heidi the truth," Thomas says.

"Seriously?"

"Can we agree that something hinky went on with your adoption?"

"Hinky? . . . Yes."

"Heidi was involved. If we come at her directly, she probably won't let us in the front door."

"What do you suggest?"

"I'm a reporter doing a story on the unsung heroes of the foster care system in Oregon—caseworkers. Heidi's name came up during my research as a champion for children. I'd like to talk to her about her work."

He really is a good liar, quick on the draw. "Then why am I here?"

"You're my girlfriend. I promised to join you and our dog at Manzanita for the day but this was on the way, so you agreed to stop."

I sniff. "What happened to your journalistic integrity?"

Thomas shrugs off the jab. "First, we don't know if Heidi has that much to do with your story."

With a smirk, I say, "Go on. Your rationalizations are fascinating."

"Second. You might not believe this, but I actually want to find out the truth about your past for both of us. Okay?"

I consider. For the moment we're on the same side. Once Thomas gets what he's after, he'll use it against me. But this isn't over. Hana used to read me fairy tales. Her favorite was "Hansel and Gretel." The siblings, left to starve in the woods, were lured into the home of a cannibalistic witch. Gretel ultimately tricked the witch into climbing into her own oven, bolted the door, and let her burn to death. My mother thought the moral of that story was, *Never go inside a stranger's home, even if you're starving.* But to me, it was always, *Use your wits.*

"Okay," I agree. "Tell Heidi your little story. But Max might've already warned her about me."

"It's possible. We'll know pretty quickly. Do you still want to do this?" he asks.

My gut sizzles. "Let's go."

We follow a curved path of stamped concrete dotted with bearded garden gnomes in red hats. Heidi Hiddleston warily opens her front door after our third knock. She's taller than me, well over six feet, very thin, and her wavy, dyed red hair has a quarter inch of white roots that runs the length of a middle part. Her eyes are dark blue, the white on the right side marred by a squid-like broken blood vessel. She's put together neatly in tan slacks and a pink collared shirt but purple dishwashing gloves that reach almost to her elbows detract from the look of a retired teacher. Deep lines stretch from her nostrils to the corners of her mouth. They remind me of the old man in my snow globes who gleefully worked his marionettes. I'd peg her age as mid-sixties. *Will she recognize me?*

"I'm a happy Catholic," she firmly says to Thomas and me, clearly mistaking us for proselytizers. "But I'm so glad you've found comfort in your religion." She starts to close the door.

"Ms. Hiddleston? We're not from a religious group," Thomas says.

He holds out his business card. "I'm Thomas Holmes, a reporter with the *L.A. Times*. I'm doing a story about the heroes of Oregon's foster care system and your name came up as one of the most dedicated caseworkers."

Heidi reads the business card, and a slow smile spreads across her face. "Well, gosh, I've been retired for eighteen years. Hard to believe anyone remembers me!"

"They do," Thomas says. "Might we come in, chat for a few minutes?"

Heidi glances at our car in the driveway. Moose's head pokes out of the window. She plucks at her gloves, looks at me, and says, "Well. You've caught me in the middle of spring cleaning."

She doesn't recognize me. Why would she? It was almost two decades ago and I was a little kid, one of dozens of cases she juggled. My nerves buzz like a beehive that's been kicked. It's hard to think, focus. *This woman knows everything.*

Thomas says, "We should've called. Apologies. This is my girl-friend, Syl. I promised her and our dog a day at the beach but since you were on the way, she was game to stop in case you might be willing to talk about the great work you've done."

"Well . . . if it'll shine the light on the importance of those dedicated to foster children," Heidi says and peels off her gloves, "then of course I can spare a few minutes. Goodness, it's not like there's a timeline for housework, but I do like to keep a schedule, otherwise we retirees can lose track of time and our sense of purpose."

"Totally understand." Thomas smoothly steps into Heidi's home.

The single-story house has a small entryway with a wooden coat stand in the corner. There's a closed door to the right, probably her bedroom. To the left is a combined living and dining room with a door at the far end that opens into a sea-foam-green-accented kitchen. A glass cabinet just inside the opening to the living room is filled with china, gold-etched floral plates on display.

"Those were my mother's," Heidi says when she sees me looking. "My sister wanted them, but Mom knew I was the better cook and love to entertain."

"They're beautiful." I follow her into the living room, where the walls are one shade darker than the beige carpet. A two-foot-high cross with a very real-looking Jesus peers from the wall behind the couch. *Bless you for taking little Sylvie Peters into your home.* There's a brightly colored painting of the Last Supper hanging to the right of a highly polished dining set. *I believe with your love and GOD's guiding hand, Sylvie will have a good life.* And the side table dividing the living and dining room has two rows of votive candles lined in front of a statue of the Virgin Mary. *Give justice to the weak and the fatherless.* This is definitely the Heidi who wrote Mom that letter.

An upright piano stands tight against the right-hand wall. I stop to admire the photos lined along the top. Max was right. Heidi was a beauty. In one picture she's in her twenties, wavy red hair halfway down her back, high cheekbones, deep-blue eyes. She wears a white halter and a purple hippy-style skirt slung low on rounded hips. Beside her is a woman who must be her sister, eyes the same color but set deep in a square face capped with spiky red hair. The sister sports a white collared shirt and plaid shorts.

The rest of the photos show the two girls at the beach, on a sailboat, hiking in the woods; they range from childhood to the present. *They've been best friends their whole lives.* A pang of jealousy strikes and the vibrations ripple through me. *What would it have been like to have a sister?* Only one photograph has a man in it—he's turned sideways, broad shoulders, jet-black hair, arms casually wrapped around Heidi's waist, hands on her bare belly. *She might not have married, but she definitely slept with that guy.*

Heidi lifts a frame—two barefoot little girls on a dock. "My sister, Briella," she says.

"You look close," Thomas notes.

"We are . . . when she's capable." Heidi's eyes fill. "Briella has Alzheimer's. On good days she remembers me. Not so often now. Her husband died a few years ago. I'm thankful I can be here for her. 'It is the Lord who goes before you. He will be with you; he will not fail you or forsake you. Do not fear or be dismayed.' Deuteronomy 31:8."

Once Thomas and I are settled on an overstuffed floral couch with cups of tea on cork coasters and a plate of Pepperidge Farm Milano Mint cookies, Thomas pulls out his notebook. "Why don't we start with your decision to become a foster care caseworker?"

Heidi slides to the edge of her chair and takes a nibble of cookie then a sip of tea before placing them carefully on their respective plates. She blots thin lips with a paper napkin. "Both Briella and I were so very lucky. We were *called* to our respective careers. Honest-to-goodness. Probably on account of beautiful childhoods—mother and father were strict but kind and instilled a deep love of God and the importance of giving back to our community. After graduating with a degree in social work, I was an administrative assistant for the Department of Human Services. I saw, firsthand, all the important work done by DHS and the special role of foster caseworkers."

"What was it, specifically, about foster care that called to you?" Thomas presses.

Heidi's cheeks flush. He's good at playing into her emotional needs.

"Children. They're my life's work, God's work, truly, and it was always my heart's desire to see every child loved and happy. My family wanted me married with offspring of my own. Those were the times when a woman's place was definitely in the home, barefoot and pregnant, ha-ha. They didn't understand that each child I helped was one of my own. That it took every free moment and iron-willed resolve, no time for marriage, honest-to-goodness, to make sure my kids weren't let down by the system, that they were shepherded to a good life."

Thomas asks, "How do you become a caseworker?"

"My parents didn't support my career goals so I worked full time at DHS as an executive assistant while taking night classes for four years to earn my master's degree in social work. The day I became a caseworker was the proudest of my life."

I lean in. "Did anyone in your family support you?"

"Briella. Always. No questions asked."

Thomas takes a bite of his cookie. "Isn't it difficult work? Most kids in the foster system are there because their parents neglected or abused them, right?"

"Not necessarily," Heidi says. "Some have been raised by a loving grandparent who can no longer care for them. Others were given to the system at birth by a mother who didn't have the life skills to cope, or two loving parents too young to properly raise a child. Of course, there are cases of drug-dependent parents, and worse. Babies born with addictions because of their birth mother's disease are heartbreaking. There are also cases of emotional and physical trauma . . ." She trails off, watches a robin feed at the wooden birdhouse hung outside her bay window.

"Can you tell us about some of your more difficult cases?" I push.

"Oh, dear. No, I really can't do that," Heidi says with a little frown. "They're confidential."

The prim way she tucks her lips at the end of *confidential* grates. I slide to the edge of the couch. "What if one of those cases, one of those children, came to you for information?"

Heidi reaches for her teacup, takes a neat swallow. "You're too young to understand this," she says. "But it's best for those children to look forward, never back."

Thomas gives me a warning look. "What if they want to know?" I press.

Heidi holds up one hand, palm out, and says, "'For I know the plans I have for you, declares the Lord, plans for welfare and not for evil, to give you a future and a hope.'" She finishes her cookie and darts a pointed tongue to remove a crumb on her upper lip. "I'm so glad we could have this chat, but it's time for me to get back to cleaning. Idle hands are the devil's workshop."

"I'm one of those children who was your life's work; one of your own."

Heidi's brows rise. "My-oh-my! Really? What's your name, dear?"

"Sylvie Peters."

Her face transforms from confusion to shock, and finally fear, in a single second. She puts her cup down, misses the coaster, it clatters, and tea slops over the edge. Quickly, she wipes the spill off the polished wood, doesn't even bother to look at me, says, "That name doesn't ring a bell, dear, but then age has dimmed my memory."

Frustration, fury, and the unfairness of it all rise like bile. "Let me help fill in the blanks. From age four-and-a-half to almost six, I was in foster care, but there's no information in my file about that time. And I can't recall a single thing about it or anything from my life before. In 2002, I went to live with Hana and Wess Young in High River. A month later my adoption went through and I became Sylvie Young."

Heidi unfolds her skinny limbs like a praying mantis and stands. "I'd like you to leave. Now."

TWENTY-EIGHT

Thomas

I have to steer Sylvie through the living room and out Heidi's front door. It closes firmly behind us. The bolt scrapes into place.

Furious, she shakes off my hands. "Fuck you!" She stalks toward the car. The guy trimming his hedges looks over.

"Fuck me?" I say, voice low. "You just blew us out of the water. If I didn't know better, I'd say you did it on purpose!" She whirls. Moose growls, half his body now out the window. *Great. Cerberus is going to attack me.*

"Stay," Sylvie tells her dog. "I did it on *purpose*? For the past forty-eight hours I've been picked at like I'm roadkill. I've had to defend what I do, who I am, while you and my parents sit on thrones like the arbiters of morality. Who are you to judge me?"

The man in the next yard has given up his work and now watches us. Pretty soon he's going to call the cops. "Sylvie, calm down—"

"Calm down? I've had to beg for information at DHS about *my* life. MY life! Smile, cajole, and wheedle for the chance to find out who I was before my adoption—"

"I don't—"

"That woman KNOWS. She knows what happened to me," Sylvie

says, jabbing her finger toward the house. "She knows what happened to my real parents. And she won't tell me. That's not fair! She has no right to keep my past from me! It's MINE."

The guy now has his phone out. I'm not sure if he's taking a video or calling the police. "Sylvie, we need to get out of here," I say with a nod at him.

She ignores me, face red, eyes wild. "How do you think it feels to want to know about my past and at the same time be terrified of what I'll find?"

"I never—"

"That's right! You've *never* put yourself in my shoes. Did you ever consider that something horrific might've happened to me? I could've been abused, molested, raped! Maybe I don't recall it because remembering could seriously screw me up!"

Sylvie pants like she's run a race, fists ready to hit something, someone. I close the distance between us. Blows rain against my chest. When they weaken, I pull her close. She struggles for a second then goes slack, her face pressed against me.

Voice muffled by my down jacket, she says, "Mom thinks I'm *literally* going to hell. Dad is ashamed. I loved them, still do, but I'm not allowed to exist, be their daughter, unless I choose their world. But their world isn't right for me. I don't fit."

I hold her tight as her body shudders and wonder how she's kept it together this long.

"And you've spent the past year working to destroy my reputation and career!"

"Sylvie—"

"You think I'm scum—"

"I don't," I murmur into her hair. Sylvie leans back, face tear-streaked. I don't let go, can't help it. On impulse, I lean down and kiss her and she kisses me back. Electricity surges, mouths hungry, bodies pressed tight. If we were back in the hotel room . . . "Let's go," I say, voice rough.

The man next door watches us get into the car. So does Heidi, by the twitch of her living room's curtains. She does know the truth, but we won't get it from her.

Sylvie shifts on her seat to face me. "You just kissed me."

I focus on the road. "I shouldn't have."

She's quiet for a few minutes then says, "I've screwed up my chance. Heidi will never tell me the truth now."

I tamp down the heat from our kiss. "There's always another avenue. Let's go back to Clementine."

"She doesn't know anything."

"I agree. But the names of families who foster kids have to be on file, right?" Sylvie sniffles. I ignore the desire to put an arm around her, pull her close.

She says, "Maybe. Probably."

"So we'll ask for a list from 2000 to 2002. Call every single one of them and see if any remember you. They might know your story." I glance over. Sylvie is wrecked—smudges of gray beneath red eyes, face drawn. "Get some sleep while I drive back?"

Sylvie finds a paper napkin, blows her nose. "Are you just being nice to me because I cried like a big baby?"

No. "Maybe."

Eyes closed, she asks, "Why did you kiss me?"

Heat courses through my body. I have to concentrate to stop its downward path before I get hard. "Why'd you kiss me back?" I'm relieved when, a few minutes later, Sylvie's breath steadies. *The kiss was a mistake.* Any good journalist knows when they're on to a bigger story than the original one. It's like a wolf scenting blood. The evidence I already had about Sylvie and her shows, added to the information from time with her parents is good, but this deeper layer plus bombing at her show without research will knock the ball out of the park. I promised all of it was off the record unless Sylvie agreed I could use it. *Will I keep that promise?* I'm even less sure now.

What about Madison's brother? Everything has an explanation. I just haven't found that one yet. Maybe it's as simple as people winning the lottery despite a billion-to-one odds. I glance at Sylvie, now slumped against the window. Asleep, she looks fragile. I can't let myself get distracted. In a few days, I'll be back in LA and on to the next story.

Why did you kiss me?

If I'm honest, I've wanted to kiss Sylvie ever since she walked out on that LA stage. Again, each time we fought. I've wanted to since she got Chris to eat and was so sweet with her; as I watched her twist, braid, and knot her hair; when her parents were cruel; after her panic attack; during our fight on the train, her face inches from mine; I wanted to kiss her and more when we shared her childhood bed, the moon's reflection a silver streak along her shoulder's curve. I had to move to the window seat to stop myself.

Why did you kiss me?

Sylvie is intelligent, beautiful, and ferocious. I get how it feels never to be enough for family. I see the way her eyes gleam when she thinks she's helping someone, flash in resentment, or fill with tears. Despite the fact that I hate what she does, that's not who she is . . . *Yes it is. Fuck.*

But who am I to cast stones? I've planted traps in the audiences of each of these frauds. I've bribed a janitor at ODHS, used good folks, and been unnecessarily harsh, told countless lies to get this story off the ground.

Did you ever consider that you're the one using people? That you're the vampire?

Sylvie is right. We both feed off other people for our own benefit. But she is conning people to make money and that's a crime. And what I did on Facebook, lying about a dying wife so I can write an exposé, further my career, garner awards, and bump up my salary? In the rearview mirror, Moose sits in the center of the back seat like an overgrown child. Chris sleeps beside him. Curled, she's the size of a kitten. The dog studies me with eyes that shine with accusation. I look away.

TWENTY-NINE

Sylvie

It's the same dream—the sand castle behind me, wave rising in the distance. *Time has almost run out.* When the wave hits, the treasure will be lost. *I'll be lost.* A sharp wind sends a shower of crystals that burn. The wave growls my name. My fingers glance off something hard, smooth, and I wrestle the treasure free . . . The wave strikes. Greedy fingers rip my prize away. "NO!"

One of my hands smacks the window hard, the other Thomas. He swerves and the car in the left lane honks. Thomas jerks the wheel, swerves again, and we skid on the wet asphalt.

"Hold tight," Thomas mutters.

A split second later we're safely back in our lane. In the rearview mirror, Thomas checks to make sure Chris and Moose haven't been hurt.

"What the hell was that?"

My heart slams against my chest. "Just a dream."

"Seriously?"

I rest my sweaty forehead against the cold window. "It's . . . I've had the same one before."

"When?"

"It first came as a vision two days ago, onstage at the start of my show. I saw a sand castle with a moat, tiny sailboats. And I was there, too, on the beach. A massive wave rose in the distance. I knew that when it reached the shore, it would destroy the castle and what was inside."

Thomas glances at me. "What was inside?"

"A treasure. The next time, everything was the same but I was digging for the treasure and the wave was coming to destroy me, too."

"And today?"

I press my index fingers against throbbing temples. "I finally dug the treasure free."

"What was it?"

I hesitate, twist my hair into a knot, and consider whether this information could hurt me. "An old snow globe."

"What was inside?"

There's a hacking sound behind us. Chris vomits onto the seat. I look back at the chunky mess. It's bright red. "Thomas, it's mostly blood," I say. The stricken look on his face tells me everything. Chris coughs again then vomits more blood. "Give me your phone." I Google "Veterinarians." "There's a vet ICU fifteen minutes away." I call and tell a receptionist our situation while Thomas grips the wheel. "They said to bring her in, they'll be waiting." I set the phone on the dash and Google Maps says: "Follow Route 26 South for twelve miles . . ."

I climb into the back seat, wipe the mess up with leftover Starbucks napkins, then hold Chris on my lap. The old cat's eyes are squished shut. Moose rests his muzzle on Thomas's shoulder. *Good boy.*

When we arrive at the vet's, Thomas carries Chris like a baby through the clinic's doors. She's whisked away by a vet tech while Thomas is given forms to fill out, one of which is a list of costs for the tests Chris might need. When he's done, we're ushered into a tiny exam room. Thomas paces the white box, peers outside. Moose's head hangs out the open window, his expression morose. *Animals can sense things we choose to ignore.* It starts to rain again and Moose retreats into the car.

Thomas agonizes, "She's old. I know she's old. But we've been together most of my life. She was there through Dad's death. I don't have . . . My mom didn't cope well after she was widowed. Chris is my family. I didn't . . . I should've . . ."

His shoulders hitch. There's nothing right to say so I stand behind him, wrapping my arms around his torso. His hands find mine and hold tight. There's a soft knock on the door. "Come in," I say while Thomas pulls himself together.

"Hi, I'm Dr. VanVoorhies."

The vet wears a white coat over green scrubs and her sandy hair is cut short; brown eyes in a gently lined face devoid of makeup focus on Thomas. "So. Christopher Robin." She motions us to sit, pulls up a stool, glances at her clipboard. "You said she's twenty."

"Chris's almost twenty-one," Thomas says. "In a month."

"That's a long life for a cat. And I can tell she's been loved."

Thomas's jaw muscles clench. "She's . . . yes."

"Right now we have her on an IV—mostly to hydrate but also to deliver pain meds."

"She drank a lot of water a few hours ago," I say.

Dr. VanVoorhies nods. "That makes sense. We took some blood to check her creatinine levels and a few other things. I'm sorry to say that Chris has chronic renal failure."

"What does that mean exactly?" I ask.

"That Chris's kidneys have failed. Probably have been failing her for a while."

Thomas clears his throat. "Any options?"

"I'm afraid not," the vet says. "We can put her on a low-protein diet, atenolol for hypertension, but Thomas? There is no way to fix renal failure, just support life."

Thomas twists the hem of his shirt. "Is she in a lot of pain?"

"Not anymore, and we can ensure she's comfortable with the right medications, but—"

"I'm not ready," Thomas admits.

The doctor nods. "I understand. We'll fill Chris's prescriptions here. When you are ready? We can come to you, if you'd like. A favorite place . . ."

"I kept her indoors," Thomas says, his voice breaking.

"Her favorite place is a person," I say. A tear dribbles down Thomas's cheek, and the urge to wipe it away is hard to suppress.

"She'll feel much better with meds on board," the vet says and stands. "But just to be clear, she is living on borrowed time."

The vet shakes my hand. I hold hers for an extra moment. *She was a single mother . . . is about to become a grandmother. Her son will name the baby after her.* I don't know if any of that is true, or if it's an attempt to find light in this dismal moment, but my mind, without the pressure of shows or the crutch of research feels more . . . facile, receptive.

It's dusk by the time we drive back to Portland. The monochromatic day darkens without ever releasing a single ray of sunshine. I drive and Thomas holds Chris on his lap. She does seem better, more alert, and bats Moose's nose when he drops his head over the seat to check on her.

Thomas sighs. "I can't recall the last time I cried."

What about when your dad and Deacan died? I hesitate then opt to help him regain his composure. "Not even when your last girlfriend broke up with you?"

He gives me a side-eye. "How do you know that I didn't break up with her?"

"Just a guess."

"Why do you think she dumped me?"

"You're emotionally unavailable?" I venture.

"Bingo."

He rubs beneath Chris's chin and she purrs. Once again, I'm drawn to his hands.

"What about you?" Thomas asks.

I admit, "I can connect with total strangers, yet intimate relationships ultimately elude me."

"Maybe," Thomas says, "if you let people get too close, you'd have to answer the hard questions, and they'd really know you."

Seven different therapists who never lasted more than five months, only a few casual boyfriends, no good friends, a handful of one-night stands. "Maybe."

We're both quiet for a few minutes as the truth settles. "Can you grab the envelope Dad gave me, show me those figures again?" I ask. Thomas reaches into the glove box, empties the envelope onto my palm. A woman in a straw hat, a little girl in a white sundress dotted with pink flowers, and a broken swing set. "They were in the snow globe, in my dream."

"What do you think that means?"

If you let people get too close, you'd have to answer the hard questions, and they'd really know you . . .

I close my fingers over the plastic woman, little girl, fractured swing set. "I don't know. But that snow globe, these figures? They were my *real* life."

THIRTY

Thomas

By the time we get back to the hotel, it's almost 8:00 p.m. We're both exhausted. "Room service?" I ask. Sylvie finds the menu. I settle Chris on the couch and immediately Moose climbs beside her. She gets up cautiously, like her bones might snap, and curls in the curve of the dog's thick neck. He moves his head closer, so she's encircled. "Thank you," I say and, for the first time, run a hand along Cujo's silky black head. He allows it, one brow cocked as if asking, *What took you so long?* I sit beside him, scratch behind each ear and his belly when he lifts one massive haunch for a rub.

When the food comes, Sylvie whisks off the silver domes to reveal breakfast for dinner—Belgian waffles, banana pancakes, orange juice, and a platter of fruit. "Breakfast?" I ask.

She grins. "When I was a kid and got into a fight with Mom, Dad would make me apologize."

"Even if it wasn't your fault?"

Her smile dips. "In our house it was always my fault. Anyway, on those nights Hana skipped supper so it was just the two of us. Dad always cooked breakfast—chocolate chip pancakes, blueberry waffles. Whatever I wanted. It was his way of saying he was sorry." She smothers the waffles with maple syrup, takes a big forkful, and says between bites, "It made me feel better."

Unconvinced, I take a bite. Sugar floods my mouth. It does taste good. We share both the waffles and the pancakes. I'm too full for the fruit plate but Sylvie dusts it. When she's done, she reaches out, grazes my lower lip, and holds up a finger dotted with syrup.

"You saving this?"

"Thanks."

"Don't mention it."

She licks her finger and heat travels its natural course. I gulp down some cold orange juice. "I'll take the couch if Moose will share it."

"If we could sleep in my childhood double bed without a problem, we'll be okay on a queen mattress," Sylvie jokes.

I smile but there was *definitely* a problem in her childhood bedroom. That's why I ended up on the window seat. "Are you just being nice to me because I cried like a big baby?"

Sylvie shrugs. "Maybe."

By the time I come out of the bathroom in my T-shirt and boxers, Moose is snoring, Chris asleep beside him. Sylvie climbs under the down duvet. She wears only the white flannel top of her pj's, and her long legs gleam in the lamplight. My body instantly responds and it takes serious effort to keep things under control. When I check the closet for an extra blanket, there isn't one. Sylvie watches me. "I'll stay on top of the covers."

She puts a pillow in the center of the bed then folds back the duvet on my side. "My safety is ensured."

"Thanks." I turn off the lamp, climb in, silence settles, but I can tell Sylvie isn't asleep. I ask, "What really happened last night in your parents' bathroom?"

"Why do you want to know?"

Why do I? "To understand you better."

"You've already decided who I am."

I ask, "What if I haven't?"

"Tell me what happened the night *your* father died."

"I already did. It was wet out, dark, his car hit a guardrail, went off a bridge."

Sylvie rolls to face me. My eyes have adjusted and in the dim light I can see the contours of her face, the curve of her lips.

"Why was *she* right about the rain?"

"What?"

"The male spirit that came forward during your reading said *she* was right about the rain."

"Do you remember *everything* you've ever said?"

"Most of it. Was it your dad talking about your mom? Maybe she didn't want him to drive that night?"

My chest squeezes. "Stop it."

She presses, "Tell me and I'll tell you what really happened in my parents' bathroom."

She won't share if I don't . . . "It was Saturday night. We were watching our favorite movie—"

Sylvie murmurs, "You take the red pill, you stay in Wonderland, and I show you how deep the rabbit hole goes."

My muscles clench. She wrote that on her skin when we met in her dressing room. *Those were Deacan's favorite lines in the movie.* Sylvie watches me. I can smell the mint of her toothpaste; see the outline of her hips beneath the covers; feel the electricity between us. I'm suspended in this moment. The forces of gravity, relativity, elasticity, cause and effect, that there's no such thing as a psychic-medium——fill a glass. *Am I willing to throw it onto concrete, shatter everything I believe to close the distance between us?* There will always be a rational explanation for what Sylvie says, writes, hums, and knows. I'm a journalist, my career is based on logic, facts, and unequivocal truth. Over the past forty-eight hours I've wavered, but in the end, I can't let go of that glass for the chance to hold her.

"Thomas? What do those words mean?"

Despite my decision, I tell her. "It's what Morpheus said to Neo in the movie *The Matrix* when he gave Neo the opportunity to know what was really happening in their world. I wanted to pause the movie, do an ice cream run. Mom said it was raining too hard. Dad went out anyway, he died that night."

"Why didn't you go with your dad?"

Because Deacan and I played rock-paper-scissors to see who got to go with Dad. Deacan won. They both died. I roll onto my back, stare at the ceiling. "I just didn't. Now tell me what happened in your parents' bathroom."

THIRTY-ONE

Sylvie

I can tell Thomas's resolve is beyond shaky. This is my chance to drive him over the edge, *make* him a believer. I could say a young spirit has come forward and exact revenge by telling him that Deacan is ashamed of him and that his father is, too . . . and more. *Thomas's article will destroy everything I've built. It will erase me. I have the right to protect myself.* But if I do that, it'd make me guilty of every crime he's heaped on my shoulders. I no longer want to be Montresor to his Fortunato. If he chooses to tell me about Deacan, I'll listen. If not, it's his secret to keep. *But then why should I tell him mine?*

"You don't have to," Thomas says like *he's* read *my* mind.

I step onto a dark country road, the past a heavy pack strapped to my back. To open it in front of Thomas is a risk—I'm not sure exactly what's inside. "Do you believe in repressed memories?"

"I get the idea, but it always seemed like a cop-out, a way to blame others for adult hang-ups."

"I was in that camp, too, but I didn't remember much about what I'm going to tell you . . . until last night."

Thomas props his head on one elbow. He asks, "What did you remember?"

My body tenses. "I vaguely recalled the showers, but last night the reason why came back to me."

"Showers?" Thomas asks.

I gather my thoughts. "When I came to High River, I wet the bed every night. I was almost six, way too old for that. Mom decided to sleep in my bedroom. The plan, I think, was to wake me up after a few hours, take me to the toilet, and get me in the habit of doing it myself. I'm pretty sure that she thought the problem was the new house, different routine."

"Makes sense," Thomas says.

"I guess. Yeah. That night, she read me a story before lights out . . . and then she was shaking me. The look on her face . . . She was scared, but disgusted, too."

"Why?"

My cheeks burn. "I thought it was just that I'd peed the bed. She dragged me up the narrow staircase to her bathroom. My legs were hot, sticky, and she forced me into a cold shower, scrubbed the pen off my skin—"

"Pen?"

I twist the edge of the bed's blanket. "In the mirror last night, a vision of a naked little girl on the tiles of my parents' shower appeared. That girl was me. There were letters and numbers written on her skin . . . *my* skin. I'd forgotten that part."

"Was that the only time?" Thomas asks, his tone middle-of-the-road.

I'm relieved that he's put on his journalist hat. If he gave me any sympathy in this moment, I'd probably cry. "No, though I can't say how many more times it happened. Mom would read me a bedtime story. At some point, I'd pee the bed. She'd shake me out of whatever stupor I was in, drag me upstairs to shower. Then she'd wait in a leather chair outside the bathroom door while I dried off, put on the clean pj's she'd left folded on the counter. I'd apologize then go back to bed."

"What about Wess? Did he ever step in?"

Suddenly cold, I pull the covers higher. "I think Dad argued with her at least once, said they should find a therapist, not douse me with cold water. But Mom believed the cold showers would do the trick."

Thomas says, "It's a harsh punishment."

"She didn't spank, hit with a belt, or worse. It was just water. And it worked." My mind struggles to put the memories into context. "On the train you asked if my gift began when I was a kid. If I knew when the telephone was going to ring, or if someone had died."

"You said you didn't grow up in the kind of house where magical thinking was encouraged," Thomas recalls. "That your life was pretty regimented."

"Maybe . . . maybe when I lost time, wrote on my skin? Maybe that was the start of my abilities and what Mom, what she did to me, taught me to cram my gift down."

"Have you ever asked Hana what you said and wrote that freaked her out?"

I shake my head. "In fairness, until last night all I remembered was wetting the bed, those showers, and my apologies." Thomas rests his head back on the pillow. This close I can smell the slight musk of the hotel shampoo and the clean scent of shaving cream.

"When you left home, the fugue states, for lack of a better word, started again?"

"Yeah. The first I can recall was when I spoke with that pregnant woman, Bethany."

"And the panic attack?"

"When I went up to my parents' bathroom and saw the shower where Mom used to scrub my skin, had the vision, I got dizzy, took a seat, reached out to grip the bathroom door. My nail gouged a paint bubble and a scab tore free. Beneath the white paint, the door was red."

Thomas is quiet for a few moments then admits, "I don't understand."

"The door I open to the other side is the *exact* same as my parents' bathroom door."

THIRTY-TWO

Thomas

I want to tell Sylvie that she's not damaged from whatever happened to her before High River, and after she arrived. That she has an inexplicable gift. There have been moments over the past few days I was starting to believe it, but given what I now know about her past, repressed memories, the red bathroom door, it seems more likely that she's both a talented mentalist, extremely intuitive, but also suffers from some sort of early psychological wound.

"Thomas?"

In this vulnerable moment I can't bear to wound her, so I tell her *my* whole truth. "My big brother was killed that night with my dad. Deacan was only fifteen. He wanted to be a journalist." I rarely share this and each word drops like a stone.

"*Sorry* doesn't seem like a big enough word, but I am, so sorry, for your loss." Sylvie says. "Could Deacan have been . . . Could he be the younger spirit that came through during your reading? The one with the journal?"

Sylvie's eyes are silver moons. I could lose myself in their glow, enter a mystical world where talking to my dead father and brother is possible. But the laws of nature overwhelm my desire. *For every action, there is an equal and opposite reaction.*

"It was my idea to get dessert the night my dad and brother died. Mom said no. Dad was the pushover. He worked long hours, traveled, tried hard to make it up to Deacan and me. My brother and I played rock-paper-scissors to see who would go with him to pick the flavor. Deacan won."

"Why didn't you both go?"

"Mom said only one of us could, the other had to help clean up from dinner while we waited for the ice cream delivery. That night ruined her life and took away theirs."

"You were a kid who wanted dessert," Sylvie says gently. "What happened next was an accident. You're not responsible. They don't blame you."

Despite everything, this woman is kind. "Deacan didn't get to live his dream."

"You can't live it for him."

"If not me, then who?"

She shakes her head. "None of them want that."

She doesn't understand. I have to ask, "With everything you've re-membered about your childhood, how can you still believe you're a psychic-medium?"

"There will always be people like you. Doubters. And I will always wonder at times if I'm an impostor. It's true," Sylvie admits, "I do. But there are moments of clarity, unexplainable and pure, when I'm certain."

Residual anger from growing up with my mother sparks within me. "So what you do is *entirely* selfless?"

Sylvie nibbles her lower lip, considers. "You're right, what I do isn't entirely selfless. It fills *me* in a way I can't really explain." Her eyes shine. "But I do help people. And I'm willing to face critics who don't have faith, who despise me, want to humiliate and ruin me, for the opportunity to help the ones that do believe and need me."

"I don't want to humiliate you."

"But you can't believe."

"No."

Sylvie is quiet for a bit, and when she finally speaks, her voice is resigned. "Still, we actually are on the same side."

"How so?"

"We both want the truth."

"What if it destroys you?"

She presses her palm to my cheek. "What if it doesn't?"

Maybe it's Sylvie's honesty or the fact that I'm raw from the past forty-eight hours, her childhood story, Chris's diagnosis . . . I bring her hand to my mouth and press the soft skin inside her wrist to my lips. She watches me, preternaturally still, a deer caught in the headlights of an oncoming truck.

I find my voice and say, "This can't be about my article."

Sylvie half smiles. "Thomas, are you trying to make another deal with me?"

I hold her wrist, where the pulse beats a steady tap beneath my fingertips. *I'm the one that's afraid.* I should sleep on the couch. Instead I throw the pillow between us to the floor. She moves closer, until our bodies are inches apart, lips close enough to share breath. "This shouldn't happen."

"Why not?" Sylvie asks.

I snort. "Should I list the reasons?"

"Give me your number one."

"It's not fair," I say.

"To whom?"

"You."

She laughs, musical as wind chimes, and the skin around her eyes crinkles with genuine mirth. "I could say the same thing."

"What's your number one reason?" I ask.

"You might fall in love with me."

I chuckle. "And that would be a bad thing."

One corner of her mouth crooks up. "Very bad."

"Why's that?"

"I'll break your heart."

Despite myself, I ask, "What if I want to take that risk?"

"You don't strike me as a guy who lives dangerously."

The slip of air between our bodies is electric. "It won't change my article."

"I'm not asking you to change it," Sylvie says.

"But you want me to."

A little smile plays on her lips. "Yes."

"I won't."

"I know."

"Should we have the requisite conversation about protection?"

"If I get pregnant, I'm going to keep our baby."

My expression must be somewhere between shock and appalled.

She laughs. "Kidding. I was tested three months ago. Clean bill of health and I'm on birth control. You?"

"Tested a year ago. That was my last relationship."

"No Tinder dates?"

"Never."

Sylvie gets out of bed, carries Chris along with a pillow into the bathroom. Moose follows and she shuts the door, slides between the sheets. She's thrown out a dare and now waits to see if I'll bite. Her eyes gleam in the dark and I can see the slope of those full lips, feel the heat of her body and an invisible pull. *It's wrong. Unfair. Dangerous . . .* But my fingers trail down the petal-soft skin of her long neck to the pronounced bones of her clavicle and the hollow between them. I don't pull off her pajama top though every cell in my body sings out for skin-on-skin contact.

There are lines that shouldn't be crossed . . . I slip one hand between the buttons of her pajamas, and trace her breast. All the while she watches, dares me to go further. When the tips of my fingers find her nipple, her breath hitches and the nerves in my body respond, send off hot tendrils of desire. We kiss slowly, tentatively, like we're rolling down a hill, picking up speed and intensity with each rotation.

I've been with a number of women, and the first time we're intimate is always filled with breathless anticipation, but this? There's no comparison. Sylvie pulls off my T-shirt and trails her fingers down my bare skin. Our kisses become hungry . . . *I can still stop this before it's too late.* But my hands slide over the curve of her hips, silk panties, round ass, and the honeyed skin of her inner thighs. The need to be inside her overwhelms me. If we were already lovers, I'd pull the scrap of lace between her legs aside and slide in. Instead, I run my hands under her pj's, across her belly, and travel slowly to her breasts, squeeze until a sigh escapes her lips.

I unbutton her top and slide it free. She tries to pull me close but instead I get up, open the curtains so that the city's golden lights glance off her bare skin. Straddling her lean body, I begin to kiss her, my lips traveling from her navel upward, my tongue tasting the slight saltiness of her skin, encircling small nipples, her breasts in my hands. I nip and suck until her back curves. Again she reaches to pull me down. Instead, I weave our fingers together at her sides, slide down and kiss her thighs, the heat between her legs. My tongue drifts inside the elastic of her panties, swirls along the soft folds. She sighs and her legs slowly open. *I can't stop this.* "Yes?" I ask.

In answer, Sylvie pulls free, rolls over, now on her hands and knees, and pushes herself against my erection. "Yes," she says.

I consider taking her that way, plunging inside; one hand on her hip while the other tangles in her hair. I'm so hard, it will be over fast. We can take it slow the next time. I slide her panties off, part her legs. Sylvie reaches back, pulls me forward until the tip of my cock begins to penetrate. Fighting my desire, I pull back and use my fingers, slide them inside her and find the most sensitive spot, slip over it again and again as she gets wetter until her legs tremble . . .

"Now," Sylvie beckons.

I withdraw my fingers. "I want to see your face." She doesn't turn. Again I bring her to the edge of orgasm but stop short. I'm not sure why I don't take her this way . . . I want to, almost to the point of losing all rational thought, but it's like there's some animal part of my brain warning that if I slip inside her from behind, I'll have gone down the wrong road. "I want to see you," I repeat, my voice rough.

She rolls onto her back, wraps her legs around me, and we both groan as I enter. For a moment we're still. When I kiss her, the spell is broken and we begin to move together. Her hands grip my back, while mine cup her ass as I drive deeper and deeper, my eyes never leaving her face, until we buck, quake, cry out. Our orgasms ricochet, going on and on until we fall into each other.

Burying my face in her hair, I whisper, "I don't want to hurt you."

"You will," she replies. "It's the human condition."

THIRTY-THREE

Sylvie

I watch Thomas sleep. He knows more about me than any man I've ever been with. When he smiles in his dream, tears slip down my temples. The past forty-eight hours have been grueling, out of control, as I've fought for my career—my right to exist, as Sylvie Young, a legitimate psychic-medium—while at the same time trying to discover a past that may hurt or even destroy me. I turn my face into the pillow to stifle sobs. I told the truth and for a short time Thomas liked me anyway. But the pressure and his kindness are not the only reason I'm crying. Sex with Thomas, our emotional and undeniable physical connection, will give me power. Does that make me a bad person?

I think so.

Before sleep, I move Chris and Moose back to the couch. My dog gives me the look—he's been relegated to the bathroom before. "Don't judge." I tuck both animals beneath a throw blanket. I slide back into bed and Thomas spoons me in his sleep. Tomorrow he'll probably be sorry we had sex. He was in the dominant position over my career and me. Now he's professionally compromised and I have newfound power. The question is: Am I going to use it?

When I first spoke to Lucas about Thomas, I was unsure if I was

Fortunato or Montresor. And when I had the chance to be the latter, to use what Lucas had told me about Deacan to manipulate Thomas, I repeatedly balked. *But don't I have the right to survive?*

A female praying mantis kills and eats her mate so she can use his energy to produce more eggs and provide for her offspring. Shark embryos cannibalize littermates in the womb to ensure their nutrients. Male hummingbirds use sharp bills to stab each other in order to secure a mate. Meerkat mothers kill the offspring of other females to maintain their dominance. Every organism on earth does what's necessary to survive. I dig deep for resolve. *If need be, I will, too.*

Moose noses my hand at 6:00 a.m. He needs to go outside. Quietly, I dress and head down the elevator. It's dark, cold, and the air has the chemical stink of rain on asphalt. I forgot my coat and shiver. Moose takes pity on me and quickly does his business. In the elevator he gives me a side-eye. "We all have needs," I tell him. "Remember that cute Labradoodle at the dog park? You were twice her size. And what'd I say when we had to leave because you wouldn't stop humping her?" Moose looks away. "I said way to go, buddy. She was hot."

I pause at the door, keycard in hand. "What if Thomas isn't sorry?" I quietly ask Moose. He lifts a paw in the air. "I didn't think you liked him, but I'll take that as a high five."

Thomas is already in the shower. He's locked the door. When he comes out in a towel, he doesn't look directly at me. I didn't expect a relationship, but detachment from a man I was *truly* intimate with makes my insides wilt.

"I won't be long," I say, then grab a change of clothes and my coat and close the bathroom door. In the shower, I run my hands over the body he kissed just a few hours ago and soap the soreness between my legs. In the moment, sex with Thomas felt like more than a one-night

210 · Nan Fischer

stand. I shouldn't have kissed him or let him see that moment of total vulnerability when I came. If I hadn't done that, this would hardly rate more than a slight emotional sting. *Focus.* If I take too long of a shower, Thomas might become suspicious that I'm up to something. *He'd be right.* I crouch in the corner, my back to the spray. I'm done in a few minutes then turn the shower off and quickly towel dry.

By the time I'm dressed in a clean pair of jeans and black cashmere sweater, breakfast has arrived—scrambled eggs, bacon, fruit, and coffee. *Is that a message that we're back to being adversaries?* We focus on our food, forks and knives clattering, coffee is poured, sipped. When we reach for jam at the same time, we both recoil. Moose watches from the couch. The invisible bubble over his head reads: *Duh.*

"Should we talk about it?" I tentatively ask.

Thomas finally meets my eyes. Politely, he says, "Yeah. Yes. I'm sorry. I shouldn't have. The power dynamic—"

"It was just sex." I take a bite of eggs, swallow without tasting them. "ODHS opens at eight." Thomas pops a Prilosec out of its pack and hands it to me. "Still trying to make me well before popping me in the oven?" He doesn't laugh. I wash it down with cool water that does nothing to quell the increasing heat in my gut.

Thomas pushes his chair back and stands. "I need to feed Chris, give her the meds."

In the end he can only get her to nibble her new food and I have to help him with the pills, which requires that he hold a surprisingly strong Chris as she squirms and hisses while I pry open her mouth, push the pills down, try to avoid a bite. I'm not sure who is more upset by the process, Thomas or his cat. Moose doesn't seem pleased, either. *Well, grow up, everyone. This is reality.*

"Shall we?" I ask, and grab my coat.

Thomas makes sure Chris is comfortable and we hang a DO NOT DISTURB sign on the door so the maid doesn't have a heart attack when she sees Moose. In the elevator only inches separate us but we're miles apart. Outside it's spitting rain and steel gray clouds press down on the city. By the time we reach ODHS, the thighs of my jeans and my hair are damp. Clementine is at the front desk, this time in an electric blue blouse and black pants.

"Ms. Young, back so soon?" Clementine asks.

Thomas says, "We'd like the names of families who fostered Sylvie from 2000 to 2002."

Clementine adjusts one of her chunky gold hoops. Her entire ear is pierced, top to bottom, each hole filled with a colorful gem. "If that information wasn't in Ms. Young's file, I'm not sure where to find it."

He pushes, "Could you ask the current caseworkers if they recall families who fostered back then? We're happy to sort through the names, call them ourselves."

Clementine takes a swallow of coffee, the rim of the mug stained with crescents of lipstick. "Yeesh. Twenty years ago. My guess? Those families have come and gone."

"Some could've been young at the time and are still fostering," I say.

"Sweetheart, being a foster parent isn't easy. Most of 'em only last a few years." She clicks her red nails together. "I knew your name rang a bell. Googled after you left. You're a psychic with a show at the Schnitzer this Sunday, right?"

I nod.

Clementine's grin reveals the slight gap between her front teeth.

"Good for you! The Schnitzer is a big theater. Child, you exited the foster system fast. Got your forever family. Made something of your life. That's what matters. Focus on the future."

My chest is so tight, it's hard to draw a full breath. "What if . . . what if I can't until I know what happened to me?"

"Honey, very few of us get out of our childhood unscathed," Clementine says with a slow shake of her head. "That goes double for foster kids. More than sixty percent of the children in foster care spend at least five years in the system before being adopted. Those years usually aren't a picnic. You're one of the lucky ones. Don't go borrowing trouble. Enjoy life *now*."

There's nothing left to say. My parents don't know anything. Heidi does but won't talk. If I can't find my foster parents, there's nowhere else to turn. And Clementine is right. I need to concentrate on the present to make sure I actually have a future.

We head outside, the drizzle now solid rain. Max, the security guard, smokes a cigarette under the overhang, back curved against the wall, head engulfed in a gloomy haze. He nods at us.

"Got a spare?" Thomas asks.

I didn't take Thomas for a smoker but then I don't really know him. Max offers a pack of Marlboros. Thomas taps one out, puts it between his lips. The older man cups the end, lights it, and Thomas takes a draw, slowly exhales, then says, "This weather gets old."

Max chortles. "That it does. I've spent every winter of my entire life in the Pacific Northwest. Surprised I haven't turned into a duck."

Thomas asks, "Heidi was a silver lining, though, right?"

What?

Max blows smoke out the corner of his mouth and says, "Surprised Heidi mentioned we dated."

"She didn't until I pointed out your photograph on her piano," Thomas lies. "You two were young. Must've been serious for her to keep that picture."

Max was the guy hugging her? I sort through the photos on the piano until I reach the one with the tall, muscular guy with jet-black hair . . . and a mole under one eye. I was too amped up to see it. Recovering quickly, I ask, "How long did you date?" The ash on the end of Max's cigarette burns bright as he draws the nicotine deep. *Heidi meant a lot to him.*

"Four years."

Beautiful woman but she never did marry though a buncha fellows tried. My eyes flick toward Thomas, silently convey that I've got it from here. I say, "You asked her to marry you."

"At least ten times. That girl loved me, but she was stubborn as a bull. Said she couldn't be married to both me and her job and the latter was a higher calling."

"But in the end she was fired," Thomas says. "Right after Sylvie's adoption."

Max grinds the cigarette butt against the wall and turns to leave.

"She wasn't fired," I quickly say then try to make the next right step. "She chose to leave . . . after what happened."

Max hesitates then lights another cigarette, takes a deep draw. "I didn't shred that file, it was just my dumb luck to catch her doing it late one night after the office was empty."

"Did she say why?" I ask.

"Something about it being the only way to make sure a secret was kept; to protect everyone involved. Then she printed out a new page and put it in the empty folder."

"You promised not to tell anyone," I say carefully.

"'Course not. I never would've told a soul. Don't know if it was me knowing 'bout it or her doing it and feeling guilty that led to her resignation. Shame. Those kids were lucky to have her in their corner."

"It was my file Heidi destroyed. That doesn't feel lucky for me."

"Do you know what was in it?" Thomas asks.

Max shakes his head then meets my gaze. "But if Heidi got rid of it, then you're better off. That woman would never intentionally hurt a child."

"'You can't go back and change the beginning, but you can start where you are and change the ending.' Do you remember telling me that?"

"Yes."

"I'm trying to do that. Tell me what you know about me. Please."

———

THIRTY-FOUR

Thomas

"No one wanted you," Max says.

Sylvie almost hides her flinch. "Why not?"

"Found Heidi crying one day on the back steps of this building. She'd tried to place you in a foster care home. Don't know why it was so hard. Kids under the age of five were always pretty easy to place. She said you desperately needed a mom and dad, even the temporary kind. Honestly, I thought she might finally be ready to say yes to my proposal. I would've taken you in."

Sylvie grimaces. "But she wasn't, so you didn't."

Max finishes his cancer stick, lights another. "I peripherally knew a guy, president of Rotary at the time. There was a young family who'd recently joined. He thought they might do the trick, just for a bit." Max coughs, the sound phlegmy and rough.

"What's their name?" I ask.

"Horsley. Scott and her name was Fay or Faith, I think. They may or may not still live in Portland. That's all I know."

Sylvie tugs her ear, hesitates, then says, "You should get a physical. Have them check your pancreas."

Max chuffs, "Too late. My pancreas *and* lungs are hosed." He drops his butt, grinds it beneath the heel of a scuffed boot, and heads back inside the building.

The driving rain eases a bit as we walk back to the hotel. At the corner, Sylvie says, "What you started, back there with Max? If the writing thing doesn't work out, you could have a promising career as a mentalist. A lot of what they do is intuition."

We leap a puddle, cross the street. "I almost lost him."

"You got excited, went too fast."

A steady stream of cars clogs the street. We wait for a light to change. A cold gust ruffles Sylvie's hair and a lock falls free. I sweep it from her forehead. My fingers remain and it takes real effort to pull them back. The light changes and we cross the street. I ask, "How'd you *intuit* that Max is sick?"

Sylvie considers her answer. "He has rhinophyma—a skin disorder that makes an alcoholic's nose swollen and red. So you could say a doctor's visit to check his pancreas was an educated guess. Or you could believe that his mother came to the red door, showed me her son's diseased organs. Asked me to help him."

Sylvie meets my gaze. The sparkle in her eyes as she watches me grapple with what's true makes me chuckle. Despite the fact that Max's answers hurt her, that he hadn't wanted to help her, she still tried to do right by him. *Again, she shows kindness.* When we step into the warm hotel lobby, in a rush I say, "I'm not sorry about last night. Are you?"

Sylvie's smile is suddenly shy and the grim day brightens a touch. "I'm not sorry, either."

Back in the room, I start with the easiest method—online white pages. There are forty-two Horsleys listed in Portland but no Scott, Fay, or Faith. I give Sylvie her phone, just for this, and we call all of them anyway, figure they might be somehow related. Neither of us gets a hit.

"What next?" Sylvie asks.

"A lot of people no longer have a landline so let's try *people search engines*." She watches over my shoulder as I type names into the free apps, TruePeopleSearch and ZabaSearch. Nothing. I agree to a fee and try BeenVerified and Pipl. No hits for a Scott and Fay or Scott and Faith.

"How about Facebook?"

"There will be hundreds of Horsleys," I say. "And there won't be any numbers." We spend the next hour looking anyway. Find a Scott Horsley who lived in the Midwest, rides motocross. A Faith Horsley who has a book club with thousands of followers. There's even a Scott and Fay Horsley who are siblings, professional tap dancers.

We order room service for lunch—grilled cheese sandwiches and tomato soup. Sylvie wraps long cheese strands around her index finger then nibbles them off like a little kid while Moose and Chris play with his fuzzy toy.

Suddenly, Sylvie exclaims, "Rotary!"

I mentally kick myself, embarrassed that I didn't think of it, quickly pull up the website, scan the list of past presidents and the years they served. Two short calls later and Sylvie has spoken to Mr. Jones, gotten a number for Faith Horsley, who uses the last name *Benson*, and set up a six-thirty meeting with Faith for tonight at her home. Giddy, she spins in circles then falls onto my lap. I kiss her. Maybe it's wrong to do this again, given, well, everything. But people do the wrong thing for all sorts of reasons. I'm not trying to manipulate Sylvie. I haven't demanded sex to shelve my article. The truth is what started as a mutual need for an emotional release has shifted. My attraction to her now runs deeper. Our kisses intensify. We're both adults. We're both making this choice. Sylvie unbuttons my jeans. I ignore the warning bells signaling that I'm in danger of losing objectivity and pull off her sweater and lace bra. The sound of bullfrogs loudly croaking breaks through the moment. I reach behind her, send the call to voicemail.

Sylvie stands, wriggles out of her pants, almost trips getting one leg off, giggles then straddles me, only a silk scrap of panty left between us. She yanks off my flannel shirt, nails skimming along my sides. Nerves scream, every inch of me erect.

The phone rings again. Bullfrogs. I throw my phone and it hits the wall. Sylvie pulls me free from my boxers, slides a hand down my shaft. I'm desperate to be inside her—

Again bullfrogs. *Shit*. "I'm sorry, I have to get it." Sylvie retrieves the phone, hands it to me. Breathing hard, I say, "Hello?"

"I'm sorry to bother you," my mom says. "I know you're busy."

Voice tight, I ask, "Can it wait?"

"Old lady problems. I fell. Doc says my hip is broken. I'm having surgery to pin it—they're getting me ready now. Just wanted you to know, in case . . ."

She's talking too loud, sounds scared. "What hospital?"

"Legacy."

"I'll be there when you wake up."

"You don't have to come all the way—"

"I'll be there," I say and hang up. "I'm sorry." Sylvie tugs on her jeans, tosses my flannel shirt over.

"Let's go," she says.

"Where?"

"The hospital."

Taken aback, I say, "You don't have to come."

"I know."

I button my shirt. "Are you just being nice to me because my mom is hurt?"

"Maybe."

We leave Chris and Moose in the room with food and fresh water, hang the DO NOT DISTURB sign for a disappointing reason, and head to the hospital. In the Uber, Sylvie holds my hand.

THIRTY-FIVE

•

Sylvie

When the elevator doors open to a brightly painted pink hallway, it's clear that the elderly woman at the information desk has sent us to the wrong floor. We follow signs to the nurses' station, past murals of birds, mountains, and children swimming in a river beneath a cloudless sky. At the main desk Thomas asks for directions to the adult surgical wing, his tone impatient. He might not like his mother, but he loves her—enough to interrupt sex. What game am I playing anyway? He's made it clear that the exposé will still be published. *Isn't it time to turn the tables?*

"There's a shortcut. Take the right-hand elevators down the hall there to the fourth floor," a nurse in scrubs spotted with smiling daisies says. "Then take the skyway across to double doors that lead to the surgical wing."

We skirt a family that walks a little boy down the hall. There's a cannula under his nose and his Superman hospital gown can't hide the jut of sharp collarbones. Behind him a man, probably his dad, wheels a green oxygen tank; his jaw is set in a smile, eyes rimmed red. Mom and the boy's little sisters make small talk, point to the mobiles of neon-colored butterflies overhead.

When we reach the elevators, Thomas presses the up button three times. At the end of the hall are double doors with a sign: INPATIENT CHILDREN'S PSYCHIATRIC UNIT. ALL VISITORS MUST BE BUZZED IN.

The elevator doors slide open and Thomas steps in. "Sylvie?" he asks.

I can't move. The elevator dings. My pulse jacks sky high. Each breath I take slams hard and fast into the next one. An arm wraps around my waist. Strong hands knead knotted muscles. *Shit-shit-shit.*

"Slow it down," Thomas says. "Slow and steady."

I can't. It's like trying to stop a runaway horse with no reins.

"Do you need help?" a woman asks.

"She's having a panic attack," Thomas says.

The woman crouches in front of me—white sleeves, black hair, a gold ring on her index finger. "Can't—stop," I gasp. "Feels . . . heart . . . explode." Hands tingle and my head fills with helium. Spots rain across my vision.

Calmly, the woman says, "I'm Dr. Prim Acharya. A panic attack is an episode of intense fear that triggers a physical reaction. But you're *not* in danger. You *won't* have a heart attack even though it feels like the big one is right around the corner. And you *won't* die."

Tell that to my body.

She continues, her voice melodic, "The hormone adrenaline has flooded your bloodstream. It puts your heart on overdrive. But it won't last long. Focus on an object in your mind—let's use a tree. A beautiful aspen tree whose leaves have just turned golden. Can you see it? You're under the tree and it rustles in the wind, listen . . . each muscle will now slowly relax, release. Think of the adrenaline as a line of ants that march out of your body, up that tree. Purse your lips and take a slower breath . . . good. Another one? There you go. Do it again . . .

and again . . . and again . . . now one more time. Good girl. Think you can stand up? I do. I know you can."

I slowly stand, my fingers still numb, breath ragged. Dr. Acharya is a willowy Indian woman with wavy black hair, salted at the temples, and dark eyes behind round glasses. She takes my wrist, checks the pulse.

"That was a doozy," she says.

My face burns. "I'm sorry."

She stage whispers, "I get them, too. They're scary as fuck. Find a therapist, develop a coping strategy; they'll happen less frequently. Maybe even go away." She squeezes my hand. "What set it off?"

"Thomas's mom is having surgery. That was probably it. I'm squeamish."

"Off you go, then," Dr. Acharya says.

An elevator arrives. We step into the empty car. Thomas squeezes my shoulder. "What really happened?"

"I have no idea." But I do. I don't know where or when, but I'm certain that I've been behind the locked doors of a psychiatric unit.

We cross the sky bridge, then head down the curved hallway until we reach a white desk. A nurse in green scrubs named Levi tells us Thomas's mother is in surgery and leads the way to the waiting area, a collection of regular and oversized chairs and couches upholstered in dark green. Low tables showcase an array of magazines—*National Geographic, Cooking, Sunset, People, Architectural Digest*, and *The New Yorker*. In the far corner, a mother and teen daughter sit on a couch. The daughter is slumped against the arm, texting, while her mom scans the hallway, waiting for whatever doctor will give her news.

"How long will my mom be in surgery?" Thomas asks Levi as we sit.

"Hip replacements take one to two hours. It's a very straightforward procedure." Levi glances at me, does a double take. "Hey, wait a minute, I saw you advertised in the paper. You're a psychic, right?"

I give a little nod.

"I tried to get a ticket to your show," he says, "but it was sold out."

The red door blasts open. A female spirit rushes out, her energy all sharp edges. She shows me an elaborately tattooed arm.

Quietly, I say, "There's a spirit present . . . Do tattoos mean anything to you?"

Levi quickly sits beside me, his expression hungry. "Mom had a bunch. She died a year ago. Is it her coming through?"

"Maybe . . . Are the letters P, M, or L important?"

"L is Levi, my name, obviously. M could stand for my mom's middle name, Mary. And P is definitely Penny, my girlfriend."

"She's showing me a stomach, signaling that it's round."

"Dang! Our baby's due in six weeks."

"The spirit is pointing to the same tattoo—it's an emerald green serpent coiled around a black stallion? There are scabs along the serpent's body. Does that mean anything to you?"

Levi glances away. "Mom died from a heroin OD."

He's lying about something. The spirit's energy has morphed to sticky fear. She shows me the tattoo one final time. The scabs have torn open. Blood runs down the arm, pools in a curled hand.

The beeper clipped to Levi's scrubs buzzes. He jumps then glances at it. "Sorry. Gotta run. Mr. Holmes, the surgeon will be out to talk to you as soon as your mom's in recovery." Levi sprints down the hallway.

I reach for Thomas's hand but he pulls it away. "What's wrong?"

He scowls. "Could you *not* use my mother's surgery as an opportunity to forward your case?"

The woman across the waiting room slaps her thighs like she's made a decision, and walks over. Exhaustion and worry spool off her body as she says, "I couldn't help but hear . . . No judgment, bless your heart, but I don't, we don't . . . practicing Catholics . . . but . . . Do you know how my husband is doing in surgery? He had a heart attack, a big one. Died twice on the way to the hospital. The surgeons said . . . It's a quadruple bypass."

I glance at Thomas. He stares straight ahead, lips compressed. "I'm sorry. But I don't know." Shoulders drooped, the woman returns to her daughter. There's a tang of metal in my mouth. A spirit lightly taps on the other side of the red door . . .

Twenty minutes later two men in surgeon's caps and white coats appear, and the air in the waiting area turns dense. They approach mother and daughter, speak softly, and the woman's body folds in two from the blow. Her daughter helps her stand, their roles suddenly reversed as they're escorted out of the waiting room to begin the process of mourning.

Thomas pretends to read a *National Geographic*. I buy two really bad coffees from the machine down the hall and neither of us can stand more than a few swallows. Despite the Prilosec, a rodent with razor-sharp teeth dines on the lining of my stomach.

An elderly man shuffles to the couch and settles. Soon after, a young couple in typical Pacific Northwest fleece, jeans, and waterproof boots gets comfortable in the far corner. They hold hands and talk quietly. I don't want to know anything about any of them. An hour later, Dr. Bernstein, early fifties, bald, kind eyes, and his resident, Dr. Shayghani, at least ten years his junior, dark hair in a ponytail halfway down her back, step into the waiting room.

"Mr. Holmes?" Dr. Bernstein asks.

Thomas shoots to his feet. "Right here."

"Your mother's surgery went very well. She's in recovery now. You should be able to visit in about an hour. A nurse will come get you once she's been transferred to a room."

"When will she be able to go home?"

"Given her age and that she lives alone," Dr. Shayghani says, "a social worker will be in to talk with you. They will suggest that your mother transition to an assisted health facility for a week or two, until she's able to care for herself."

"Thank you," Thomas says. The surgeons move on and he turns to me. "About before . . ."

I shrug. "You're worried about your mom."

"That's no excuse. It's just . . . I was afraid you were going to open that red door and say my mom was on the other side. We haven't been close for a while, but still . . ."

A burst of pure happiness fizzes through my body. *He believes it's possible.* "I wouldn't have done that, called to her, unless you asked."

Finally meeting my gaze, Thomas says, "I just didn't want you to go through the motions."

The worst blows, even when they're not intended to harm, are the ones we don't expect.

THIRTY-SIX

Thomas

Mom looks so much smaller. Her skin tone matches the hospital bed's dull white sheets, and an IV snakes from the back of her hand, which is mottled with an ugly, purple bruise where she's bled beneath the skin. She still dyes her hair brown, but patches of gray show at her temples. Her skin is dappled with irregular reddish spots, and deep lines seam her cheeks. Folds of loose skin have replaced a once pronounced jawline and now connect it directly to a saggy neck. She's lightly snoring.

Uncomfortable in my own skin, I cross to the window, watch gunmetal clouds travel across an even darker sky. Levi came to get me a few minutes after Sylvie went down to the cafeteria to see if she could find something edible for our lunch. On the way to Mom's room, he asked me to thank her.

"For what?"

He pretended to read notes on the clipboard he carried. "I've been . . . Basically, I need to get into a program before my son is born." Nervously, he scratched at the long-sleeved shirt he wore under his scrubs. I saw the swirl of a colorful tattoo beneath the white fabric and caught a glimpse of what looked like a horse's black legs.

Levi exhaled hard. "That Sylvie is really something, isn't she? You better stay on the straight and narrow, dude, 'cause she'll know if you step over any lines."

I press tented fingers against the hospital room's cold glass window. *Did Sylvie see that tattoo?* A jet from the nearby airport climbs steeply into the sky then disappears behind the clouds. Here one minute, gone the next. *It's not magic, it's science, engineering, know-how.*

"You came," Mom says, her voice hoarse.

I slide a metal chair close to the bed. Her eyes are still the same shade of indigo, but now red veins spider across a cloudy surface. "Hey, Mom."

She sniffs. "Thank you for being here."

We sound like strangers. "Sure." She fumbles for the glasses that rest on a side table and knocks them to the floor. When I retrieve them, our fingers make contact. Her knuckles are swollen, the skin chapped. She used to get manicures, pink polish, but now her nails are yellowed, ridged. She slides the round black frames on. *When did she start wearing glasses?*

Mom inspects me, her eyes magnified behind the lenses. "You look tired, and you need a haircut."

I joke, "I'm not the one who just got a new hip. How's it feel?"

"Like I got kicked by a mule." Her rusty laugh devolves into a cough. I pour water from the plastic pitcher into a cup and guide the straw to her lips. It's a strangely intimate moment and uncomfortable. Mom was never overly affectionate, and our last contact, a brief hug, was years ago.

"The doctors said your surgery went well. You won't have to stay here for long, but you'll spend a week or two in a care facility. When you're ready to go home, I could come for a few days to help with things?" *Why did I just offer that?*

"No need. My friend, Bernie, can look in on me and pick up anything I need."

It takes a second to identify the twist of my gut as disappointment. *Did I actually want to take care of her? Or did I just want her to want me to do it?* "Bernie?"

"Next-door neighbor. His wife died a few years ago. We spend time together. Dinners, dominoes, and Netflix series—my picks are better but I try to be fair. He's the one who found me on the floor. Such an old lady cliché, I've fallen and can't get up. Humiliating, but we had a laugh about it while we waited for the ambulance."

"Sounds like you've got a boyfriend," I joke.

Mom actually blushes. "He'd like that, but your dad is the only man in my life."

He's been dead over twenty years. A memory of my parents dancing in the kitchen rises to the surface. They loved to dance together, jitterbug mostly. Mom would laugh as Dad twirled her around. When he died, the music in our home died, too.

There's a knock on the door. Sylvie, balancing sandwiches and Starbucks coffees, stands in shadow, just outside the threshold. "Thought you might want this now," she says and holds out a sandwich. "I'll wait in the lounge."

"Come on in," Mom says.

Sylvie shakes her head. "Thanks but I'll let you two visit."

There's a line drawn in the sand. I hesitate then cross it. "It's okay. Mom, this is my friend Syl. This is Eve."

Mom struggles to sit up, winces. I quickly reach for the controls on her bed and raise the back. "That okay?"

Mom says, "Yes. Thanks." Her eyes take in Sylvie, top to bottom. "Aren't you a pretty gal. I've never met any of Thomas's girlfriends. Sit down. Tell me everything. How long have you two been dating? Do you live in LA or is it a long-distance thing? You young people are so modern. In my day we didn't date via hookup apps."

Hookup apps? "She's not . . . Sylvie's just a friend," I say.

Mom looks down her nose at me, like she did when I was a kid, caught in a lie. "Thomas Henry Holmes, don't tell fibs to an old woman."

"He's not," Sylvie says.

"Girl like you won't be on the market long."

Sylvie chuckles, "You'd be surprised."

Mom rubs her hands together, winces when her IV needle pulls. She always did like to gossip. I recall listening to her talk for hours on the phone with friends. My dad called it *chirping.* She asks Sylvie, "Why's that?"

Sylvie takes a swallow of coffee.

"She works a lot," I say.

"Doing what?" Mom looks back and forth between us. "You can tap boots but not answer a simple question?"

"Your mom would've been a good investigative journalist, given you stiff competition," Sylvie says.

I'd forgotten how direct and determined my mother could be. When we were kids, she never let us skate on homework, chores, or commitments, and she could sniff out a lie like a bloodhound. Behind her back, we called her *Sergeant Eve.*

Sylvie heads for the door. "I'll let you two visit in private."

"Hold your ever-loving horses! I know who you are! You're Sylvie Young! I have a ticket to your show this Sunday at the Schnitzer. Won't make it now, but holy cow!" She slaps me on the arm. "You're dating a psychic-medium? After telling me for years that what they

230 · Nan Fischer

do is horseshit?" Mom cackles, "Doesn't this just beat all? Bernie will die laughing." She looks from me to Sylvie. "If I'd known all it took was a pretty face to change my son's mind, I would've made a private appointment, tried to set you two up on a blind date."

Sylvie backs through the open door, cheeks rosy. "He hasn't changed his mind."

"Well, you're here now. Let's prove it to him." Mom pats the bed, beckons Sylvie. "You may not know this, Thomas, but this young lady is going to be really famous. People *in the know* say so. Then folks like me won't stand a chance to get a personal reading!" Sylvie doesn't budge.

"I hate to use the old lady card," Mom pushes, "but hell, I'm an old woman who could die of a blood clot in the next twenty-four hours or fall, hit my head, and never come out of the coma. You and my son clearly have something going on, so I'll use that to try to sway you, too. Sylvie, would you read me, please? I can even pay . . . but not until next month, depending on the doctor bills."

Sylvie asks, "Why is it so important to you?"

"I've spent the past twenty-plus years trying to contact my husband and son. There have been times when I thought maybe I had, psychics and mediums that *almost* had me convinced. But despite my son's be-lief that I'm a dotty old bat, I know those connections weren't real. That's why I've kept trying. On plenty of occasions, I was ready to toss in the towel, but I just can't."

Sylvie tips her head and fans her ear like there's a fly buzzing near it. "I'm sorry." She turns and disappears down the hallway.

I catch her halfway to the lounge. "Stop." She doesn't, so I grab her arm.

Sylvie shakes free, backs into the wall, and demands, "What do you want from me?"

Why didn't I tell Sylvie to steer clear of Mom's room? I consider all the people I've seen her read—at her shows, strangers, Madison, Max, Levi. My mother has two feet buried deep in the past. Does it matter how she moves on, whether it's a trick, a show, or Sylvie's desire to provide closure? I've accused Sylvie of robbing people of a natural and necessary process that follows the death of a loved one. But that assumed everyone has the ability to get on with life. My mother doesn't—she never has.

"Thomas?"

I rest the flats of my hands on the wall to either side of Sylvie's head. She tips her chin to meet my gaze. Anyone looking might mistake us for a couple. *Is that what I want?* I can't destroy Sylvie's reputation *and* expect to be her boyfriend. I gently run my thumb along her cheek, capture an eyelash, make a wish. *No matter what happens, please be okay.*

"What do you want?" Sylvie repeats.

"Will you . . . will you give Mom a reading?"

"Thomas. I might . . . there's no guarantee . . . or that it'll help."

"I know that."

"Are you sure?"

"Yes."

THIRTY-SEVEN

Sylvie

I settle in the chair by Eve's bedside, place my marker on the rolling table next to a mauve-colored plastic water pitcher. "Do you have something for me to hold?"

"In the closet." Eve waves an impatient hand. "There's a pin on my sweater."

Thomas withdraws a hunter green wool sweater. The scent of mothballs and lavender, old lady smells, tickle my nose. Carefully, I remove the pin, put it in my left palm. It's a black oval locket with a single diamond in the center that looks like a star. If I opened it, there would be two photos inside—her husband and dead son. *I'm sure of it.* Thomas leans against the window, watches. *This could change everything.*

"Full disclosure," I say. "I know how your husband and son died. That your family was watching TV, Deacan and your husband went for ice cream. It was raining and their car slid on a bridge, broke through the guardrail, and plunged into the river."

Eve nods. "They died on impact."

My nerves jitter as I fold my fingers over the pin, close my eyes, approach the red door, and unlock it . . . A metallic tang instantly floods my mouth and a spirit steps forward. "A male energy is here . . . Does the initial G or O mean anything to you?"

"My father's name was Gordy," Eve says.

"He's showing me a wooden rocking horse with bright blue eyes."

"Daddy was a cabinet maker. He carved that rocking horse for me. It was so tall, Mother was afraid I'd fall off, get concussed. He painted the glass eyes blue to match mine!"

I tug my earlobe. "Was he musical?"

"No, but he loved to listen to all kinds of music."

"There's an old-fashioned radio, curved on top, woven silver-and-black speakers with shiny knobs . . ." My adrenaline surges as I'm catapulted beyond this bridge. "He's hitting the top of it with his hand, twisting the knobs, like he's trying to get it to work, then pointing at you." I open my eyes, glance from son to mother. Silence. "Eve?" Her lips press into a tight white line. "Thomas?"

"Mom broke her father's radio the night Dad and Deacan died."

"What was your dad's name?" I ask him.

"Matthew."

I silently call to Matthew through the open doorway. Nothing. I use what I know. He comes across the threshold fast, like he's been waiting for the right invitation. A younger male spirit joins him. They show me a dark night—pounding rain—two pints of ice cream on the front seat of a car—a narrow bridge—bright headlights—a skid—crash—metal on metal—the car plunges—weightless—bone-jarring impact—hands fumble to unbuckle seat belts—open doors—break windows—water floods—boots kick—fingers scrabble—screams—*Help me, Dad—I love you, Deacan*—frigid water surges into mouths, nostrils—*I can't-breathe-can't-breathe-can't-breathe!*

My heart thrashes. I gulp for air. Sweat tracks down my spine. *Eve*

234 · *Nan Fischer*

lied to Thomas all these years. "It took a while," I say once my pulse has slowed. Eve's chin trembles.

Thomas looks from his mother to me. "What are you talking about?"

I wait for Eve to explain. She twists her arthritic hands, looks away.

"Sylvie?" Thomas presses.

He deserves the truth. "Your dad and brother didn't die when their car hit the water. They showed me . . . They both tried to get out but couldn't open the doors or break any windows. It took time for the car to fill with water. They drowned." *The last thing your father heard was your brother begging for help. The last thing Deacan heard was your father saying he loved him.*

"You're wrong," Thomas says, his tone dismissive. "They died on impact. Tell her, Mom."

Eve sniffles, wipes her nose with a wadded Kleenex, stares at the sheet covering her bony legs like a child determined to avoid punishment.

Thomas repeats, "Tell Sylvie they died on impact."

Eve flinches. "I . . . They didn't." She finally looks at Thomas, the corners of her mouth tugged down, eyes shiny. "According . . . according to the medical report, Matthew and Deacan didn't have mortal injuries . . . other than drowning. You didn't need to know that. No one should know that."

Thomas steps back, absorbing the blow. I take Eve's hand. The skin is parchment-thin. "You keep living it, over and over again. Rain. Bad tires. The crash. Their panic as the water level rose. The questions never stop: Could you have kept them from going? Should you have gone yourself? What if you'd been less stubborn and had dessert in the freezer instead of only buying it for special occasions? But there's no answer to any of those questions just like there's no reason for a tragedy."

A sob rips free from deep in her chest. I want to stop, comfort her, but she needs to hear this; they both do. "The bigger tragedy, for them and for you, is that you can't let go. Instead, you've tried to pull Matthew and Deacan back, again and again. But they can't come back, not in any *meaningful* way. They want you to know that they were more than those terrifying minutes. They lived full lives, both of them. And they're at peace."

The old radio appears again. Gordy's spirit forms a question mark in the air. I ask Eve, "Why did you break your father's radio that night?"

She draws a ragged breath. "I was mad with grief—the unfairness of it all. Matthew was the love of my life. Deacan didn't even get to have a girlfriend, go to college. He was going to be a journalist and was such a gifted writer. I just know he would've won a Pulitzer."

I recall what Thomas told me about his mother when I asked if she was proud of him. He said that she'd had bigger dreams. *They were for his brother, not him.* Thomas has retreated to the window. Hands pressed to the glass like a prisoner behind bars, he watches rain fall in sheets from a lead sky. *You're better than good enough.* I wish I could tell him that. But he's not, for his mother, and he probably never will be.

Eve begs, "What is Matthew saying?"

I turn from Thomas. "That he wants you to move on so that they can, too, and—"

. . . Thomas grips my shoulders so hard that pain spirals beneath my skin. I look around to get my bearings. The pin is on the bed, marker clenched in my hand. Beneath the fluorescent lights of the hospital room, I read the message scrawled on the inside of my palm. *I still believe in you, kid.* The look in Thomas's eyes is equal parts pain, accusation, and betrayal. He's out of the hospital room in three strides.

"Bring him back," Eve begs.

At first I think she's talking about Thomas. But she holds the pin out, begs me to take it, call Matthew and Deacan back from the other side. *What about Thomas?* "They're done. Now you have a choice. You can either continue to live in the past, pour your heart into that bottomless pit, or you can love the son who is still alive."

I find Thomas in the exit stairwell at the end of the hallway. He's slumped against the cinderblock wall, head in hands, fingers burrowed in his unruly hair. I sit down facing him, lean close.

"Is she okay?" he asks.

I rest a hand on his leg. "Yeah. Are you?"

"Depends."

I know what he wants—me to tell him that my knowing about Eve's father, the radio, and the truth about the drowning was all a trick. "Thomas, I can't."

He pushes my hand away. "In 1964, the James Randi Educational Foundation issued a one-million-dollar challenge to anyone who could demonstrate a supernatural or paranormal ability under agreed-upon scientific criteria. The competition ended in 2015. Do you know the result?" he demands.

His cheeks are pink blotches in a chalky face. I shrink back from his anger. "No."

"There were thousands of applicants and not a single person could prove their supernatural abilities."

"Thomas—"

"Over the years hundreds of scientists have repeatedly tried to prove that people are capable of perceiving something happening on the other side of the world, in a different room, on another plane, or events in the future. Do you know what every single one of them has found?"

I slide to the wall, press my back against it. "No."

"Zero evidence." His tone is sharp as broken glass.

"Thomas."

He bites his lower lip. "You're a liar. You deceive old women like my mother. Feed on grief. Steal their money. You no more spoke to my grandfather, Dad, and Deacan than you could fly to the fucking moon."

My stomach ignites like it's filled with gasoline and Thomas has flung a lit match. "Then how did I know?"

"Clearly, Lucas told you about the medical examiner's report when he called. I don't know about the rest, but that doesn't mean there's no explanation."

I hold up my hand, where the message is written over the heart line on my palm. *I still believe in you, kid.* "What does it mean?"

Thomas glares at me. "The thing I stole when I was a kid? It was a journal. Dad made me return it, but later Deacan bought it for me, hid it under my pillow." He nods at my hand. "That's the message my brother wrote on the first page minus the word *still*. Nice touch," he sneers. "I can't explain that one, either. But there *is* an explanation."

His derision leaves me carved out, empty. I get to my feet, bones aching like I'm eighty.

"Where are you going?"

"To meet Faith Benson."

Thomas rubs his face hard. "I'll go with you."

I cram down my hurt and calmly say, "I think we're done, don't you? But just FYI, there's an emotional angle for your exposé that you missed."

"What's that?" Thomas challenges.

"You never asked me how knowing other people's secrets affects me." I glare down at him and will my voice to remain steady. "The wife who approached me in the waiting room? The one whose husband had heart surgery? I knew he'd died; knew her world was about to crack open and had to watch that happen. Levi's in trouble—I'm not sure he'll live to see his baby born." I consider stopping there but can't slow my roll. "And Deacan and your dad? I *felt* their terror, drowned *with* them. That's what it's like, for *me*."

Beneath a calm exterior, my body quakes. Thomas's face is pale. He starts to say something but I hold up a hand, cut him off. "Don't forget your cat at the hotel and do leave my phone, iPad, and computer. As you've pointed out, I need them. Good luck with everything. I hope you win a Pulitzer to make your mom proud."

I leave the stairwell and Thomas behind. Have to force myself to walk, not run, to the elevator and to try not to wish that Thomas would follow me. He doesn't. I'm alone . . . but not quite. An invisible kiss brushes my temple. I hear the increasingly familiar woman's voice and finally make out the first word she says: *Come.*

THIRTY-EIGHT

Sylvie

"I'd recognize those eyes anywhere."

I stand there at the end of a stone path before a lacquered white door that was opened in a rush, Faith's arms held wide. *Does she expect a hug?* I opt for a handshake and she ushers me inside a three-story Tudor perched at the top of a steep, manicured lawn. I take stock as I follow her—chin-length auburn hair, black leggings, and a long-sleeved top with slits along the arms that reveal toned biceps.

We walk through an elegant front hall with wood floors covered in Persian carpets. At the far end, a curved stair climbs to the second floor. Black-and-white photos of children, framed in silver, adorn the walls. Faith follows my eyes, points at a little girl with similar freckles to her own that dust a round face.

"You remember Bennett? She was seven when you came to stay with us. The other two popped out after you'd moved on. Twins." She rolls her eyes. "That was quite the hitch in my giddy-up. Three months of bed rest for yours truly while I was an associate. I'm surprised the firm kept me on. Kids are a blessing but no one tells you what a crimp they put in your career."

I'm still stuck on her phrase, *moved on*, like I was a guest in her home, or it was my choice. I don't recall anything about Faith, her husband, or her daughter. "Sorry. I don't remember Bennett."

"Probably a good thing. She was a prima donna until the twins put her in her place."

Faith leads me into a large kitchen with a farmhouse table in the center. Glass cabinets line the walls, filled with china and crystal, marble counters, two stainless steel refrigerators.

"When the kids were young, this was where all the action happened," she explains. "Now they're in grad school and rarely come home." One corner of her smile hangs on.

"Is your husband going to join us?"

She shakes her head. "Scott and I have been divorced for three years. Heart problems did us in."

"Was he sick?"

"No. He thought I was missing mine." She gestures to a chair. "Can I get you anything?"

"Water would be great."

Faith pours two glasses then sits across from me. She glances at her Apple Watch. "Apologies, I only have about fifteen minutes. Yoga class. It's my sanity. You said on the phone that you had some questions?"

"Yes." I dive in. "Did you foster a lot of children?"

"You were the only one."

"Was I that bad?" I mean it as a joke to break the ice, but it sounds pathetic.

"How could you be bad? You didn't speak when you arrived."

The ground shifts beneath me. "What do you mean?"

"You were with us for about a year but only spoke the last two months." Faith toys with the gold signet ring on her pinkie. "I've always wondered why you didn't talk at first."

"I don't know," I admit. "The first six years of my life, until I was adopted, are a complete blank."

Faith sits back. "Complete?"

I dig out the plastic figures in my pocket—the woman, the girl, and the remnants of a swing set—and spill them onto the table. "All I know is that when I arrived in High River, I brought these. Did you give them to me?"

"You came with them." She points at the woman in the yellow dress. "The only time we ever saw you upset was when Bennett tried to play with that figure. Scott had to hold you back—he thought you were going to claw her eyes out."

My cheeks warm. "That's embarrassing."

"You were just a little kid. God only knows what was taken from you before you arrived at our home."

The skin on the back of my neck tightens. "Did my caseworker ever mention my past?" Faith shakes her head. I take a sip of water to hide my disappointment.

"What do you do now, if you don't mind my asking?"

"I'm a psychic-medium." Faith's brows arch high. I've been judged enough for one day and push back my chair. "Thanks for your time."

"I'm actually not surprised you're a psychic," Faith says.

"Seriously?"

She grins. "Yes! Every single time Scott, Bennett, or I lost something in the house, you'd find it! Can't believe I forgot this. Car keys, a ring, her favorite toy. At first, Scott thought you were hiding stuff.

You know, as a way of making yourself more . . . valuable. God, that sounds awful. Like we only would've fostered you if you could make our lives easier. Anyway, he decided to test you. To be perfectly honest, Scott didn't want a child around who would be that . . . mischievous, thought it wouldn't be a good influence on Bennett. He hid one of my shoes, a key to the shed, and some of Bennett's costume jewelry. You found it all. Straightaway."

It takes effort to chuckle. "Well, if my career doesn't pan out, it's nice to know I have something to fall back on."

Faith walks me back through the hallway, opens the front door. It's almost dark. She snags her keys from a hook and follows me down the stone path.

"Where are you headed?"

"Back to my hotel on Broadway."

"Did you drive?"

"I walked."

Faith nods at her sedan. "I've got time. I'll drop you before yoga."

Happy hour is in full swing in the hotel lobby. There's laughter, the cacophony of different voices, and the clink of tiny forks on small plates. A hotel employee offers me a glass of red wine but I decline. When I reach my room, I pause. My phone, computer, and iPad will be inside and Thomas will be gone. I'll try to forget about him and what it felt like to be honest, seen, and for a moment, even liked for *me*. But I know that's not really possible. Once the genie is out of the bottle, she'll fight, tooth and nail, to keep from being forced back inside it. Still, now that Thomas has left and I've hit a dead end in my search, I'll phone Lucas and then start preparing for the show. Maybe I can't forget what's happened, but I can choose to move on.

A growl rumbles on the other side of the door. It's prolonged, and so unlike Moose that I drop the key card, quickly scoop it up, and trigger the lock.

In the center of the room, Moose stands over Chris, legs splayed, lips pulled back in a snarl. Thomas crouches a few feet away.

THIRTY-NINE

Thomas

Moose and I are at a standoff. I came to grab my bag, give Sylvie back her electronics, and return to LA, where I'll continue to investigate the mystery behind Sylvie's birth parents and adoption. If I use what I already have, go back on my promise to Sylvie to keep things off the record, I can turn that new information into a story about both Sylvie as a fraud and the lies from her childhood that led her to be a con artist. Annie might run that article, but I'd rather keep investigating, solve the bigger mystery. My instinct tells me it's where the beating heart of the story lies. If Annie demotes me to obits, I'll quit, find another newspaper once my exposé is finished. It'll sell—it might even garner an award.

"Why are you still here?" Sylvie demands.

I wanted to be gone before she returned from Faith Benson's, but Cujo barely let me in the hotel room. The closer I got to Chris, the louder his growls. Full snarl, he truly could guard the gates of hell. And I'm pretty sure, if I touch my cat, he'll rip my arm off. The look on Sylvie's face now—surprise and disappointment, underlined by hurt—is hard to take. I'd hoped never to see her again; or more accurately, never again see a look on her face like the one in the hospital's stairwell—like I'd spit on her. I don't know what to feel anymore—*furious-ashamed-desperate-enraged-insulted-uncertain*—and so fucking drawn to her.

Warily eyeing Moose, I stand. "He won't let me get near Chris."

"It's okay," Sylvie tells her dog and he hangs his head low, whines. She kneels beside my cat. "Chris's breathing is all wrong."

Sharply, I say, "I know. I spoke with Dr. VanVoorhies. She's waiting at the clinic." Sylvie carefully carries Chris over, Moose at her heels. She weighs next to nothing in my arms. Now that I have her, that I can leave, my chest collapses and it's hard to breathe. "I don't know . . ." My voice breaks.

Sylvie waits a beat then asks, "Do you want me to go with you?"

". . . Please."

She drives. Chris curls in my arms, her body trembling. Moose hangs over the seat, watches us. "Why wouldn't he let me near her?"

Rain pounds. Sylvie turns the windshield wipers to high and passes a pickup truck, stays in the faster lane. "My first dog lived to sixteen," she says. "One day I couldn't find him. He'd crawled under the porch to die. I was devastated he'd been alone but Dad said animals know when it's their time to go, and my dog hadn't wanted me to watch him suffer or prolong his life. Animals are intuitive. I think Moose was honoring Chris's wishes."

My heart might splinter into a thousand shards. "I loved Chris from the moment we brought her home. Deacan did, too, but when we did homework, she'd curl in my lap, not his. At night, she'd pick me; sleep in the crook of my arm. She *always* chose me."

Sylvie stares straight ahead. The car's beams stretch beneath an oppressive, starless sky. "What happened with your mom the night Deacan and your dad died?"

Why is she asking me this now?

Sylvie passes a semi and a sheet of water hits the windshield, momentarily blinds us. She doesn't flinch. "When Eve broke the radio, what'd you overhear?"

She's driving well over the speed limit and we hydroplane across a deep puddle, lose traction for a moment. I grip the armrest. "Why does it matter?"

"It matters to *you*."

I shrug like what I'm about to say means nothing. "Mom said it should've been me. She wished *I'd* died instead of Deacan." The words I've never said aloud taste like poison. I wait for Sylvie to tell me that it was grief talking, but she doesn't. *She wouldn't lie to me about that.*

"Your mom may *never* choose you first," she says. "But Chris always did. Now it's your turn."

The truth of it all is a punch to the gut. Sylvie could've bludgeoned me with it or manipulated. Instead, in this moment when I'm most vulnerable, she's kind. *I haven't been.* Shame for the way I treated her in the hospital stairwell floods me. "I was such an asshole. What I said—"

"Is what you believe, right?"

"Yeah," I admit. "But I was also humiliated and really fucking sad."

Again, Sylvie doesn't try to convince me I'm wrong about my mother's love. Instead, she says, "Guilt has a thousand different faces."

Our conversation from the previous night flows back . . .

I told Sylvie that *Deacan didn't get to live his dream.*

You can't live it for him, she pointed out.

If not me, then who?

None of them want that . . .

I didn't think Sylvie understood that embracing Deacan's dream of being a journalist was a way to make up for my part in his death. But she had understood that, and more, all along. "Mom and I aren't so different, are we?" Sylvie waits for me to say it. "In our own way we both wanted to keep Deacan alive."

"It's not a crime," she says with a tiny shrug of one shoulder. "It's just human."

I take a breath. "After you left, Mom said that she's done trying to connect with the dead. I don't know if she'll go back on that, if it'll stick. But if it does, I'll have you to thank." Sylvie pulls into the vet clinic's parking lot, puts the car in park. Rain pounds the car's roof. "I'm sorry. Truly."

She turns off the engine and the dash lights go out, leave us in shadow. "For what?"

"How I've treated you. Regardless of what I think, I should've asked how it felt being on the other end of all that need and raw emotions." Heat climbs up my neck. "It must be brutal."

Sylvie's eyes glow like beacons. "Sometimes it is. But it's also a gift. Do you believe in *anything* I told you?"

I swallow the tangle of emotions jammed in my throat. "Can you forgive me anyway?"

". . . Yes."

Chris manages to purr for a few seconds. Softly, I say, "Sometimes the smallest things take up the most room in your heart." *It's my turn.* "Will you come in with me?"

Sylvie unbuckles her seat belt. Again, I'm floored by her capacity for kindness. We leave Moose in the car despite his whimpers. When we get to the front desk of the veterinary clinic, I can't say the words and step away as Sylvie quietly confers with the receptionist.

We're ushered to a different room than before and there's no steel exam table. Instead it looks like a small living room with leather chairs, a plush couch, and throw pillows in warm greens. A wide-planked oak floor is partially covered by a braided rug. The lighting is soft; paintings on the walls are of mountains, oceans, and a forest. Sylvie lights the candle on the table and soon the scent of pines fills the small space. There's a soft knock on the door and Dr. VanVoorhies steps inside. She's taken off her white coat and wears jeans and a pink turtleneck.

"Hi, Thomas," she says then runs a hand along Chris's back, rests it momentarily on her chest. "I'm glad you brought Christopher Robin in tonight." She meets my eyes. "Chris won't feel any pain. I'll give her a mild sedative to make sure she's comfortable, relaxed, and then a shot of pentobarbital, which will bring on unconsciousness. Within two minutes Chris's heart and brain functions will shut down. You can hold her in your arms the entire time."

My brain screams *NO!* But my heart takes over. I sit on the couch while the vet gathers the medications from a wooden cabinet by the door. Chris gazes at me like she knows.

Sylvie sits beside me, close but not touching, and murmurs, "Chris doesn't know. She just loves you."

Tears soak into Chris's fur. "I love you, Christopher Robin," I tell her. "Thank you for choosing me. It means the world. I chose you, too. I'm still choosing you." I nod at the painting of a forest. "Imagine walking through that forest," I say. "We're together, soft dirt and pine needles beneath our feet . . ."

"Ready?" the vet asks.

"Yes." I bury my face in Chris's neck and murmur, "We're together in that forest and the air smells of evergreen and sap. There are birds, every color, and their songs float through the air. We listen to them; happy because we're together . . ." Slowly, Christopher Robin's eyes close for what I know will be the last time . . .

In the end, her death is peaceful and about her, not me. The vet leaves me to sit with her while Sylvie takes care of the paperwork. Chris will stay here, be cremated, and then I'll take her ashes into the forest we imagined together so that she can be at rest outside.

On the drive back to the hotel, Moose puts his blocky head on my shoulder like he knows I just lost my best friend and I cry into his fur. When Sylvie turns off the car, neither of us gets out. Unsure, I ask, "What do we do now?"

"I guess you get your things from the room and we go our separate ways."

"What if . . . What if I'd rather not? Go our separate ways."

She firmly shakes her head. "One of my many therapists told me that I avoid intimate relationships because I believe intimacy, kindness aren't deserved. Maybe she's right and I should stop avoiding it, but I would rather be alone than judged."

"What if I promise not to do that anymore?"

"Can we decide next steps tomorrow, when we can both think more clearly?"

I nod. "I'll get my things and book another room."

She opens the car door, gets out, then turns back to me. "It's been a really rough day. We can stay together, if you want company."

That night we sleep in the same bed. Before dawn Sylvie's arms wrap around me while I cry for the pain and terror my dad and Deacan felt drowning, the truth about my mother, and the loss of Christopher Robin, whom I chose.

———

FORTY

Sylvie

The dream is much the same . . .

The ocean wave, ornate castle, and a treasure I don't understand. Except this time when I free the snow globe, there are tendrils of blood inside it. The wave hits. The globe is torn from my hands . . .

When the water recedes, I'm on the familiar street of past dreams, the snow globe nestled in the crook of my arm. The honeyed scent of roses is carried on a warm breeze, but beneath their perfume I now smell rot . . .

I turn the corner, past the shingled house, the dog, Boone, and the neighbors. All watch with wet eyes as I continue down the sidewalk to the house at the end of the street, each slow step punctuated by the staccato of my pounding heart . . .

I stop in front of a gate fashioned from pieces of driftwood, unlatch it, and walk to a gray door, reach for a dented bronze knob. Terror snakes around my body, loosens my bladder. The globe slips. Before it hits the ground, invisible hands grasp my shoulders and the now recognizable woman's voice beseeches: *Come out* . . .

I sit up, sweaty, disoriented. *I'm in a hotel.* Moose sleeps beside the bed. Thomas is next to me. I finally heard both words: *Come out.* But who said them? All I know for certain is that I recognized the gray door from childhood nightmares, but this time . . . *NO*. I tear myself free from the bad dream's sticky web, cram down irrational fears, and rest a hand on Moose's rib cage, match the rhythm of our breaths. The dream's images turn to sepia then scatter like leaves in the wind.

Rolling onto my side, I watch Thomas sleep. I've got the upper hand and can go to his editor, kill my section in his exposé. He's way too compromised at this point to be objective or believed. So why haven't I done it already? Ended this? He's my enemy, adversary, one-time lover . . . *and friend?* Is that what's stopping me? The idea that we might continue on in any capacity, after all of this, was never possible, even if he'd believed. *Right?*

If you let people get too close, you'd have to answer the hard questions, and they'd really know you . . .

I'll miss Thomas. Having someone who demanded more, challenged me, and made me want to be better, do better. So what's next? *I'm safe right now.* When Thomas wakes, I'll send him away and then call his editor. Over the next few days I'll prep for my show. Then I'll return to LA, get ready for the next stage of my career.

Quietly, I get up and dig the plastic pieces from the pocket of the jeans that hang over the back of a chair. The figures are hooked together, the woman's hand caught in the little girl's braid. *This* was *my life.* I pad to the trash can, hold the pieces over it, and tip my palm to let them slide away. But at the last second I close my fist.

"Hey," Thomas calls. "You okay?"

I turn and place the figures on top of the duvet. Frustration strangles my voice. "I need to know."

His eyes are somber. "Let me help you?"

"All Faith remembered about me was that I didn't speak when I arrived. I've reached a dead end."

Thomas shakes his head. "There's no such thing. We can figure it out together."

A better person would say no. "Okay." Moose stretches, brings me his leash. "Order breakfast?"

"Sure. What do you want?"

"You choose."

I shrug on my dad's old down coat, clip the leash to Moose's collar, more to make the people we meet on the street feel safe than for him. In the lobby I stop by the concierge's desk. She's early forties, clad in a silk blouse and dark blue pants, name tag: ELLIOT.

"Can I help you?" Elliot asks.

"Yes, I'd like to send a package. Do you have an envelope?"

"Let me check." She pulls open a drawer, withdraws a four-by-six-inch manila envelope. "Would this work? If not, I can send out for a different size, bring it to your room?"

"It's perfect." I reach inside the lining of Dad's coat for the small flip cell phone and charger he put there. In the orchard, when he stopped me from hugging him a second time, he guided my hands back to my sides and I felt the bulge inside the down jacket. Later, in the hotel lobby bathroom, I finally had the chance to look. The lining had been slit, nylon edges neatly tucked and sewn so they wouldn't fray and a tiny snap added to keep the pocket closed. Dad doesn't sew. Mom is an expert. The phone was fully charged and he'd turned off the ringer. I used it to call Lucas from the shower the morning after Thomas and I had sex—when he wouldn't look at me. I told Lucas everything and he shared what little information he'd been able to dig up.

I slide the charger, phone, and a scribbled note, *Love always, Sylvie*, into the envelope, address it to Dad *and* Mom in High River, then hand the concierge a twenty. "Snail mail is fine."

Elliot glances at the address. "I can't imagine it'll cost that much. I'll have the change sent to your room."

"Please don't. Consider it a tip."

"Thank you," Elliot says. "Oh, Ms. Young, you have a card. I was going to send it to the room but since you're here." She hands me a thick white envelope with the hotel's name embossed in one corner. "It's from one of the hotel employees. It's not our policy to message guests, but she explained the circumstances and I hope you don't mind?"

"Not at all. Thank you."

"My pleasure."

Moose and I walk outside. It's not raining yet, but the sky is a dingy smear of gray. We walk toward a patch of grass a few blocks down and I take off his leash, let him wander while I open the envelope and withdraw the note.

Dear Sylvie,

You may have heard that my brother, Brian, was killed in Iraq by a suicide bomber. I think that you already knew. When we talked, you referenced him in the past tense. What you said, about him being at peace with the choices he made, has been a comfort to my mom, sister, and me. Maybe that message was directly from him? I will still be at your show on Sunday. I don't expect you to pick me for the final reading. There are other people who haven't heard from

their loved one and need you more. I just want to thank you and
bless you for sharing your gift with us.

Love,
Madison

We take the long way back to the hotel. In the elevator, I say, "If I told Thomas about the phone, he wouldn't believe in anything I've said as a psychic—and some of it was real." Moose licks my hand, as usual bestowing unconditional love.

Thomas has ordered banana pancakes. We drench them in syrup. When we're done, I give him Madison's note. He doesn't say anything, but that's better than shooting holes in it. When the hotel room's phone rings, I don't move. There's only one person who'd call me. Thomas raises one brow. I say, "It's Lucas."

He reaches over and picks up anyway. "Hello? Yes. Yes, she's right here. Hang on." Thomas holds out the phone.

I hesitate then take it. "Hey, Lucas—"

"Nope. This is Dr. Anthony Johnson. Is this Sylvie Peters?"

There's something familiar about the deep timbre of the man's voice. "It is. Can I help you?"

"I think I'm meant to help *you*. Faith Benson called me this morning."

I sit back. "Sorry, I'm lost."

"Faith apologizes for not thinking of me last night. I'm a child psychologist. I was *your* psychologist, years ago. Faith thought you might have some questions for me?"

My nerves tingle. "I do."

Dr. Johnson can't share patient information over the phone so we agree to meet at a park on the waterfront near his office between his patient sessions. Thomas reaches out, squeezes my shoulder when I tell him.

"See? There's no such thing as a dead end."

Thomas glances at Chris's carrier, and his eyes fill as the enormity of his loss hits. I lead him into the bathroom and with apologies to Moose shut the door. When the shower water is hot, we peel off our clothes and step under the spray. I draw Thomas toward the teak bench. He rests his hands on my hips as I shampoo his hair, knead his neck, then take the showerhead from its chrome hook to wash away the suds and hopefully a tiny bit of pain. Thomas pulls me onto his lap. We kiss, his unshaven chin both rough and sensual.

"What do *you* need?" Thomas asks.

The answer surprises me. "To be seen."

With his hands gripping my waist, he lifts until he's inside me. I wrap my legs around his torso. We kiss, my fingers tangled in his hair, his arms tight enough that I can feel the pounding of his heart. When we're both on the edge of orgasm, Thomas meets my gaze and then we cling to each other until our bodies shudder then settle. There are times when sex is an act of kindness, passion, apology, absolution . . . it was all those for me.

I tip my head back and the spray washes away my tears before Thomas can see them. Given our situation and the choices I must make to protect my career, I won't have this kind of intimacy again. The fact that it will soon be gone is painful enough to steal my breath.

"You good?" Thomas asks.

There's a starry look in his eyes that won't last. "Yeah." *I just want to remember this.*

FORTY-ONE

Sylvie

We take Moose with us to the waterfront to meet with Dr. Johnson. I settle on a metal bench across from a marina dotted with small boats that rock in the waters of the Willamette River while Thomas plays with Moose. He tosses the orange rubber ball we brought into the air and Moose lets it bounce once then catches it. They begin a game of fake chase, neither quite himself, both feeling Chris's absence but distracting the other. *We have come a long way in five days.*

"Sylvie?"

A tall man, sideburns dusted gray, in a tan raincoat and plaid beret, umbrella tucked neatly beneath his arm, strides over. I stand. "That's me."

"I'm Dr. Johnson."

He reminds me of the narrow spine of an old, leather-bound book, its edges comfortably worn. *I don't recognize him.* We shake hands and settle on the bench. Thomas joins us and I make the introductions while Dr. Johnson scratches Moose's chest.

"Okay, first things first. Since we're going to talk about a past patient, that's you, and the information is privileged, protected, I need to see some identification." Dr. Johnson slides on round glasses with thick lenses.

I pull out my driver's license and he scrutinizes the plastic square before handing it back. "Do you, um, have my file?" I ask.

"I read through it." He taps his head. "Now it's in here."

Thomas cocks a brow. "Photographic memory?"

"Much like your friend," Dr. Johnson says with a head tilt at me. "Though mine has faded a bit."

"How do you know about my memory?"

"You and I played many games. You were a whiz at Go Fish! At first I thought you just had an elastic mind. But I decided to test it by showing you detailed photographs. For example, I showed you a tall building, took away the photo after ten seconds, then asked you how many windows it had, doors, awnings, et cetera. You'd close your eyes and it was clear you were seeing an image, counting. Then you'd write down the number of each item. Perfect every time. Do you still have an eidetic memory?"

"I do," I say, "but it starts at age six. That's not normal for someone like me, is it?"

Dr. Johnson's index finger traces the long slope of his nose. "No, but I'm not surprised. Clearly there was some sort of disturbing trauma in early childhood. You didn't speak when you came to my office and your caseworker, Heidi, said you arrived in foster care that way after a hospitalization. You have absolutely no recollection about what happened, or your time in the hospital?"

"I don't." It's not a total lie. After visiting Eve, it's clear that I was in a children's psychiatric ward, but I don't remember it, or know the reason.

Thomas asks, "What did you focus on during Sylvie's sessions?"

"At first, getting her to speak."

"How'd you do that?" I ask.

"I would like to say it was my incredible skill as a therapist," he chuckles. "But in actuality, it was a fluke. In my practice I see many different children and have a vast library, some books chosen for their stories and messages, others for characters that might interest a specific client. One never knows how a breakthrough will occur." Dr. Johnson slides off his beret. He scratches closely shorn gray hair then replaces the hat. "One day I asked you to choose a book from my shelves. You wandered along the rows and touched the spines but didn't pull one out. I thought that you weren't interested but suddenly you ripped a book free and read the first line aloud."

"What was the book?" Thomas asks.

"*The Broken Ear*. Fascinating choice."

Moose noses my leg for an ear scratch. "Why?"

"It was in French! The main character was a man named Tintin."

A white dog bounds through my mind. "He had a dog . . . Snowy?"

Dr. Johnson slaps his thighs. "Exactly! Tintin was an adventurer who traveled with Snowy."

"Did I speak French to you?"

"Other than that first sentence, no. But after that, the dam was broken."

My memory is still blank. "Did Heidi mention anything about my past?"

"No, she was rather skittish about it, and I wasn't encouraged to dwell on it."

"What do you mean?"

The doctor pats the pockets of his raincoat, pulls out a Nicorette pack, and pops a square of gum into his mouth. "Don't ever smoke," he warns. "I went to see Heidi, told her that to best help you, I needed to know your history. She showed me a judge's order that said your files were sealed."

The promise I felt this morning fades.

Dr. Johnson pops a second piece of gum free and chomps down on it. "I still went down to the county courthouse and petitioned to see your records. Waited a month with no response. I had a friend who worked as a court clerk. Didn't ask her to do anything illegal, just track where my request was in the queue. Turned out it'd been tossed because there was no information in the system for Sylvie Peters. Must've been some kind of filing snafu—it happens," he explains. "The system is overtaxed."

Another dead end.

"What was Sylvie like?" Thomas asks.

Dr. Johnson smiles at me. "You were a sweet child, but very lost. You reminded me of that children's story *Are You My Mother?* by P. D. Eastman. Do you know it?"

I shake my head. "What's it about?"

"A baby bird that hatches while his mother is off finding food. He leaves the nest to look for her. He asks a kitten, hen, dog, cow, even an old car if any are his mother. Finally, he's returned to his nest by a crane operator."

Except I was never returned to my mother. Why? Despite my disappointment, I ask, "Once I was talking, what'd we work on during our sessions?"

"Ways to anchor you to the present, discover things you liked. You enjoyed craft projects, made a lot of jewelry with beads. Oh! And you had an obsession with the numbers 9 and 2. Expressed them in watercolors, charcoal, chalk, even made a macaroni collage with those numbers glued to a sheet of construction paper." He laughs. "It was very creative, actually. I wouldn't be surprised if imagination plays a part in whatever you do now?"

I glance at Thomas but he has his journalist's face on. "It does," I admit.

Dr. Johnson looks at his watch. "Ah. I need to get back to my office."

Thomas says, "One last thing? You said Heidi showed you a letter from a judge. Any way you'd remember his name?"

Dr. Johnson closes his eyes. "The first name started with a G . . . maybe Greg? No, it was longer." He opens his eyes. "Sorry. Old age can be an unkind fellow."

I force a smile. "Thanks so much for making the time."

"My pleasure."

He tips his cap then strides off and, with him, the last of my hope. "Let's head back to the hotel."

Thomas reaches out, squeezes my hand. "We'll think of something."

"Gabriella!" Dr. Johnson shouts in the distance and hurries back. "Her name was Gabriella H. Bryant."

My brain flips through the photographs along the top of Heidi's piano. Almost all of them were with her sister.

Heidi said . . . *Both Briella and I were so very lucky. We were called to our respective careers . . .*

I asked . . . *Did anyone in your family support you?*

Briella. Always. No questions asked.

The bottom of the letter my dad gave me flashes. *PS G is on board.*

I meet Thomas's questioning gaze. "Briella is Gabriella. Gabriella Hiddleston Bryant. She's G. Let's go."

FORTY-TWO

Thomas

There's a four-block square near our hotel with food carts that sell Mexican, Greek, Korean, Indian, Southern BBQ, Thai, and every imaginable kind of fusion. We buy sushi for lunch and bring it back to our room so we can eat while we work. I Google "Gabriella H. Bryant," find her immediately. "She went to University of Oregon, honors program, graduated summa cum laude, then Lewis & Clark Law. Practiced family law for seven years before getting elected to serve as a family court judge for Manus County, Oregon. She retired in 2015 after serving forty-two years on the bench."

Sylvie finishes her unagi then says, "Briella has Alzheimer's. Heidi said *on good days she remembers me.* If she's that far gone, she's in a care facility. Heidi visits so it must be pretty close."

I search for Alzheimer treatment centers within a few hours' drive from Tillamook and find twelve. Four of those are in Tillamook. Sylvie chews her lower lip. "What's wrong?"

"What if she doesn't remember?"

"It's possible," I have to admit as I dial the first number.

"You can't just call them," Sylvie says.

"Why not?"

"Patient confidentiality issues."

"Cherry Lane Memory Care," a woman chirps on the other end of the line.

"Gabriella Bryant's room, please."

"One moment . . . I'm sorry, sir. We don't have a resident by that name. You might have us confused with Cherry Walk Retirement?"

"You're right. Thanks for your time." I hang up, nod at Sylvie's phone. "You take half the list. Divide and conquer." She grabs two Cokes from the mini-fridge, pops the tops, and hands me one then perches on the arm of the couch. I watch her dial the first number. Her knee bounces and her eyes shine with excitement. She nibbles her lower lip and my chest cinches. How can I have these kinds of feelings for someone who's so wrong for me?

Whatever I think is happening, or might happen, between Sylvie and me is impossible. We've been working together the past few days, but we are adversaries. Nothing has changed. I don't believe in psychics, and if Sylvie, and people like her, are allowed to continue their scams unchecked? People like my mom, who can't accept reality or process grief, will be victimized.

On top of all that, I'm a journalist. This is my job. Annie has given me enough rope to either hang or save myself. I prefer the latter. I owe my boss for the chance and still believe in the value of this story. Sylvie glances over at me, offers a smile. She is fighting for self-preservation, but if she wins, a lot of people lose. *I lose* . . . My brain searches for a way out and a memory leaps forward . . .

———

Do you hate your mother? Sylvie asked on our drive away from her childhood home.

I feel sorry for her. She thinks that people like you can bring back the dead.

What if people like me could, at least for a few minutes?

Then, assuming you always believed that your bio parents were dead, why didn't you ever try to connect with them?

I told you on the train, it felt like a betrayal.

Doesn't ring true.

. . . I can't.

Why not?

I don't know.

———————

The reporter in me abruptly wakes up. Everything falls into place. This search is a carefully orchestrated charade. Sylvie already knew the plane crash was a lie; that her birth parents were still alive. She's constructed all of this to make me feel like I'm the hero that saves a damsel in distress. The past five days have been an elaborate ruse to soften my stance, get me to omit her from my exposé. My face burns. *That's why she slept with me.* I've been so blinded by her act that I let her admission of guilt slither away.

"You said you couldn't contact your biological parents, on the other side."

Sylvie finishes her phone call and turns. "Why are we going back to that?"

I stand up, pace the room. "I let it go. You'd just been through hell with Hana and Wess. But it was either an admittance of guilt, that what you do is a scam, or you knew all along that the plane crash story was a lie; that they were alive." Sylvie's face drains of light, the smudges of gray beneath her eyes now visible. This week has been brutal—me, her parents, the pressure. But a lot of it is her fault.

Warily, Sylvie admits, "Yes. I lied that it felt like a betrayal to Hana and Wess. But I didn't lie when I said that I couldn't contact my biological parents. Not because I knew they were alive, but because every time I opened the red door, tried to reach them, I had a panic attack—it felt like dying. One of my therapists said it meant childhood trauma. So I let it go."

I stop pacing, meet her gaze. The gray of her irises has darkened to the shade of storm clouds. "I don't believe you."

Sylvie grimaces. "So we're back to me being a liar?"

"Yes."

"Are you recording this conversation?"

I toss up my hands. "Seriously?" Moose, curled on the dog bed the hotel provided, gets up and stalks to Sylvie's side. They watch me.

"If you don't trust me," she says, her voice flat, "I can track down Gabriella myself."

"I know you can," I say. "The question is whether you *want* to do this alone." She looks away, disconnects. Despite everything, it registers like a blow. "Okay. I'll be out of here in five." I quickly toss clothes into my bag, head toward the bathroom for my Dopp kit.

"What do you want?" Sylvie demands.

"The truth!"

Her chin trembles. She bites her lower lip to stop it. "What if I don't know the truth?"

"Then tell me what you *do* know."

Sylvie's hands shake as she twists her hair into a knot. "I have a recurring dream," she finally says. "It started when I moved to San

Francisco—a tree-lined street, small bungalows. I'm a little kid again, wave to a cute dog; smile at imaginary neighbors. I always woke before I walked too far. Last night I dreamt that I was there again, except the snow globe was in my arms. I reached the end of the street. There was a small house and a path beyond its gate led to a weathered gray door. I . . . I've seen that door before."

"Where?"

"In childhood nightmares—monsters waited on the other side of it. Last night, standing in front of that same door, I was petrified. The globe slipped. I woke before it shattered. But I think it did shatter, in real life . . ." Sylvie rubs her forehead hard enough to leave a streak of reddened skin. "That I opened a gray door and there was a monster; that something horrific happened . . . and it was my fault."

"What?"

Tears trickle down her cheeks. She whispers, "I don't know and I'm terrified to find out."

FORTY-THREE

Sylvie

Thomas squats in front of me, brow furrowed, and asks, "What do you want to do?"

Run away. "What do you think I *should* do?"

He hesitates. "Finding out that Dad and Deacan drowned was brutal."

"Are you sorry I told you?"

He shakes his head. "But it's like ripping off a bandage. The wound beneath it is ugly but the best disinfectant is sunlight."

My gut releases a shower of acid. A few days ago the burning in my belly was uncomfortable, sometimes painful, but Tums quelled most of the heat. Despite the Prilosec, it's getting worse. I could *try* to escape this . . . but I can't outrun it. "I want to know the truth."

I find Gabriella on my sixth call. She's a resident of Hillcrest Memory Care in Tillamook, just a few miles down the road from Heidi's home. The operator connects me to her room.

"Hello?" a woman says, her voice watery.

"Gabriella?"

"What?"

"Briella?"

"Yes. Who's this?"

"An old friend. I'd like to come for a visit, is that okay?"

"Certainly. I like visits."

"See you soon."

We grab our rain shells and head out into the late afternoon. I rest a hand on Moose's head through the lobby. Thomas takes my other one. I can't recall the last time a man, especially one I've slept with, has held my hand. "Don't be nice to me just because I cried like a big baby."

He holds my hand tighter. "Never."

We pass the concierge who mailed back my phone. When Elliot approaches, I look away and she takes the hint and passes by. Thomas grabs an umbrella from a silver urn by the door and the three of us crowd beneath it and cross the street to the parking lot as the skies unleash a rainstorm that could sink Noah's Ark. I sit in the back of the SUV with Moose, who hates thunderstorms. He shakes with each loud crack and boom, hides his head beneath giant paws. "Do you know what makes that sound?" I ask my dog. "It's the rapid expansion of air surrounding the path of a lightning bolt."

"High school science class?" Thomas asks.

"Dad taught me."

"Parenthood must be a hard job. My mom was only a few years older than I am now when her husband and son died. Yet I expected her to cope. Demanded it."

There's a deafening rumble. Moose whines. "Do you want children?" I ask.

Thomas slows to stop at a red light. "Always been ambivalent, probably because I can recall what it was like to have a relatively happy family. And there's also the shrapnel when it was blown to bits. You said before that you don't want kids?"

The light changes and Thomas navigates onto the highway. Rain turns to hail and hits the windshield with tiny mallets. When Moose whimpers, I wrap my arms around him. "I've never wanted them. Ever."

"Why?" Thomas asks.

The truth, anchored deep, tugs free. "I've always been certain that having a child will somehow invite death." I sound ridiculously dramatic and my face burns.

He's quiet for a few minutes then says, "That's a strong belief. Is it based on anything concrete?"

"You mean like a vision?"

"Yeah."

"No."

"Could you be wrong?"

". . . I don't know." The rest of the drive we're both silent, lost in our own thoughts.

When we get off the highway, we find Hillcrest Memory Care at the end of a street filled with two- and three-story apartment buildings and a low-slung shopping mall with a Dollar Tree, Walgreens, and PetSmart. The one-story facility is painted bright yellow with white trim around the windows in a bid to look cheerful. Cherry trees bordering the parking lot are in bloom but the rain has beaten their blossoms senseless and they droop from the branches. I snap on Moose's service dog vest.

"Ready?" Thomas asks.

"I have to be."

FORTY-FOUR

Sylvie

The three of us make a dash through the downpour to the glass front doors of the building and step inside the entryway. "What if Heidi's here?" I ask as we shake water from our jackets and Moose does a shimmy, head to tail, to get rid of the cold drops.

Thomas's eyes glint. "I'll threaten to publish a story about her shredding your file."

I open the facility's interior door. The warm air inside carries the scent of disinfectant and stale air freshened by flower-scented deodorizers. The walls are painted a sunny orange and the floor carpeted with gray squares shot through with streaks of reds, blues, and yellows. At the front desk I inform the receptionist that I've brought my service dog to visit Gabriella Bryant at her sister Heidi's request. He asks for my ID but is so distracted by Moose that he doesn't bother checking for my name on his list of approved visitors.

The receptionist reaches over the counter to pat Moose's head. "Wow, he's giant! Gabriella's room is I-117. Follow the red arrows past skilled nursing. When you reach the double doors, use code 2929 to open them, and you'll enter the memory care wing. Please make sure you don't allow any residents out of that wing. They tend to wander and get lost. Enjoy your visit!"

On our way to memory care, we pass two women in rocking chairs. They gape at Moose. One beckons and we pause for a quick pet. When we turn the corner, a man hobbles toward us with two canes, eyes trained on the floor. He's surprised by Moose and almost falls. Thomas grabs his arm, steadies him.

"I used to have Danes," the old guy shouts. He giggles when Moose kisses the back of an arthritis-gnarled hand.

"He likes you," I say.

"I'm a great guy!" He pets Moose again then moves on.

We pause a handful more times for residents to greet Moose. Smiles light up their scoured faces, and each time I see the flicker of their inner child. Moose eats up the attention, prancing like a prize horse, head held high. He gives even more kisses than he gets.

When we reach the double doors at the end of the hallway, I put in the code, the doors unlock, and we enter the memory care wing. Here people drift in various states of dress—some in slouchy robes and furry slippers, others mismatched clothing, but a good number are well put together, the women's hair dyed, combed, and set; nails painted; men in V-neck sweaters, slacks, and shiny shoes. Some chat with employees who wear name tags, others drift, occasionally redirected by the staff like go-carts momentarily stuck in a corner.

Gabriella's door is open. We pause on the threshold—the room has a kitchen sink, a counter, and a half-fridge on one wall, a twin bed covered in a sky blue quilt on another. A rectangular table for two and a leather couch fill the rest of the space along with a large-screen TV. The walls are off-white and undecorated, but framed pictures are scattered around the room. I've seen the photograph on the bedside table—Heidi and Briella on the dock. *Better days.* Beside it is a photo of Gabriella posed on the bench in her black judge's robe with gavel in hand, a look of calm authority on her face. For a woman used to mental acuity, success, authority, Alzheimer's seems especially cruel. *She wiped out six years of my life with a signature. Isn't her disease poetic justice?* Still, I wouldn't wish her fate on my worst enemy.

We find Gabriella curled in a corner of the couch. A game show plays on the TV. Someone has maintained the red of her hair, and the style is still short but no longer spiky. She's dressed in an oversized green sweater and black leggings. Pink bunny slippers cover her feet, their long ears drooping. She's much heavier than she was in those earlier photos. I knock on the doorframe.

"Come in!" Gabriella says, blue eyes sparking. "Two guests. Lucky me!" She leaps to her feet when she spies Moose. "And a dog! I love dogs!" Moose pads over and she scratches him from head to butt. "Heidi and I used to have a dog. His name was Happy. You're a good boy, yes you are." She kisses the top of Moose's head.

Thomas takes the chair while I sit on the sofa. *Please remember me.* "Gabriella—"

"You must be lost, dear," she says, retaking her corner of the couch. "Shall I ask my clerk to help you?"

I adjust. "Briella?"

"Yes? I don't mean to be rude, but my docket is full today. On your way out, you can ask my clerk to make an appointment."

"She already did. I'm right on time."

"Oh good. They're on me like flies on shite if I get behind. What are we discussing today?"

"A foster care case," I reply. "Sylvie Peters."

Gabriella taps her temple, lips pursed. "Peters. Peters. I don't recall that name. Give me the basics. Chop-chop."

Thomas quickly explains, "She was a foster child between 2000 and 2002. Hospitalized after a trauma. You sealed her file."

"Heidi asked you to," I add.

"Heidi who?" She nibbles a nail already bitten to the quick then darts a look at Thomas. "Is he the opposing counsel? Looker, that one, but don't get distracted. Your job is to protect the children."

"We're all on the same side," Thomas says, "working for the best interest of the child."

Gabriella nods. "Foster care—important system, but terribly flawed. If I had my way, it'd run smoother."

I ask, "What would you do?"

She leans in. "The problem is that nobody wants a *problem*." She taps her forehead like what she just said was brilliant.

I repeat, "Do you remember Sylvie Peters?"

"You have stunning eyes—don't see that shade of light gray very often. What was your name, dear?"

"Sue. I'm the lawyer assigned to Sylvie Peters. She was the little girl who didn't talk for a year. She was hospitalized then placed in a foster home. Eventually a couple named Hana and Wess Young adopted her. The adoption went through very quickly."

"Ah, the skids were greased," Gabriella says with one finger held in the air. "I'm reminded of an old case. Bear with me, there is always an important moral to my stories. God loves a moral. He also enjoys fucking with us."

Her eyes dim then lose focus like a cartoon character under hypnosis. Briella returns to the game show on TV. "Choose curtain number three, you dolt," she shouts at the contestant. Thomas crosses the room, blocks the screen.

"You were saying, about an old case?" I prompt.

"Oh. What? Ah, yes. Every case is different. Each requires focus, commitment. There's a caseworker I used to know. Committed with a capital C. Retired early, though. Nerves shot. Always told her, law isn't for sissies."

"Was that Heidi?"

"Who's Heidi?"

I bat away frustration. "Can you tell us about your foster care cases?"

"Ah. Foster care. There were some happy times. Adoptions were the best days. B-E-S-T ever!"

"Were there difficult cases?" Thomas probes.

"They're all difficult. Drugs. Abuse. Violence. Death. You name it. My job was to do whatever I could to protect the children. It was my calling, my sister's, too. Some situations were so horrible, I'd lose sleep, have nightmares. Can't un-see crime photos. Nope. Not possible. Best never to see them at all . . ." She falters, looks around the room like she's searching for a word, memory, her mind, desperate to pluck it from the air.

"What kind of crime photos?" Thomas asks.

"Do I know you? Court is in recess. Where's my clerk?"

I get up, look around, desperate to find something to create a bridge . . . but even if I could? Gabriella probably wouldn't understand the messages.

"There were some cases impossible to forget," Gabriella says, eyes still trained on the TV. "Alzheimer's is especially brutal in that way, it has left me with the horrors. A brother and sister beaten by Mom's boyfriend—one died, the other left paralyzed. Mom retained custody. The law is the law. A baby born addicted to crack, blind. Dad got custody, molested her when she was six months old. Mom killed the bastard. She went to prison for life. The law is the law. Little girls burned by cigarettes, placed in scalding water, chained to a radiator. Most of them ended up back with their abuser after court-appointed mommy and daddy classes. Those classes are BS in most cases. But the law is the law." She rambles on, "Mom murdered, little girl stayed with her. A delivery guy noticed the smell, called the police. Media was on that one like buzzards to roadkill. Sometimes the law needs a swift kick in the a-s-s."

A shrill voice demands, "What are you two doing here?"

Heidi's eyes dash from me to Thomas and then to Gabriella, who has returned to the TV. In the bend of one arm is a silver pan of lasagna, hot from the oven; the smell of tomato sauce and melted cheese wafts into the room.

My body clenches. "We came to talk to your sister, or should I say the Honorable Judge Gabriella Bryant, about sealing my files."

"Who are you, dear?" Gabriella asks.

Thomas interjects, "She's Sylvie Peters."

"You should be ashamed," Heidi snaps. "My sister is in no condition to speak with you two. Briella was once an esteemed judge. What you're doing could ruin her reputation! A reputation built on the unwavering desire to help children. Get out. Both of you."

Moose follows me to the door. Despite his calm presence, the thermometer inside me is close to boiling point. "You didn't give us any other choice," I say through gritted teeth.

"What you're doing is a sin," Heidi states. "Isaiah 43:18: 'Do not call to mind the former things, or ponder things of the past.'"

"'And you will know the truth, and the truth will set you free.' John 8:32." I'm so furious at this woman who stole my past and place in this world, who hid my real mom, at her audacity to judge me, that spit flies from my lips with each word. "We can trade Bible verses all freaking day. You chose Hana and she made sure I went to church. So bring it on!"

Gabriella pounds her fist on the armrest and shouts, "'Sanctify them by the truth. Your word is truth.' John 17:17. My sister and I loved church. I've forgotten her name. Do you know her?" she asks Heidi.

"You should thank us both," Heidi levels at me, her body rigid. "Without us, you would *never* have been adopted."

"Why?" I demand. "What was so wrong with me?"

"If you don't leave, I'll call the police," Heidi threatens.

Thomas touches my shoulder. "Sylvie, we should go."

Heidi waves us through the open door. "And don't come back. I'll make certain the staff here knows that if you do, they should call the police."

Gabriella shouts, "Order in my court."

I cross the room, kneel, Gabriella's bunny slippers between my feet. "Please, please tell me about Sylvie Peters."

She stares down her nose with pursed lips then a smile blooms and she pats my hand. "Let me simplify it. Imagine a child is a house. There was a horrific crime in that house. Who'd want to buy it? But if you repaint the house, oil the system so it runs lightning fast. Voilà. A sale."

"Out!" Heidi shrieks.

"Bye, bye, birdie," Gabriella calls with a wave as we walk out the door.

─────

FORTY-FIVE

Thomas

Sylvie thinks Gabriella understood enough of our conversation that there's something we can use. I'm not sure. Still, it's what we have to work with. I order room service for dinner. Sylvie feeds Moose then joins me on the couch with two beers from the minibar.

"What was your biggest takeaway?" she asks.

I go through the conversation in my mind, pluck out the highlights. "Gabriella believed the foster system was flawed. Heidi admitted that they did something to get you adopted. We know that was sealing hospital records, destroying your foster file, and a quick adoption to folks who agreed not to ask questions."

Sylvie takes a sip of beer. "Whatever was in my files must've been really bad." She taps a hotel pen on a pad of paper, thinks aloud. "Dr. Johnson petitioned to see my records even though they were sealed—"

"His friend the court clerk said there was nothing in the system for Sylvie Peters. He guessed that your information was misfiled." I drink some beer, peel the paper label—in college whoever could peel their label cleanly off first was owed the next round. Rolling Rock was easiest, then Pacifico . . . *Imagine a child is a house . . . there was a horrific crime in it . . . paint the house . . . voilà, a sale.* The truth smacks me between the eyes. "Your records weren't misfiled. Heidi and Gabriella changed your name!"

Sylvie grabs my arm. "They must've. So how do we find out who I was?"

Room service arrives. Pizza and two salads—we both dig in. "Heidi's a dead end," I say between bites. "For argument's sake, let's assume Gabriella was tracking. She said some situations were horrible . . ." I tip back my beer and drain it. "She listed a bunch. Brother and sister beaten by a boyfriend, crack-addicted baby . . ."

"Molestation, children burned, chained." Sylvie grimaces. "But we don't know if any of those situations involved me. I don't have any burns. The scar on my hand is from some sort of cut."

I hate my next thought. "Can't rule out that there might've been sexual abuse."

Sylvie blanches. "Agreed. Let's move on. If I was born addicted to drugs, wouldn't I have some learning disabilities?"

"You didn't speak for almost a year. Maybe you didn't talk before then, either?"

"Dr. Johnson said I read the first line in a book."

"In French."

"How could I do that if I'd never spoken aloud?" She nibbles a pizza crust. "'The law is the law,' that's what Gabriella said about those cases. Like there was never anything she could do to save those kids—"

"Except for the last one," I point out. "She said, *Sometimes the law needs a swift kick in the ass.*'" I scratch the stubble along my jaw. "It gives the impression that the last case was somehow different, right?"

"'*Mom murdered, little girl stayed with her . . . a delivery guy noticed the smell, called the police . . . media was on that one like buzzards to—*'"

"'Roadkill,'" I finish. "But we're hanging on to the memories of a woman with Alzheimer's. Sylvie, what she said? It might all be fiction." My phone vibrates. Bullfrogs croak. "Something could've gone wrong." Sylvie nods and I pick up. "Hey, Mom. Everything okay?"

"I-I just wanted to see how you're doing . . . after hearing about Dad and Deacan?"

"Yeah. I'm okay. Can I call you back?"

"Are you planning to come by again?"

There's a note of neediness in her voice that repulses me. She's spent the last twenty years basically living for my dead father and brother. *Guilt has a thousand faces.* It's going to take a while to adjust, if she's truly determined to repair our relationship. "I'll swing by tomorrow. Gotta go now, though."

"I do love you," she says.

My thumb hovers over the red disconnect button . . . "Hey, Mom, you still there?"

"Yes?"

Sylvie holds up her empty beer, nods at mine to see if I want another. "Yeah, thanks." She crosses the room to the minibar on the far side. Quietly, I ask, "Do you remember a big story in Oregon, early 2000s, about a woman who was murdered?"

"I'd need more detail than that."

"The body wasn't discovered for a while. A delivery guy noticed the smell, called the cops. They found a little girl—"

"In the house with her!" Mom exclaims. "Of course I remember. It was a big deal until something knocked it from the headlines—the funeral of Queen Elizabeth, the Queen Mother, I think that's what it was. It was held at Westminster, I watched the whole thing on TV. More than a million people turned out—"

"What about the murder?"

"Sorry. Let me think . . . I'm pretty sure that the child stayed in that house with her mother's dead body for, maybe two weeks? Poor thing was starved . . . and there was something about words or numbers painted all over her skin in dried blood. Horrible. There were rumors of satanic worship, maybe a cult. A lot of people thought that the little girl was part of it; that she'd killed her own mother."

Ice trickles through my veins. I glance at Sylvie, who's riffling through the mini-fridge. "Seriously?"

"If I remember right, the police didn't have any leads or suspects and the girl's fingerprints were on the handle of the knife. Journalists, mostly from the tabloids, ran with the most salacious stuff. They camped out at the hospital, followed people involved in the story, dug through garbage cans, harassed neighbors for information. I could be wrong, but I don't recall the case ever being solved."

Sylvie pops the tops off our beers. "What about the little girl's father?"

"He would've been an obvious suspect but I can't remember him being mentioned. Always wondered what in the world happens to a kid like that," Mom muses.

Was Sylvie that little girl? She crosses the room, hands me a cold bottle. A loud knock on the door makes us both jump.

"Probably turn down service," Sylvie says and heads to tell the maid we don't need our sheets rearranged or a mint.

"The girl's name was unique," Mom continues. "It was an animal . . . Squirrel, Cat, no, Sparrow, Wren . . . nope, that's not it . . . Bird. Her name was Bird, but longer . . . Birdie? That's it! Birdie . . . and the last name was French but you know I'm horrible with foreign languages . . ."

Gooseflesh breaks along my skin. *Bye, bye, birdie* ... Gabrielle was more with it than we thought.

Sylvie opens the door, steps back. "Lucas! What are you doing here?"

Her agent looks over her shoulder. "Saving you."

"Gotta go, Mom, thanks."

Lucas Haughter strides into the room like he owns it. Moose sits up but doesn't go over to him even though they must know each other well. *Good dog.* I study the agent who refused to return any of my calls—dark blond hair, square face, blue eyes, leather boots, expensive jeans, cashmere turtleneck, and a black leather jacket stained with rain. He hugs Sylvie tight.

"Get out," Lucas says with a jerk of his head at me. "Now."

─────●─────

FORTY-SIX

Sylvie

"Lucas, it's okay," I argue.

He holds up one hand. "It's Brooklyn's third birthday and Melody is furious that I'm missing our daughter's party—an entire petting zoo in our backyard, plus magicians, clowns, Disney princesses. Belle Village catered for two hundred—"

"Your three-year-old has two hundred friends?" Thomas asks.

"Shut up," Lucas says.

I wince. "You shouldn't have skipped it. Seriously. I'm fine."

Lucas throws his hands in the air. "You haven't returned a single call! I've left a dozen messages. Syl, what else could I do? This guy is clearly holding you hostage. He's taken your computer, phone, and probably done a number on your head, am I right?"

I sink onto the desk chair and Moose settles beside me. *I'm not sure.* Lucas is here, I should be relieved, and yet . . .

"What have you told him?" Lucas asks. "Because whatever it is, I've already spoken to his editor, threatened to sue if it's printed. And I won't stop with the paper," he says, finger pointed at Thomas. "I will bankrupt you, your children, hell, your grandchildren will still be paying long after you're six feet under."

"I'm here because Sylvie wants me to be," Thomas says from his seat on the couch. "If she doesn't, I'll leave. Sylvie, what do you want me to do?"

Lucas warns, "You're playing with fire. Tell the reporter to go."

He's always had my back. "Thomas, maybe you should—"

"You know that she has panic attacks and probably an ulcer?" Thomas interrupts, eyes drilling into Lucas.

"Whatever is going on with Sylvie's health is none of your business. If there's a problem, I'll take care of it."

"You haven't so far," Thomas says.

Lucas waves a dismissive hand. "You don't know what you're talking about."

Thomas stands. "I know that Sylvie has no friends or meaningful romantic relationships. That she's seen half a dozen therapists, none for long. Was the plan always to isolate her so you'd maintain total control?"

"Stop talking about me like I'm not in the room! Lucas didn't—"

"Sylvie," Thomas explodes, "he told you he'd cancel your next appearance if you didn't cheat!"

"Get the fuck outta here," Lucas growls.

Thomas's eyes bore into mine. "You said you wanted the truth. If you meant it, then start here."

I'm stretched to breaking between them. Lucas has always protected me; he believes that what I do helps people, that I'm one of the good guys. His objective from day one was to make me a star. And I wanted that because being a psychic fit. Thomas started our relationship lying to me; his goal is to expose me; ruin my career. But one thing about Thomas has remained steadfast—he's *never* lied about believing in me. His reasons for that have been complicated, some he didn't even understand, but he's only had one goal—finding out the truth.

"Sylvie, pack up," Lucas says. "I've gotten us a suite."

The question is out before I know that I'm going to ask it. "Lucas, you've never asked me why I didn't try to contact my biological parents, on the other side. Why?"

"What are you talking about?"

"She's talking about her birth parents, Becky and Seth Peters," Thomas says. "They *supposedly* died in a plane crash. Turns out, the crash story was a lie."

Lucas ignores him. "Syl, whatever he's rambling on about doesn't matter. It's the past. The future is what matters and yours is limitless. I'll make sure of that."

I rest a trembling hand on Moose's head. "Lucas, do you believe in me, as a psychic?"

His brows fly up. "Of course I believe in you, even when I was the only one. You make this world a better place." He points at Thomas. "And this jerk wants to shut you down. We've worked too hard, there's too much at stake to let him do that."

"You didn't answer her question," Thomas says. "Do you believe in Sylvie's *gift*?"

Lucas crouches in front of my chair, palms hot on my knees. "No matter what this guy has said, how he's preyed on your insecurities, I've always been in your corner."

"I know. But I need you to answer that question."

"It never mattered to you before."

His face blurs. I blink and tears track down my cheeks. "Now it does."

"He's done a number on your head." Lucas walks toward the door.

"Let's go, Sylvie. I'll stay with you through the show and take you back to LA. We can talk all this through later, in privacy."

"What if I do my show in Portland without any prep?" Lucas's silence is my answer. I dry my cheeks. "Please leave."

He stares, incredulous. "You're not coming with me?"

"I need some time to think."

"Syl, I've always been straight with you. And I've always explained that every dream has a price."

The familiar words make my insides ache. "Yeah, but I'm not sure if I can pay it anymore. I need some time to figure out who I *really* am and what I want."

Lucas runs a hand through his hair. "Is there anything I can do for you?"

"No . . . Yes. Do you remember the kid who came with me to LA? Danny?"

"I never met him."

I wince. "His last name is Archer. Could you try to find him? Please?" Lucas nods then glances at Thomas. Regardless of what he believes, he's worried about me. "I'm good, really." He looks back one last time before he leaves, his expression forlorn. *What have I done?* Lucas has been my only family for years. A lifeline when I desperately needed one. *This is how I repay his kindness?* My face burns. And is he right? Has Thomas twisted my mind? Has the stress and pressure warped my perceptions? Am I about to throw my career away? Maybe. But my world has changed.

Lucas thinks I just picked Thomas over him. Only I didn't. I picked *me*.

"Does the name *Birdie* mean anything to you?" Thomas quietly asks.

He has a strange look on his face. I join him on the couch. "Should it?"

Thomas types the search: Birdie Murder Oregon Police Neighbor Smell. Top hit . . .

The Oregonian
April 4, 2002

CHILD FOUND BESIDE MURDERED MOTHER

Monday afternoon, police discovered the body of a woman in her northeast Portland home after a UPS delivery driver reported the smell of decomposition emanating from the house.

The deceased, Olivia Ravanelle, 34, succumbed to a fatal stab wound to the heart. Police pathologist Dr. Irving Gebhardt estimated Ravanelle expired within minutes of the assault. Decomposition of the body placed the murder between eight to ten days prior to discovery.

The home's thermostat was turned to 95 degrees, which significantly sped up the decomposition process that ultimately alerted the UPS worker.

In a macabre twist, Ravanelle's daughter, identified as Birdie Ravanelle, age four, was discovered with her mother's body. In addition to a deep wound on one hand, dehydration, and the onset of malnutrition, words and symbols in her mother's dried blood were scrawled on

Birdie's skin. She was taken to Legacy Hospital for observation while Oregon Department of Human Services attempts to locate a family member.

Police Chief Dwayne Cottle asks that anyone with information about Olivia Ravanelle contact the Portland Police Department. A source within the department has stated that there were no signs of forced entry and the only prints on the knife, besides the mother's, were Birdie's.

Ravanelle was a clairvoyant who had worked with the Portland Police Department, most recently on the case of a kidnapped child, Donald T. Danzigger, age eight. Danzigger's body was recovered in March in an abandoned building in the northwest industrial district five weeks after his abduction. He had been tortured, raped, and strangled. Police have no suspects at this time.

I pull Thomas's computer onto my lap, drink in the photo beneath the article; trace the lines of my birth mother's heart-shaped face and the black hair that curls past her shoulders. She has light gray eyes. "I look just like her." My early life has so many holes. The name *Birdie* fills one. *My name was Birdie Ravanelle.* "I'm Birdie?"

Thomas nods.

Ghostly fingers sweep the hair from my eyes and the woman's ethereal voice implores: *Come out.* Her inflection is French. I scan the article again, slow at the part that reads: A source within the department has stated that there were no signs of forced entry and the only prints on the knife, besides the mother's, were Birdie's.

The next few articles I click on are from tabloids, and the head-lines are a gut punch:

CHILD KILLS MOTHER IN SATANIC RITUAL!

5-YEAR-OLD MAKES PACT WITH SATAN!

CHILD BRIDE OF THE DEVIL!

BIRDIE RAVANELLE KILLED FAMILY PET THEN MOTHER!

Heidi's furious words return . . . *You should thank us both! Without us you would* never *have been adopted.*

"I get why Heidi destroyed my file and Gabriella changed my name and sealed my medical records," I say, my voice paper-thin.

"Sylvie, it doesn't mean—"

"They knew that there were tabloid journalists digging for infor-mation," I interrupt. "That no family would agree to foster me if they were given my real name; that if anyone, including my foster family and their kids or my psychologist, realized who I really was, sold that story to the tabloids, or even mistakenly leaked it to someone who wanted to make money, no one would want to adopt me." I reread those horrible headlines. CHILD KILLS MOTHER IN SATANIC RITUAL . . . "They wanted to give me a chance; a fresh start."

"Yeah. And they didn't want to get into trouble for bending or breaking any laws."

I meet his eyes. "At the very least, I witnessed my mother's murder. And at worst, I committed it." I shiver, suddenly very cold. *Did I kill my own mother?*

"Sylvie, there's no way that you could've—"

"Don't. Please," I say. "Neither of us knows for sure."

There are more articles . . .

In one, Ricky Boylan, the UPS deliveryman, is quoted: "Soon as I got on the front porch, I was hit with the smell of death. My daddy worked as a butcher in a slaughterhouse. Smelled worse than he did when he came home at night."

In another, a source at Legacy Hospital said: "The child can't speak. We're not even sure if she hears us. Who knows what she witnessed? I don't think the little girl will ever come back."

Thomas tries to slide the computer away. I hold tight, scroll through more articles, read how the police had no leads; that the case went cold; that ODHS hadn't found any living relatives and my father, Edward C. Ford, was a Navy pilot who died before I was born in a training accident off the coast of Coronado, California. There's a group called Mothers Against Satan who called for an exorcism . . .

A related obituary pops up:

The Oregonian
April 11, 2002

Ms. Tally Danzigger, 39, single mother to son Donald Danzigger, who predeceased her, has gone home to her Lord and Savior. Family members say her son's kidnapping and the discovery by police, with the help of clairvoyant Olivia Ravanelle, that he was brutalized and murdered, left Ms. Danzigger despondent. Her sister, Gina Finney, asks that in lieu of flowers donations be made in her name to The Suicide Prevention Hotline . . .

I've heard the name *Tally* before. "How do I find out where Olivia Ravanelle lived?"

Thomas takes his computer, taps away for several minutes, then says, "The address is 29 Hydrangea Lane. That's in—"

"Laurel," I say.

"Do you remember *any* of it?" Thomas asks.

"Not yet," I reply. *But I will . . .*

FORTY-SEVEN

•

Sylvie

We park by a two-story shingled house on the corner of Hydrangea and Fourteenth. I remember it from my dream, though now there's a white portico built off the front and the yard has been heavily landscaped with rows of roses, lavender, and several Japanese maples. Despite the hailstorm, a few early tulips remain, their thick green stalks bent but unbroken.

The rain has dwindled to a typical Pacific Northwest April drizzle. It's after seven but twilight hasn't given up its hold and I can see down the entire street. *Our house was the last one on the left.* "Let's go," I say.

Memories trickle, like a tap slowly being forced open. The second bungalow on the right, where Boone the dog lived, has been repainted from green to slate, but the white-framed bay window remains. A family is inside at their dinner table—mom, dad, and three little girls. The Baileys' place is diagonal across the street. They seemed very old when I was little, and might be in a senior center by now, or passed on. I don't open the red door. *That's not why I'm here.* What about Vince and Ted? They were probably only a few years older than I am now.

In answer, a Range Rover pulls into their driveway and a mom and two teen boys climb out.

"I lived on this street," I murmur.

When we walk by the Haycoxes' house, I recall that it was blue when we were kids. Their son, Sean, and I went to the park together, played on swings. Each of us tried to swing the highest. Fearless, I usually won. *He died of cancer. Mom said he wasn't really gone . . . just on the other side.* Memories flow faster—hopscotch on the sidewalk, a lost kitten we found but couldn't keep, the baskets of fresh veggies Mrs. Bailey brought by in summer, Ted's birthday party, games of hide and seek . . .

What is something no one can ever take away from you?

"You," I murmur. But someone did. *Was it me?*

We stop in front of a black iron gate. *It was once driftwood.* The wall bordering the small lot is now made from solid planks of wood instead of chicken wire filled with stones. This new fence is smooth and impossible to scale, a 29 burned into it. I trace the familiar number then peer through the gate. Behind a giant magnolia tree I can just see the corner of a single-story white bungalow.

"We planted that tree together," I tell Thomas.

"Do you remember her?"

"Not yet."

They're evergreen.

What does that mean?

It means even when it isn't covered in beautiful flowers, there will be green leaves.

But that wasn't true. Windstorms denuded the tree in winter. Mama promised the leaves and flowers would come back, though.

And they did. Now the tree is taller than the house and blocks it from the street. *She'd be pleased.*

A brass bell hangs from the gate. I ring it. No one comes. I ring it again and again and the jingle-jangle echoes into the oncoming night. *I have to get inside. I have to know it all.*

"Can I help you?" a woman politely inquires.

She stands a few feet away. Mid-thirties, workout clothes, a rip-stop red computer bag slung over one shoulder, dark hair, hazel eyes, a snub nose. I ask, "Do you know who lives here?"

"It's an Airbnb," she says. "I can give you a link if you're interested in renting?"

"I need to go in."

Her eyes click from casual to uncertain.

"She used to live here," Thomas explains.

"I seriously doubt that," the woman says. "My parents have owned this place for almost twenty years."

I hear myself ask, "What are their names?"

The woman shifts her bag to the other shoulder. "Cindy and Randall Bailey."

"Kathy?"

Chin tucked in like a turtle uncertain whether to leave its shell, she asks, "Who are you?"

There are moments when you know, with absolute certainty, that if you take a step, utter a word, or make a decision, nothing will ever be the same. There is no return to *before*—and for better or worse, your life will begin again from that moment on. "You used to babysit me," I say, my voice strangely calm. "I'm Birdie Ravanelle." *I am Birdie Ravanelle.*

Kathy closes the distance between us. Hands grip my shoulders. She studies my face. "Your eyes. They're the same!"

That's how Gabriella recognized me, too.

Kathy hugs me hard. *She used to let me ride on her shoulders. We did craft projects, played board games, and watched* Mary Poppins.

"Oh, Birdie! We wanted to visit you. The police wouldn't let us. Mom and Dad even talked about adoption after we learned you didn't have any family left. But then you just . . . You disappeared. Mom tried to track you through the foster system but the caseworker she spoke with said that your information was private." Kathy's eyes shine. "Birdie, if we'd only known."

I have to ask. "Do you think I did it?"

Kathy's mouth falls open. "What? No! We never thought that. Tabloid bullshit. Those hacks even went through our garbage, looking for God knows what. Birdie, you were such a sweet child. The disgusting stories that were run—those journalists should've been ashamed."

"Why didn't anyone check on Mama?" I ask, my voice small. That's what bothers me most. My mother rotted in our house for ten days and no one cared. *She didn't have any friends, either.*

"I don't know," Kathy says. "I was just a kid back then. But I remember all the neighbors being really shocked and upset. I don't even think they knew what Olivia did for a living. A clairvoyant? I would've heard about that. Mom and Dad shared that kind of secret stuff in the basement and I listened through the laundry chute."

"How'd they end up owning Sylvie's home?" Thomas asks.

Kathy looks confused. "That's my name now," I say. "Sylvie Young."

Her eyes go wide. "Seriously? The psychic? I have a coworker who's going to your show." She whistles under her breath. "Just. Wow. That's so flipping wild. Did you know that's what your mom did, too?"

I shake my head. "Until today, I couldn't remember her at all. There's still a lot that's missing. That's why I need to go inside."

Kathy reaches into her bag, pulls out a ring of keys. "Nobody wanted to buy the house. When the price dropped, my parents bought it, figured that eventually the story would be forgotten. It was and they kept it as a rental." Her hands shake a little as she searches for the right key. "No one has rented for a few weeks so it's probably stuffy, dusty," she rambles as she fits the key in the gate's lock and turns it. "I never go in—the place has always given me the creeps." Her mouth presses into a grimace. "Sorry. It's just. You know they never caught the murderer?"

My heart hurts. "Yes."

Kathy hesitates. "I did sneak in, one time, with Billy Jacobs from the next street over. Had a crush on him so clearly I'd do anything for a chance to be alone." She blushes. "Anyway, this wasn't in the news . . . maybe I shouldn't say?"

"Anything that will help me remember is important."

"You sure you want to? Remember?" Kathy asks. "I mean it was pretty gruesome . . ."

"Yes."

"Okay. There was yellow tape over the door. Your mom had given mine a spare key for emergencies, so I swiped it off her desk and Billy used it to open the door. We slid under the tape." She swallows hard. "The place was a mess. Chairs knocked over, broken glass, splotches of dried blood, and a huge wine-colored stain on the floor where they found your mom." She cringes. "Sorry."

I gently touch her arm. "It's okay. Go on. Please."

"I freaked, yanked Billy out of there. But not before we saw the wooden dining chair that'd been dragged beneath the round thermostat. There were tiny red handprints on either side of it. Dried blood."

"She was cold," I say. "So I turned up the heat."

Thomas and Kathy stare at me.

"But she was dead," Kathy finally says.

I hitch one shoulder. "I didn't know that."

Kathy takes an involuntary step back. "How could you not?"

"She kept talking to me."

Little bird?

Yes, Mama?

Come out, little bird. Come out.

It was Mama all along. *I'm here*, I say and walk through the open gate.

FORTY-EIGHT

Sylvie

The house is dark, but I know my way. *Hook just inside the right door for my coat. Shoes off, that's what separates us from the horses. The kitchen is straight ahead. That's where Mama bakes snacks. Today it's pain au chocolat—a gooey chocolate croissant hot from the oven. I eat while she does her work. It's on the telephone. Sometimes the people on the other end cry. Mama tries to help them.*

I flick on a light. The Baileys have decorated in shabby chic style. To the right of the front door, plush couches covered in off-white canvas form an L in front of a wood-burning fireplace. A perfectly threadbare Persian rug is centered beneath a glass coffee table made from the frame of an old warehouse dolly with an iron handle and rusty wheels. There's a tan leather chair and ottoman in the corner with a curved brass lamp. When we lived here, the sofas and chairs were soft and worn, but it's hard to recall what they looked like. I was so young when Mama died. *Was murdered.*

To the left of the front door is the kitchen, and ten feet past its soapstone counter is an antique dining table with upholstered chairs. The only thing that remains from my time here is the crystal chandelier over the table—a cascade of teardrops that once made shimmery rainbow prisms that I chased along the walls. Mama found it in the antique shop around the corner. It's similar to the one I bought for thousands and hung in my LA apartment.

Come out, little bird, Mama says. Her voice is now rich, the words French-inflected. And so I find the spot on the far wall and slide down it, curl on my side. I open the red door and Mama takes me back . . .

———

She stands at the kitchen counter, carves a steak, her long hair swept into a chignon. The meat is too red for me, so she puts several slices back in the oven, even though she calls overcooking it a crime. While we wait, I sit at the counter and play with the snow globe she bought for my birthday. A *little* mama is inside it and a *little* me is on a swing, hair in braids. When I shake the globe, Little Mama pushes me, and snowflakes fall. It's my favorite present ever.

Mama makes a salad. There's a knock on the front door. "That's probably the woman."

"What woman?" I ask.

"Mama tried to help someone who lost her little boy."

"Did you find him?"

"Yes. But it was too late. She asked to stop by. Go ahead and answer the door."

Bare feet pad across a soft rug, onto floors Mama calls *bird's-eye maple*. I reach up to the bronze knob and open the gray door. A woman pushes past me. She has frizzy blond hair, wears a yellow coat, matching gloves, and her face is pinched like she bit a lime. Brown eyes float in a sea of squiggly red lines. She smells sharp, wrong, and she's much bigger than Mama, both higher and wider. I close the door to keep the rain out. The woman tracks water and mud toward the kitchen, her steps unsteady.

Mama looks up from slicing carrots with the big steak knife I'm not allowed to touch. "*Bonsoir*, Tally. I'm so very, very sorry for your loss. The police said I shouldn't contact you; should wait to see if you wanted to speak further . . . I'm truly sorry. How can I help?"

"Help?" Tally demands. "How could you?" Her voice is too loud, slurry.

"Mama?"

"Birdie, go to your room, please."

"No," Tally snaps. "Let her hear this. She should know what her precious *mama* did. Donald was my only child. My ONLY! How would you feel if someone told the police those disgusting things about your precious Birdie? I HAD TO IDENTIFY THE BODY! I know EVERYTHING that happened to him. EVERYTHING. Oh God oh God oh God my little boy . . ."

Mama holds up her hands like Tally is a wild animal she's trying to calm. "Birdie, your room. Now."

Tally rounds the counter, shoves Mama hard, and she stumbles.

Mama says, "You asked the police to contact me. You wanted help finding Donald. I found him."

"In a warehouse. He'd been TORTURED for a month. RAPED. STRANGLED five days before the cops found him. FIVE DAYS," she sobs. "You could have found him before then!"

Mama puts a hand on Tally's back. "I'm so sorry . . . I tried. What happened was horrible, but your boy, he is at peace now. That is hard to understand. It will take time. But he wants the same for you."

"Fuck you!" Tally screams and hits mama hard on her face.

Mama staggers back then lunges for the steak knife, holds it in front of her with shaking hands. "Get out of my house. Leave now!"

I clutch my snow globe, dive beneath the dining table, then watch their feet shuffle back and forth like a mad dance accompanied by animal grunts. They hit the edge of the table hard. Legs twist and they both fall. The steak knife hits the floor, clatters out of sight. Mama's lips are pressed together, eyes clenched as the bigger woman straddles her, hands around her neck. There are scratches like tiger's whiskers on Mama's cheek.

"Mama," I whimper, "I'm scared."

Mama's eyes open. She bucks her hips. The big lady falls, they roll over and over, and then everything stops and Mama slides sideways, her back to me. The lady's face rises like the moon. She reaches toward me. Her glove is covered in glistening red paint.

I crawl farther back, out of reach. "Mama, please move," I whisper. "I'm afraid."

The woman scrambles to her feet, boots slap on the floor. The door opens then slams shut.

"Mama?"

"Come out, little bird."

Trembling, I crawl from beneath the table and try to pull her up, but she's too heavy. So we crab-walk toward the wall and she manages to sit. The steak knife sticks out of her chest. I reach for it but she moans when my fingers clasp the wooden handle.

"Mama?"

"Put your head in my lap, little bird, and I will tell you a bedtime story."

I do, even though the front of her dress is hot and sticky, smells like pennies. And then I wait for the story as the meat she put in the oven burns then turns to a crisp. I sleep off and on. We talk each time I wake and she asks me to leave, find a neighbor, but I refuse. At some point I realize that Mama is very cold and drag a chair to the thermostat, climb up even though I'm dizzy, and turn the dial just like she does when there's a chill in the air. Then I return to her side, lie down until finally . . .

Mama says, *It's almost time to go.*

Can we play questions first?

Oui. What is something no one can ever take away from you?

She asks me this every night before bed. First a butterfly kiss, then the question. *You,* I say and feel her smile.

If you live looking behind you, what happens?

You trip and fall down. Her laugh is a warm breeze, like wind chimes.

Why is it dangerous to answer some questions?

This is a new one . . . *I don't know.*

The truth has two edges.

I look up at her. *I don't understand.*

You will. Little by little the bird makes her nest.

Mama?

A man and a woman are coming up the walk.

My heart is a knot tugged too tight.

Let them in.

I grip her legs. *I don't want to.*

Little bird?

Yes, Mama?

Je t'aime.

I love you, too. There's a knock on the door. Goose bumps rise. Mama?

Don't be afraid.

More knocking. Louder.

When I sit up, the side of my face sticks to Mama's dress and my hair is slicked back, dried like glue to my skull. I look into eyes the color of sea glass we collect on the beach. *Mama?* The dry red paint on my skin pinches and cracks as I throw my arms around her neck. I see the numbers 2 and 9, letters T-l-y, and the words *je t'aime* and *birdie* . . .

I will see you soon.

Promise?

Oui.

I creep toward the door, knees wobbly. It crashes open . . .

"Holy hell," cries a woman with a silver police badge on her chest and a gun at her hip.

The policeman beside her picks me up. "I'll get the girl out of here."

I struggle out of his arms, dive under the table for my snow globe. When the cop latches on to my ankle, yanks me out, it falls from my hand. The sound of shattered glass fills me with rage. *You can't take her from me!*

Kicking free, I lunge under the table as water and snowflakes pour onto the wood. I scamper farther and grab for the figures inside the globe just as the policeman rounds the other side of the table. His black boot mistakenly comes down on my outstretched hand, grinds it into the cup of jagged glass that cradles the mother and daughter. Pain bites deep. But I have them. *I'll never let you go, Mama . . .*

———————

I open my eyes in this house that is no longer my home. Knowing what happened here; that I was never abandoned but instead much loved; that opening the gray door wasn't my invitation to death, but simply a child who obeyed Mama's instructions, that what followed wasn't my fault, that all of it matters but doesn't define me. I built an elaborate castle to hide a treasure that was never buried in sand.

Mama softly says: *The truth has two edges.*

"I will wield it as wisely as I can."

I will always be with you.

"I'll always be with you, too."

·——·

FORTY-NINE

Thomas

I waited outside with Moose, both of us worried, though Moose was the only one who whimpered. When Sylvie finally emerged, dark had fallen. We left the key where Kathy had instructed, a clever hidden panel in the wooden fence, and walked to the car.

Gently, I asked, "Sylvie, are you okay?"

She looked to the sky. The night had cleared and there were countless stars. One fell, the tail a scrape of orange that glowed long after the brilliant pinpoint extinguished. "That was Mama."

"Do you know who killed her?"

"Yes. But it doesn't matter anymore."

We drove back to the hotel, sat in the car when we got there with the engine off. "Do you remember it all?" I asked.

She leaned in, kissed me. "I do. Thank you."

I wanted to keep kissing her, but it wasn't that kind of a kiss. "What will you do now?"

Sylvie looked into my eyes. "What will you do, Doubting Thomas?"

I waited for her to ask about the article. She didn't. We went up to the hotel room, I packed my bag, gave Moose a final scratch behind his ears.

"Where will you go?" Sylvie asked at the door.

"I'll get another room for the night. Check on Mom tomorrow then take a flight back to LA."

"Consider staying in Portland."

My heart hammered. "Why?"

"Maybe it's time to revisit the past and put it to rest. You're a good man, Thomas. You deserve happiness."

Again, it struck me, despite wishing for more, that Sylvie's true gift had always been kindness. I held her one last time and then walked away. Was there anything other than goodbye in the way she hugged me back? I've gone over it in my head, again and again. I'll probably never know.

I've spent the past two days in my family's old home, wandered an apartment with photographs of a happy family forever fractured on the walls. Faced my guilt about Dad and Deacan's deaths, the horror of their last moments. None of it was my fault—I was just a kid who wanted ice cream. But accepting that has been hard. I've taken responsibility for Dad and Deacan's tragedy almost my whole life. But the worst part is that Mom and I never recovered. I can't change how she feels about Deacan, that he was her favorite son, or the fact that there's a part of her that may always blame me for that night, but I can change how I react to her fragilities. I can try to be kind, too.

It felt strange to sleep in my childhood bedroom, once shared with Deacan, a sliding wall constructed in the center when he got old enough to need privacy. Mom kept his old school newspaper articles in a thick album beneath his bed. Over the past twenty-four hours,

I've read them all. He would've been a good journalist, maybe a great one. Sylvie tells her audiences that their loved ones are at peace; that they want us to be at peace with their deaths, too. That's something I'll have to work toward.

In the closet on my side of the room, I found a box of stories I'd written in elementary school, before I switched to the school newspaper in a bid to fill Deacan's shoes. I've read them, too. They were about dragons, epic battles on alien planets, animals that could speak, a sorcerer who became the white rabbit in his own top hat. Each had an element of magic. Before Dad and Deacan died, I'd been a believer in the impossible.

At the bottom of the box was the leather journal I once stole. The one Dad made me return and my big brother bought and stashed beneath my pillow. Deacan's note was on the first page: *I believe in you, kid.* The irony didn't escape me. I accused three psychics of being impostors, frauds, but spent the past two decades trying to be my big brother in a bid to keep a part of him alive.

This morning, I helped move Mom back in, met Bernie, who stepped up to take care of her while she heals so she doesn't have to stay in a care facility. He's a quirky old guy with fleshy earlobes and the bushiest white eyebrows I've ever seen. It's clear he loves Mom. While they played cards, I've continued facing my own set of ghosts—the collection of Dickens that Dad bought to instill a love of reading in both his sons, the kitchen desk where Deacan did his homework, our old radio (the one from Granddad) once again perched on the windowsill, striped throw pillows Deacan and I piled on the floor when we watched favorite movies.

I've put it off, but now it's time to call Annie. Perched at the foot of my childhood bed, I pull up her number, not certain what I'll say, or do. She picks up on the second ring.

"Hey, champ. How's it going?"

"It's been a long week," I reply.

"Do you have a story?" Annie asks, cutting right to the chase.

Yes, but it's not the one I set out to tell. An unsolved murder; a crime perpetrated by a foster care caseworker and judge, who both broke the law to save a child. Adoptive parents who continued that lie and the repercussions for a traumatized child who grew up never knowing her real story, but was ultimately determined to find the truth. It will make a great article, sell a ton of papers, and maybe even garner an award.

"Thomas?"

"Sylvie isn't a fraud." I slide back, lean against the wall, decision made.

There's silence, then: "How can you know that for sure before her show tonight?"

I hear the question Sylvie asked me in the car before I took Chris inside the vet's office to say goodbye.

Do you believe in anything I told you?

I want to . . . but.

I finally get it—it's a choice. "I don't need to go to Sylvie's show."

"Seriously?" Annie asks.

"Yes. My exposé is that most psychics are con artists but Sylvie isn't. She's the real deal. Is that something the *L.A. Times* is willing to run?" I can hear the wheels in Annie's head turning.

"Are you trying to protect Sylvie? Did you fall for her or something?"

I don't answer.

"Come on, Thomas, where's your perspective?" Annie demands. "You're a journalist. She's the subject. You do know that anything you think might've happened, romantically, is pure manipulation?"

In her own way, Annie is trying to keep me from a serious demotion, basically the end of my career. I flip through my journal, glance at the drawings of castles and wizards. I haven't risked anything, taken a leap into uncharted territory, since I was a kid. *It's time.* "I'm sorry, Annie. I'll clean out my desk when I get back to LA."

Annie blows out a loud breath of air then says, "Damn. You're a good writer, Thomas. Let me know if I can help with references."

"Will do. Thanks for everything you've done for me. And Annie?"

"Yeah?"

"Go on a real date, okay?"

She chuckles. "Good luck, T. Holmes. I hope you find a soft place to land."

I hang up, lie back on my pillow, and stare at the stars Deacan had glued to the ceiling decades ago. In the other room I hear Mom laugh at something Bernie said. She sounds like a young woman. *Bernie's got this.* I pull up the United Airlines app and find a flight back to LA for tonight. Sylvie's show is at 7:00 p.m. I consider staying in Portland, attending it, but she hasn't called. *She's made her choice.*

I book the ticket.

Surprisingly, there's no bitterness that I lost the article. I understand, now, why survival was more important than anything to Sylvie. Whatever happened in that house, she lived through it. Ten days with a dead mother who she believes spoke to her the whole time? Who am I to say it's impossible. Regardless, I don't want to be a reminder to Sylvie that there are doubters. There will be enough detractors as her career hits the stratosphere.

If I'm honest, though, there's a part of me—the guy who watched her face disappointed parents, helped her ask and answer tough, sometimes brutal, questions, let go of lies, who worked with her to uncover the truth—that doesn't want to let Sylvie go. I only really knew her for five days, but I'll never forget her. Do I love the myth, a complex web of lies, a real person, or the version she showed me? I don't know.

My duffel is already packed. I turn off the light in my childhood bedroom, say goodbye to Mom and Bernie, then head toward the unknown.

FIFTY

Sylvie

Moose watches me slide into my sleeveless black silk jumpsuit. The beads along the edge of the neckline sparkle beneath the hotel bathroom's overhead light. I fasten diamond hoop earrings and slide the sapphire infinity ring onto my index finger, sweep my hair into a chignon, apply makeup and red lipstick. When I stare at my reflection, another one wavers beside it. *Mama.* Dark hair falls in soft waves around her heart-shaped face; gray eyes the same shade as my own watch me.

Come out, little bird . . .

Moose chuffs and Mama's image fades away. For a moment I consider calling my adoptive parents, telling them the truth about my past. But they never wanted to know, and finding out that my birth mother was a clairvoyant wouldn't make my choices more acceptable to them . . . so I let go. It will always hurt, but pain doesn't mean it's the wrong decision. I recall Thomas's face as he walked out the door two nights ago. Letting him go is harder. But I do, because every dream has a price.

There's a knock and hope flutters in my belly, but when I open the room's door, it's Lucas, not Thomas.

"Ready?" Lucas asks.

He's dressed in one of his charcoal suits, narrow tie, the picture of a successful Hollywood agent. Yesterday he brought two new manila folders to my hotel room. They were filled with more research on tonight's audience. I read every page and post, chose a few to highlight during my show, and one for the final read—a woman named Reba who survived a car accident that killed her son and has blamed herself for ten years. I have plenty of bridges and have ensured that this will be a great show. It may be my last, depending on what Thomas decides to write about me.

"You look terrific," Lucas says. We walk down the hallway to the elevator, Moose at my side. The doors open and he steps in . . . but I don't.

"Sylvie?"

Little by little the bird makes her nest . . .

"I can't," I say. "Please cancel the show."

Lucas steps off the elevator. "Sylvie, come on. You've got this."

"It's not that." I look down at my jumpsuit, wave at my face. "It's this. I'm not *her* anymore." Lucas tries to hug me but I back away.

"I know who you are," he says. "You're a psychic-medium with a huge career ahead—shows, a TV series, who knows, maybe even an HBO special."

I shake my head. "You don't understand. I do know who I am now, but I have no idea what I want."

Lucas frowns. "You have contracts, a TV show in the works. You can't turn your back on that."

In this moment I see us both clearly. Lucas told me who he was that first night in his car—a man who believed in me, but not my abilities as a psychic; a man who could make me a star. And I've shown

312 · Nan Fischer

him since then that I'm a woman willing to do what's needed to survive. He's done everything he promised and more. I'm the one that's now reneging.

"I'm sorry. Truly. Lucas, I really do appreciate everything you've done for me."

Lucas gets into the elevator. "And if your career goes up in flames?" he asks.

"Then I'll have to find my way out of the ashes." The elevator doors close, and for the first time in six years, I'm on my own.

———

FIFTY-ONE

One month later
Thomas

I wasn't sure I wanted to go; that I should go. But Sylvie sent me a ticket, front row center. So I'm here tonight. Filled with uncertainty, I entered the rococo-style lobby of the Luminaire Theater in downtown LA, with its marble statues of Greek gods and goddesses and opulent crystal chandeliers. As I walk down the aisle to my front row, center seat, I spot Lucas. He's in a dark suit, his perfectly pressed white shirt open at the collar, a stark contrast to my jeans and flannel. To my surprise, he comes over.

"Glad you could make it," Lucas says with a tight smile.

"*You* sent me the ticket?"

"Sylvie asked me to."

"Why?"

Lucas fiddles with his chunky stainless steel watch then meets my gaze. "Not sure. She keeps the personal stuff to herself these days." He hesitates. "Can I ask you a question?"

"You can, but I'm not sure I'll answer it."

"Why didn't you run the exposé? You had enough, and if you'd included everything you'd learned about her past, the cover-up and lies? It would've sold a lot of papers."

I shift my backpack to the other shoulder. "It's Sylvie's story to tell. Can I ask you a question?"

"Shoot."

"Why are you still her agent when you don't believe she has a gift?"

"I believe in *her*, always have; that what she does helps people, gives desperately needed closure. When she walked out of her show in Portland, I was worried that she was done for good. We had to refund all the ticket holders and compensate the venue, but it was a small price to pay for Sylvie's peace of mind. For a minute I thought she might fire me, but Sylvie knows that I'll always have her back." This time when Lucas smiles, it's genuine. "Sylvie's TV show comes out this spring. Done *her* way. We're already filming. It's fantastic. Will you watch?"

"Probably not," I say. *It would be too hard.* Lucas holds out his hand. We shake. We'll never see eye to eye, but we agree on one thing, protecting Sylvie. When he's gone, I find my seat and dig a snow globe from my backpack. It was in the window display of a tiny jewelry shop on Sunset. At first the owner wouldn't sell it, but eventually I convinced him. I might've used the word *love*.

Inside the snow globe stands a woman in the center of a wheat field. Golden stalks sway in an imaginary wind. When the globe is shaken, orange and red wildflowers swirl, catch in the long brown hair and the folds of a white dress. I don't know if that woman waits for someone or has chosen to walk alone. I've written an address on the bottom of the globe, a restaurant a few blocks away. I have no idea if Sylvie will come after the show. Whatever she chooses, I hope she's happy.

The lights go down. The audience's excitement mutes to murmurs as they await the complex light show, inspirational symphony, and atmospheric smoke that start Sylvie's show. Instead, a single spotlight appears on the stage.

Ladies and gentlemen, please welcome Sylvie . . .

Sylvie walks out, Moose at her side, the fuzzy bone he loves drooping from both sides of his mouth. The crowd *ahhs* when they see her, and then *oohs* at Moose, the adorable monster. I've never seen Sylvie wear anything on stage but a sleeveless black jumpsuit, but tonight she's in a simple crème-colored short-sleeved turtleneck and jeans paired with the Converse sneaks she wore on the train. There's little makeup besides a pale gloss on her lips. Gone is the sophisticated chignon. Her hair is swept into a low ponytail.

The audience is on its feet, clapping and cheering. Sylvie shyly smiles, motions for them to sit. As they do, Moose joins them and she rests a hand on his head. "I never planned to be a psychic-medium," she begins. "Tonight my goal is to provide answers, but I can't promise if this will happen. I understand that you need me to connect with your loved ones, answer questions that hurt your hearts. I'll try. Truly. But first, I need to tell you a secret . . ."

The urge to stop Sylvie before she says something that might hurt her is hard to quell. My hands grip the armrests. She scans my row, finds me, and gives a little smile. I sit back . . . and trust her.

FIFTY-TWO

Sylvie

I see Thomas in the audience. He never ran his story, but that could mean anything. Maybe he only came for closure. Regardless, I wanted him here for *this* show, to see *me*.

"Every psychic has an origin story," I begin. "But I've never told my real one, until now. When I moved to San Francisco at eighteen, I met a kid named Danny at a youth hostel. He had brown curls, sparkling eyes, and a thousand-watt smile. We decided to share a basement apartment. For the first few months I didn't have enough money for my part of the rent. Danny floated me. He was a kid who'd never been given a break but was still incredibly generous and kind. His dream was to make enough to move to LA, become a famous actor, and I was trying to find myself, uncertain if I could even survive in the city.

"Danny decided to read tarot to make some extra cash, and he's the one who convinced me to do my first psychic reading. It was for Bethany, the pregnant woman I've talked about in the past whose baby was in danger. When I touched her belly, wrote *I can't breathe* on my arm, Bethany left, furious. But Danny encouraged me to do more readings. He said everyone knew it was just for entertainment, *and* if I made enough money, we could move to LA together. We made a deal. The first one who got an acting break would help the other. I didn't have a dream then, so I borrowed his."

The audience has gone very quiet and I wonder if this will be my last performance but push on. "In the beginning, being a psychic-medium was a scam—a way to support myself after my parents disowned me. But strange things happened. At first, I wrote them off, figured they were the result of my enthusiasm, the desire to meet the paying customer's needs. Deep down, though, I nurtured the hope that I was more than a fraud. I really wasn't sure. But the people who lined up in San Francisco's Haight-Ashbury believed I had a gift, and slowly I started to believe them, too."

The crowd rustles. "That's an important point. I believed in myself because people told me I was a psychic-medium. Not because I trusted in my abilities. Then one day Bethany and her husband, Matthew, came to thank me for saving their daughter's life. Matthew connected me with a talent agent in LA, Lucas Haughter, who flew Danny and me down to meet with him."

My voice shakes but I continue. "Lucas signed me that day. But the reason I've never mentioned Danny in my origin story is because Lucas only wanted me, not my best friend. So I left Danny behind." I swallow the lump in my throat. "The excuse that I was a scared kid with no prospects or family who saw a chance to do more than just survive doesn't make up for screwing Danny over. That's a shame I've carried with me all these years. My agent recently found Danny. At first he wouldn't take my call. I kept trying. We finally talked. Danny is the director of a small theater company in Seattle, has two kids and a great husband. He was kind enough to accept my apology and even invited me to Washington to see one of his plays. I'm heading there in a few weeks."

318 · Nan Fischer

I take a deep breath then slowly let it out. "But back to my origin story. Once I'd signed with an agent, successes piled up, and money, too. An elusive thing called *buzz* happened. Plus, all of you started to really trust in me." My smile feels bittersweet. "You're more powerful than you know." I walk along the stage, look into the audience. "Have any of you heard the story about a frog placed in a pot of water, the heat turned up so slowly that he doesn't realize until too late that he's been cooked alive?" A few people nod. It's a relief that I haven't lost everyone yet.

"In six years, I went from being an eighteen-year-old psychic sitting at a folding table in San Francisco, connecting one-on-one, to having a show with employees, laser lights, smoke machines, choreographed music, and hundreds then up to a thousand audience members. It happened slowly enough that I didn't realize my gift was being swallowed, eclipsed by the need to fulfill larger and larger expectations—mine, my agent's, the people who help put these shows together, and yours, too. Many times I'd stand on a stage like this one, look out at all of you, and feel like a total impostor."

The audience murmurs their disagreement but I shake my head. "I'm not asking for your sympathy. It's true. And the decisions made over those years are ultimately my responsibility. Age doesn't absolve me. I wanted to give more and more people the best of me and in turn to be validated. But in doing so, I lost touch with my gift, allowed the spectacle, the *show*, to kill off part of me. I'm sorry for that. You deserved better." I gesture to the stage, devoid of special effects, and my simple clothes. "Today the *show* stops."

Nervously, I twist the ring on my finger. "You've only ever asked one thing of me—to be honest and certain. But over the years, I haven't always been either of those things. I've come from a place of fear. A few weeks ago, I saw a doctor who diagnosed a bleeding ulcer. My stomach has been bad for over a year, but I never went to a physician because I couldn't imagine a way to fix something I knew came from the stress of all this. I'm a psychic-medium—every time I stand onstage, each reading, every question you ask that I try desperately to answer results in stress. Your tragedies sometimes hurt me *and* I'm terrified of disappointing you. I'm terrified of disappointing *me*, too. And I'm driven to survive. Above all else, to survive."

I weave my hands together to still their trembling. "Last month I met a journalist who called me a grief vampire. He said I used tricks to prey on the vulnerable for money and fame." Some in the audience hiss and boo. I shake my head to quiet them. "I've done a lot of self-reflection over the past few days. In a way he was right. I do take your money and there's some truth to the fame accusation. Who doesn't want to be admired? But it's more complicated than that. I also used your stories, questions, and tragedies, focused on you, to distract from the things I didn't want to face."

"Like what?" a woman calls out from a few rows back.

"Many of you have read that I was adopted and never knew my biological parents. Up until a month ago, I couldn't recall the first six years of my life. That might not be strange for you, but I have an eidetic memory, meaning I can recall almost everything. That same journalist gave me the courage to find out the truth about my past. Together, we learned that my birth mother was a clairvoyant. Her name was Olivia Ravanelle and she was murdered when she was only thirty-four. I was four-and-a-half and saw it happen." People gasp. "That trauma blocked all memory of the murder and life with my mother."

Moose leans his bulk against my leg in a show of support. "My foster care records were destroyed, medical records sealed, by people who thought what they were doing would help me. No one wanted to adopt a kid tied to a murder, especially one as grisly and sensational as my mother's. My name was changed to give me a fresh start. A story was made up about birth parents that'd died in a plane crash. And it all worked. But in doing so, those folks stripped me of my past, my mother's story . . . and left me with an obsession to survive with no context."

I look into the audience. "For my entire life, I've thought about looking for my birth mom, on the other side. But each time I approached the door, I was overwhelmed by panic. Now I know why. When I finally learned the truth about my past, I called to Mama. We connected . . . she's at peace and she wants that for me, too." I swipe tears away before they fall. "Sorry for being a big baby."

"We love you!" a woman yells.

I manage a half smile. "All my life I've been driven to survive, above anything, because of Mama's murder," I explain. "I began as a psychic to make a few bucks on top of the tips I earned as a crappy waitress. I used my successes to define myself because pieces were missing. But that's not why I'm here today." I take a breath, glance into the wings where Lucas stands. He nods at me. *Despite the fact that I've taken control of my career and no longer do any research, he's still in my corner.* "I believe in my gift now. I know who I am, both *because of* and *despite* my past, and my goal, above fame and fortune, is to help as many of you as possible. I hope you can believe in me, too. I'm here for you, regardless."

I cross the stage, drawn back to Thomas. He places an antique snow globe with a brass base on the edge of the stage. My pulse quickens as I pick it up. Inside the glass is a woman surrounded by a field of wheat. When I shake the globe, bright wildflowers swirl. It's beautiful—like nothing I've ever seen. I tip the globe again and spot an address written on the bottom. When I meet Thomas's gaze and nod, his blue-green eyes shine. Hope takes flight.

My hands no longer shake as I place the globe on the small wooden table set between two leather chairs, center stage. I walk forward and address the audience again, Moose at my side. "Final introductions and we can begin. This is Moose. Every time I stand up here, I'm nervous. Moose helps. Telling the truth is going to help even more. Some of these get-togethers may not be what you need, and for that, I'm sorry. All I can promise is to try my best." I smile and the audience does, too.

"So here we go. Welcome. My name is Sylvie Ravanelle Young. Let's begin . . ."

ACKNOWLEDGMENTS

We did it! And by *we* I mean the village of people who worked to make the dream of *Some of It Was Real* a reality. I know authors always say this in their acknowledgments, but it's true. I couldn't have published this novel, from cover art to the final page, without the tireless efforts, skill, creativity, and professionalism of the Berkley publishing team. I'm honored to work with them!

The first thank-you always goes to my husband, Henry. Each novel starts with a question that slowly morphs into an idea. Henry is willing to listen (a lot!) and talk through countless possibilities. He never doubts my ability to turn an idea into a story (that makes one of us!), and he's always my first reader. Thank you, H—you hang my galaxy and together with Boone you're my perfect family.

A giant thank-you to my editor at Berkley, Kerry Donovan! Every author knows what it's like to be on submission, waiting to hear if there's an editor who wants your story. It's exciting but also terrifying. Kerry, when you called I was over the moon. Despite my nerves, your kindness and love for this book were immediately evident and put me at ease. This was our first novel and I really appreciated your excellent editorial eye and keen insights. You made *Some of It Was Real* a better book. Thank you so much. I can't wait to work on the next one together!

Huge thanks to the entire Berkley team, including Kerry's assistant, Mary Baker, senior marketing manager Fareeda Bullert, production editor Jennifer Lynes, managing editor Christine Legon, copy editor Joan Matthews, publicist Tara O'Connor, and cover designer Emily Osborne.

How do I thank my agent, Stephanie Kip Rostan? With lots of compliments that don't come close to expressing how much I value her! Steph, your brilliance, wicked sense of humor, brainstorming abilities, and top-notch editorial skills make me a very lucky author. If I haven't said it lately, thanks again for picking me.

Thanks also to Steph's super-smart assistant, Courtney Paganelli— you are a delight to work with and I value your ideas and input. My thanks to Levine Greenberg Rostan's foreign rights director Beth Fisher, business manager Melissa Rowland, and contract attorney Kirsten Wolf. And thank you to Debbie Deuble Hill at Agency for the Performing Arts—working with you is a dream come true.

This whole writing thing has been a gift in so many ways. I've met incredible people in the publishing industry who love stories and work diligently to champion them. I've been given the opportunity to spend time with other authors, share our work, successes, and heartaches, and develop real friendships. And I'm part of an Instagram community that provides encouragement, thoughtful reviews, book suggestions, and gorgeous photographs.

To all my early readers—Henry Fischer, Dawn Weeman, Laurie Forest, Judy Frey, Karen Ford, Erin Burnham, Elda Orr, my sister, Sue Bishop, and my folks, Jane and Art Richardson—having your feedback and support means the world. Seriously. Thank you doesn't seem like enough, but it's all I have!

Some of It Was Real is a novel about purpose, love, acceptance, and the belief that anything is possible. I wish every reader all of those things . . .

Some of It Was Real

Nan Fischer

QUESTIONS FOR DISCUSSION

1. Sylvie and Thomas both struggle with Impostor Syndrome—the persistent inability to believe that one's success is deserved or has been legitimately achieved. Have you ever suffered from Impostor Syndrome? If so, how did you overcome your fears and embrace your abilities?

2. Early in the novel, Sylvie calls Thomas "Doubting Thomas" because he only believes what he can see, touch, and prove. Do you require proof to believe things, or can you rely on faith?

3. Sylvie has no memories before the age of six until she unlocks her past. What is the earliest memory you have? Have your first memories shaped your perception of who you are in the world?

4. Have you ever visited with a psychic, tarot card reader, or palm reader? What was that experience like, and did you leave with answers or more questions?

5. Where does the tension between Thomas and Sylvie stem from, beyond Thomas's desire to prove she's a fraud?

6. At the start of the novel, Sylvie is unsure about her psychic abilities. What was your perception of her gift at the beginning of the story? Did it change by the last chapter?

7. Sylvie convinces herself that she's still a good person because even when she researches audience members, she's helping them overcome their grief. Do you believe Sylvie's intentions make her actions ethically good, or did you disapprove because of her ulterior motives?

8. Sylvie discovers a massive lie that changes the way she remembers her upbringing. If you had a happy childhood and learned as an adult that you were told a lie that might change your perception of your life, would you want to know the truth? Or would you choose to preserve your memories at any cost?

9. If you had the chance to sit in Sylvie's audience and she called on you for the final reading of her show, whom would you want to connect with?

10. Thomas realizes at the end of the novel that believing in Sylvie and her gift is a choice. Do you agree? How has this novel influenced your thoughts on whether or not psychics are legitimate?

Continue reading for a special preview of
Nan Fischer's new novel,
coming in Fall 2023.

A woman faces an uncertain future when she unearths
the story behind the man who designed her antique
engagement ring and feels inexplicably drawn to him . . .

———

———

I walk into the house with Lucy in my arms and hope Hayden thinks she's cute *and* small. "Do you mind?" I ask. We're already fostering Blueboy, a shepherd mix that occasionally pees on the hardwood floors, and Samson, a blind tabby. "The family that was going to adopt Lucy changed their minds. She has a bad hip and needs a few days of extra TLC."

"Well then, let's build a ramp so Lucy can easily get into the yard," Hayden offers.

I kiss him. "Have I told you lately you're the best?" We head into the backyard shop and Hayden turns on the table saw he bought at a garage sale, cuts a three-by-six-foot plank from a sheet of plywood then nails on thin strips of wood for cleats. Together we carry the ramp to the back steps. Blueboy bounds out the dog door Hayden recently put in and clatters down the ramp.

I hear the click of Lucy's nails as she approaches, dig a treat from my pocket and hold it on the other side of the door. A pink nose pokes through the split plastic flap, then her head pops out. Slowly Lucy emerges, perches at the top of the ramp, entire body shaking as she stares down it. I break off a piece of the treat then wait until she creeps forward, repeating the process until she's hobbled all the way to the grass.

"Way to go!" Hayden cheers then sneezes three times.

Lucy wanders in a yard that was once xeriscaped but is now covered in grass and fenced. Hayden even put in a buddleia bush for the foster cats—they're always fascinated with the butterflies drawn to the purple blooms. These are the things my best friend, Mars, doesn't see—that my boyfriend supports my love of animals despite his allergies. He fenced in his yard soon after I moved in and he screened the back porch for Samson, so she could feel like she was outside but stay safe. Plus, he's refused to sell to the developers who want to build a fourplex on his land, no matter how much they offer. His shop and the yard are more important to Hayden than the money.

"We better get going on dinner," Hayden says.

It's game night at Delilah's, so we're making a quick pasta carbonara. I've learned that this dish is all about timing. Hayden already has the water almost boiling and the dough balls are on the counter. "I've got this." I roll the balls flat like Hayden taught me then run them through the old-fashioned pasta machine to make fettuccini.

"You're a pro," Hayden says.

I pretend to be knowledgeable by parroting him. "It's easy once you understand that the key to great pasta is the right flours. I find that half wheat, half cake flour makes the pasta more delicate."

Hayden slides his arms around me from behind and nibbles my neck. "I've created a monster."

"Hey!" I scold. "Don't mess with the chef. I need two eggs and Parmesan cheese for the sauce. Pronto!"

He pulls the eggs from the fridge and hands them to me. I fumble and drop both on the floor. With a sigh I admit, "The truth is that no matter what you teach me, I'm still a hazard in the kitchen."

Hayden returns to the fridge, pulls out more eggs, holds one above his head, and then drops it on the parquet he painstakingly restored. I giggle. "What are you doing?"

"Showing you that the mess doesn't matter," Hayden says as both dogs happily lap up the broken eggs.

"Oh yeah?" I toss a handful of flour onto his shirt and get a dusting in return that makes us both crack up.

Once the pasta is cooked, Hayden takes over the process, quickly whisking the beaten eggs with a few tablespoons of hot pasta water then tossing the pasta with the eggs and Parmesan cheese. The result is delicious.

After I wash the pots and he dries them, I search for my Vespa key. It's in one of the cubbyholes by the front door that Hayden made after he discovered I misplace, well, everything. It's still hard to believe that this is my life.

It all happened organically. When I first moved in, we'd have dinner a few nights a week. Hayden loved trying out new recipes, and I started looking forward to those cozy nights of a home-cooked meal, conversations about his students, discussions of a new book they were reading, or a Scrabble game. One Sunday I invited him on a mountain bike ride. Despite sticking to the easiest trail, we had a good time. I took a Thai cooking class with Hayden and it was cool to learn something new.

Mars always asks me for details about Hayden and his life before me. But we rarely talk about that. The truth is that neither of us wants to look back. We have talked a little bit about his past relationships. The women Hayden dated wanted more than a guy with a teacher's salary. He hasn't asked much about my past boyfriends. Like most guys, he doesn't want to imagine his girlfriend with someone else. And he doesn't need to know that Mars thinks I date incredibly selfish men who reinforce the belief that I need to go to extreme measures to be valued.

One Sunday, a few weeks into living under one roof, we went to Farley's, a neighborhood coffee spot . . .

"What do you want in life?" Hayden asked.

We weren't dating, so I told the truth. "Children—as many as my husband and I can handle—and a partner who won't leave, regardless of the challenges."

Hayden said, "That's what I want, too, and a wife who shares my passions and introduces me to new things."

"Like what?"

"Like mountain biking," he said with a twinkle in his eyes.

We had our first kiss in Farley's. It tasted like the sweet mocha lattes he'd ordered us. From that moment on, I was all in.

The cooking classes continued—sushi followed by pizza—and Hayden opened his home to foster animals and brought up the idea of making a small kennel beside his shop. When I explained the whole point was to get them out of cages, make them feel part of a family, he understood and let the idea go.

A month after I moved into Hayden's house, he taught me how to use the table saw and we made a kitchen table together out of bird's-eye maple. After our first dinner on it—homemade raviolis—he invited me to crawl under the table with him.

"What are we doing down here?" I asked.

Hayden pointed to the words he'd carved in the wood: *Constance, I love you.* "I know it's fast," he said. "But it's true."

The question escaped before I had time to push it down. "Why?"

"There's nowhere else I'd rather be when I'm with you," Hayden replied.

That night we had sex for the first time and while it wasn't the hang-from-the-chandeliers sex Mars thinks is vital for any relationship, it felt like home.

Now it seems like we've known each other forever. We hop on my Vespa and join a steady stream of cars, his hands resting on my thighs. *Is Hayden the one?* Mars is *positive* that he's not. But I thought Marcus, Damian, Nate, another Marcus, George, and even Hal might've been *the* guy. And Hal *did* steal my mattress. There's no rush, I remind myself. *Time will tell.*

When we walk into game night at Delilah's the scent of whiskey tickles my nose—*Mom's go-to.* We've brought our board, same as the rest of the crowd, but since we're late, they've already been randomly paired and begun. That means our first match will be against each other. Shouts and waves from the regular players greet us as we make our way to the last open table. Hayden pulls out my chair and I go to the bar to buy two beers while he mixes the tiles.

"Don't be too hard on our Hayden tonight," Bunker calls over.

Bunker is the retired ferry captain who started game night. He holds the record for using all seven of his tiles five times in one game, which scores an extra 50 points each time. Several of the regulars at nearby tables hold up their glasses and smile at us. Everyone is in a great mood for a Wednesday work night. Unfortunately, I still have a pile of work to do after we get home. I actually wanted to skip tonight but Hayden had his heart set on playing.

Hayden starts the timer on his phone then pushes the box top containing the tiles toward me and asks, "How was your day?"

I'm shocked to see I have a seven-letter word right out of the gate. ANXIOUS. That's 14 points on a double word score, plus 50 for using all my tiles. Hayden gives me a high five.

A memory clicks on like a light. "I used that same word in the last game Grandpa and I played before I left for college."

"Were you anxious?" Hayden asks.

"Yes. Grandpa thought I was afraid to leave home for the first time, but he was already getting more forgetful. He'd left the stove on all day, spaced on the electric bill, and twice he'd forgotten to turn off his car *in the garage*."

Hayden plays off my tiles for 14 points then asks, "Did he want you to go?"

I can still see the tears in Grandpa's dark blue eyes, the exact same shade as mine. "No one in my family had ever gotten a scholarship, let alone gone to college, so yeah, he really did." *He wanted me to escape.*

"We have that in common," Hayden says. "Struggling for something different." He squeezes my hand. "I'm excited to get to know your grandfather."

I haven't introduced them yet. Grandpa has dementia and goes in and out of clarity. And I'm afraid of what he'll say. As I rearrange my tiles, the rest of our conversation during that last Scrabble game returns . . .

"What about Dad?" I asked.

Grandpa scowled. "He's not your responsibility."

But I knew, even when I was a little kid, that Dad needed me around so he'd do better. Like the time he missed my sixth birthday dinner. He showed up two days later with a gift—a small gold locket with the inscription *I love you Becky*. Mom made fun of it, but I told him it was the thought that counted and asked if he'd stay with us this time . . .

Dad shook his head. "A full-time kid is too much responsibility for a guy like me."

"I'll be good. Promise."

He crouched so we were eye-to-eye. "You can love somebody, Constance, but not want her all the time."

"Constance? Your turn," Hayden says.

I find a spot to play my M and score 24 points. Hayden misses an obvious three-way score and only makes 15 points. Then he sacrifices a Y to spell YOU in a move that opens the board. "You sure you're okay with Lucy staying with us?"

He takes a swallow of his beer. "Of course."

I use my Q for another high score. Hayden spells ME for only 8 points. He continues to miss obvious big scores for single digit points. For a guy who usually racks up a minimum of 30 points per turn, Hayden is having a very bad night.

Since everyone started before us, they're done with their games and have to wait for us to finish to start the next one. The regulars filter over to watch as our timer counts down the final minutes. Hayden's forehead is speckled with perspiration. It's warm in here, but he doesn't usually sweat. Hayden plays off my Y to spell MARRY. The bar goes totally silent. I look up. Hayden is watching me and so is everyone else. "What's going on?" He points to one of the words he played early in the game, WILL then to another, YOU, then to the last one, MARRY, and finally to one of his lowest scores, ME.

My first thought is, How'd he get those exact tiles?

He picks up an M and holds it out to show me. "I filed notches in the letters I needed."

"What if I'd picked one of those tiles?"

"While you were getting our drinks I made sure the ones I needed were on my side of the box. Figured I'd find opportunities to make them work."

Bunker holds up a bottle of champagne, hands poised to pop the cork. "Well?"

I turn back to Hayden and there's an open blue-velvet ring box on the Scrabble board. A shiver wrings my spine and Mars's silly superstition that the chills mean a ghost is trying to control you comes to mind. Someone in the crowd whistles and I focus on the ring. It's exquisite—a square diamond set in platinum and held in place on the sides by delicate flowers made of rubies. A wave of déjà vu hits.

"Will you?" Hayden asks.

"Marry you?"

"From the first moment we met, I knew you were the one."

The silence in the bar is deafening. My mind races . . . *We haven't even known each other a year—I've never met his friends—talked to his parents—he's never met Grandpa—Mars doesn't like him—Hayden doesn't know everything about me . . .*

"Constance?" Hayden asks, a slight waver in his voice.

I take a deep breath, think about how it felt like I was meant to meet him that first night—how he makes me feel special—that he wants to share all his passions—and indulges my love of animals— how the first game of Scrabble we played together, the words LOVE, FATE, and RING were on that board. Still, there's something tugging me in the opposite direction. *My fears.*

I meet Hayden's gaze. "Yes."

We kiss to cheers. One of the regulars, Molly, catches my eye and raises her glass with a little smile. I raise mine in return.

"Way to go," Bunker says as he shakes Hayden's hand. "How many times you two been married?"

"Never," Hayden and I say in unison.

"Engaged?"

We both shake our heads.

Bunker looks at us like we're unicorns. "Then listen close, kiddies. The first wife planned our wedding for a year-and-a-half, blew thirty-thou, and it lasted six months. My advice, don't spend a lot of cash and don't wait to tie the knot."

Veronica, Bunker's wife, drains her glass then adds, "The longer the planning, the more complicated the wedding and the harder it is on the bride and groom."

"Me and Veronica had three weeks from proposal to *I do*. And we've been married forty-two years." Bunker dips Veronica then kisses her with a wet smack.

"Works for me," Hayden says. "How about May 28th?"

It's his birthday and only two months away. I joke, "Did you pick that day so you'll never forget our anniversary?"

Hayden grins. "I picked it because I can't wait to marry you. And, we're both thirty-four, old enough to know what we want."

Icy fingers tickle my neck. I smile and say, "May 28th it is."

Photo by Kelley Dulcich

NAN FISCHER is a two-time Oregon Book Award finalist for her novels *When Elephants Fly* and *The Speed of Falling Objects*. Additional author credits include co-authored sport autobiographies for elite athletes and a *Star Wars* trilogy for Lucasfilm. She lives in the Pacific Northwest with her husband and their vizsla, Boone.

Ready to find
your next great read?

Let us help.

Visit prh.com/nextread

Penguin
Random
House